The Heritage Key

BELL THE CAT
PUBLICATIONS

© 2018 – Mike Parker
Bell the Cat Publications
All Rights Reserved

ISBN-13: 978-1725919129
ISBN-10: 1725919125

No portion of this book may be reproduced, stored in a retrieval system, or transmitted in any form or by any means – electronic, mechanical, photocopy, recording, scanning, or other – except for brief quotations in critical reviews or articles, without prior written permission of the author.

The author can be contacted at: authormikeparker@gmail.com

To the person who has had one of those days which left them wanting nothing more than to curl up under a warm blanket, by a roaring fire and escape into a good book – I gladly offer you the following pages.

Sorry, I was all out of blankets.

Contents

1. THE BIG DATE — 11
2. WE'RE NOT IN KANSAS ANYMORE — 27
3. INCOMPLETE — 43
4. HOME, SWEET HOME — 61
5. WHERE DO WE START? — 77
6. TO THE TREES — 95
7. CRANK & LUG — 112
8. GOOD NEWS & BAD NEWS — 127
9. UP IN THE AIR — 145
10. ALL WET — 159
11. BEING BAIT — 173
12. PURSUED — 187
13. APPLES & ORANGES — 201
14. FROM BAD TO WORSE — 219
15. SAND TRAP — 235
16. AN UNEXPECTED WELCOME — 253
17. A TALE OF TWO TALES — 269
18. TRUCE — 285
19. A SIGN OF GOOD FAITH — 301
20. FRAUGHT WITH UNCERTAINTY — 317
21. WELCOME HOME — 331
22. TWO MORE TO GO — 345
23. ALL ON YOUR OWN — 359
24. LOWS & HIGHS — 373
25. NEGOTIATIONS — 391
26. THE EXCHANGE — 405
27. ONE LAST FAVOR — 423

- 1 -
The Big Date

The spring wind blew gently as a young man walked along the sidewalk. It was mid-May, but the weather was still rather mild for this time of year. Today the weather seemed to be especially nice. The sun was shining warmly down on the city, not a cloud in the sky. Matthew Sinclair whistled quietly and waited at the corner for the light to change. He took a deep breath of the fresh spring air as he crossed the street. His heart beat a little faster, not from the pace of his stride, but in anticipation of seeing Emma. The young man opened the door to the Jean Pierre Café and stood patiently in front of the *"Please wait to be seated"* sign.

As he stood patiently waiting, he chuckled to himself about the way his girlfriend would always ask how he could even stand to inhale the city air. Matthew was born and raised in the city. He would be the first to admit that the air wasn't quite 100% clean, but it was still home, and he wouldn't want to be anywhere else. Emma, on the other hand, loved the country. She'd rather be out in an open field or lush forest than in the middle of the city any day. Coming downtown was the worst. It would take something very special to persuade her to venture into the belly of the beast, as she called it.

Today that very special thing was lunch with Matthew.

"Have you been helped yet, sir?" the hostess' voice interrupted Matthew's thoughts.

"Umm, no," he replied. "A table for two, please."

"Certainly, right this way."

"Preferably one outside on the patio," a gentle voice called from the doorway behind him.

"Certainly, ma'am," the hostess smiled. "This way if you please."

"You're early!" Emma grinned as she fell in step with Matthew, sliding her arm around his. "That's odd," she added with an unveiled note of sarcasm.

"Actually," Matthew gave her arm a gentle squeeze, "you're three minutes late. Now, that's really odd," the young man joked back. "Glad you could make it," he smiled and kissed her cheek.

"I couldn't find a parking spot," she protested in mock defensiveness. There was no doubt that time management was one of their biggest differences. Emma was almost always casually late, but rarely more than five minutes. Matthew, on the other hand, subscribed to the view that if you want to be on time be there five minutes early.

"Will this table be okay?" the hostess asked, laying two menus on the red and white checkered tablecloth.

"Look's great," Matthew responded.

"Excellent," the hostess smiled as she pulled Emma's chair back for her. "Kathryn will be around

The Big Date

in a moment to tell you about our lunch specials today. Enjoy your meals."

"Thank you," Matthew smiled. He was glad Emma had suggested this lunch date. The Jean Pierre Café was only three blocks from his office so it was the perfect place to grab a quick bite, and far better than the greasy burger and salty fries he likely would have ended up having otherwise. Working at a big-time engineering company meant he rarely had time for more than a 20 to 30 minute lunch break. Today he had come into work an hour early just to make time for lunch with Emma. It would have been worth it on any ordinary day, but today was special.

"So, are we still on for tonight?"

"Absolutely."

"What time should I be ready?" Emma asked. She was dying to know what his plans were for the evening. Tingles ran up and down her spine as she pondered it. Spending time with Matthew was always enjoyable, but she had a sense that tonight might be something special. He had scheduled their date over a week ago. It wasn't unheard of for them to make plans that far in advance, but it usually involved purchasing tickets or making reservations somewhere. So far Matthew hadn't indicated he had done either, which only left her more curious. She had a no clue what he had up his sleeve, which she found equally exciting and irritating.

The Heritage Key

"I should be able to pick you up by six," Matthew replied.

"And I should just dress casual, right?" she asked, fishing for any sort of clue she could find.

"Yep, but you might want to bring a light coat too, just in case," he replied with a smirk.

"So, we're going to be outside?"

"Possibly, or maybe I just told you that to throw you off the scent," Matthew chuckled.

"Well, aren't you the devious one?" she inquired.

"Who me?" he said, feigning innocence.

"Yes, you. You come off like Mr. Honesty, but I know just how sneaky you can be when you want to be," she teased. She was about to ask another question about the evening's activity, but her probing was cut short.

"Good afternoon," a young woman wearing a white top and black apron greeted cheerfully. "My name is Kathryn and I'll be your server today."

* * *

After ordering their meals, the conversation resumed, but to Matthew's relief, the topic shifted. Emma was a clever girl and he knew that the longer they talked about his plans for tonight the more likely he was to give something away.

"What have you been up to today, Em?" he asked.

The Big Date

"Oh, you know, the usual," the med student replied with a gentle smile. "Dr. Stevens had me grading some of his papers this morning and this afternoon I need to work on my internal medicine paper."

"Fun!"

"Well, you know what they say, 'when it comes to internal medicine: no guts, no glory'," Emma chuckled.

"Are you sure you can take the night off?" Matthew asked out of genuine concern. Emma was an excellent student, thanks in large part to having the most disciplined study habits of anyone he'd ever met. He suddenly realized he had inadvertently turned the conversation back to the one topic he was trying to avoid.

"Absolutely," she smiled and took his hand. "I wouldn't miss it for the world."

Just then, Kathryn returned to the table skillfully carrying a large round tray which held both their meals. Matthew eyed up his steak sandwich while Emma poured dressing on to her chef's salad. She began gazing around her plate as if something important was missing from the dish.

"Looking for this," her boyfriend asked with a sly smile and holding up a fork.

"Yes, that's exactly what I was looking for."

Matthew smoothly twirled the silverware in his fingers and extended the handle to his girlfriend. Emma grasped the utensil and pulled it towards herself. The other end of the cutlery, which had been temporarily hidden from view by Matthew's hand, was revealed. Emma chuckled as she looked at the teaspoon she was now holding.

"Very funny, Houdini," she laughed. "Hand over the fork!"

The would-be magician pulled his other hand up from under the table and handed over the fork, with the tines clearly visible. He was not much of a magician, though not for lack of desire or trying. This was, however, the only trick he had really mastered. Perhaps that's why he enjoyed performing it almost every chance he got. Fortunately for both of them, Emma still found it amusing and endearing, even though she had been the victim of this sleight of hand many times.

With all the cutlery now in the appropriate hands, the two enjoyed their meals and further conversation for the remainder of the time they had left on their lunch break.

* * *

Matthew settled back into his cubicle at Finch & Steele after returning from his lunch date. He started to log in to his computer but got distracted by the photo of Emma on his screen. The couple had been dating for over a year now after being introduced to one another by a mutual friend. Their lunch together had been delightful, and a nice escape from the doldrums of reviewing schematics and writing procedures. It was, however, their date later that evening that the engineer was most excited about.

He typed in his password and waited while the computer finished logging in. Matthew gently slid open his desk drawer and discretely removed a small velvet covered box from inside. The small box sat in his hand for a few moments until he realized he was holding his breath. Matthew quickly put the box back in the drawer and exhaled deeply. It was a very strange thing, he mused. He could not be more certain that he wanted to spend the rest of his life with Emma, and yet the idea of actually speaking those four words – will you marry me? – left him utterly petrified. It was not insecurity, he reasoned to himself. He was confident that when the question was finally popped Emma would eagerly say 'yes'. Nonetheless, imagining the moment left him virtually paralyzed. If all went as planned, however, that was not something he'd have to worry about after tonight.

"Sinclair!" a loud voice interrupted Matthew's thought.

"Um, yeah?"

"Where are you at on the Harris file?" the middle-aged man asked.

"Should have it wrapped up by the end of the day, Sayid," Matthew assured.

"I hope so. I'd hate to make you come in on your day off tomorrow." The words were said in jest, but the young engineer knew that his manager wouldn't hesitate to enforce his threat if the file wasn't on his desk by day's end.

"Don't worry, I'll get it done. Oh, and by the way, don't forget I'm leaving early today."

"What?"

"I talked to you about it last week, remember?" Matthew explained.

"Oh yes, the big date night, right?" Sayid grinned. "That's fine, as long as you get the Harris file done before you leave."

"Will do."

Sayid Naveen was a good boss for the most part. He and Matthew were about as close to friends as a manager and his subordinate can be. Sayid was a pretty easy going and happy guy as long as the work got done, but he wasn't timid about cracking the whip if people started to get behind. Thankfully, the young engineer had all but finished up the Harris file before he left for lunch, so there should be no trouble completing it in plenty of time to check out early and start prepping for tonight.

"Glad to hear it," Naveen replied cheerfully and started walking away. After a few strides, he stopped and turned back around. "Hey, Matt..."

"Yeah?"

"Good luck tonight."

"Thanks."

The Big Date

"That's right, tonight's the big night," a voice cheered from out of nowhere. A head popped up over the top of the cubicle wall and asked, "Are you nervous?"

"A little bit, I guess," Matthew admitted.

"Ah, don't be. It'll be a piece of cake," Matthew's co-worker reassured. "I remember when I asked Darlene to marry me. I was so wired up I could hardly speak. I remember thinking, *'I better ask her quick before I pass out.'* Some Casanova I am, hey?"

"What did you do to get past it, Phil?"

"Get past it? Ha! I bumbled out some words that sounded something like, *'Bill, you hairy beast'* and then nearly dropped the ring in a koi pond!"

"Well, thanks for setting the bar nice and low for the rest of us," Matthew chuckled.

"It's what I do," Phil laughed. Glancing around covertly he added softly, "Hey, if you want to sneak out of here early, I'll cover for you with the big cheese."

"Thanks, but I think I'm better off staying here and keeping myself occupied rather than being at home pacing the floor and watching the clock."

"I hear you. The offer still stands if you change your mind," Phil grinned and sank back down into his own cubicle.

* * *

Matthew clocked out around four and spent the next ninety minutes or so preparing for his big date. The pressure he felt to make everything perfect came from himself, not Emma's expectations. Although she might appreciate the effort he had gone through, he knew she would not swoon over the romantic trappings, at least not enough to influence her answer. She would say 'yes' at McDonald's if that's where he asked her, but he felt compelled to give her a night to remember – not because she required it, but simply because in his mind she deserved it. He was so caught up in his preparations that he lost track of time and almost didn't have a chance to rush home to clean up before heading over to Emma's place. He pressed buzzer 212 by the door of the Carmine Housing Complex and waited for a response.

"Hello?" Emma's soft voice greeted.

"Ms. Reilly, your carriage awaits!"

"I'm on my way down."

A few short minutes later they were both in the car and heading out of the suburbs. It was only a short drive from the med student's apartment to their destination, Cat Rock Park. Matthew hopped out of the car, scurried around to the other side and opened the passenger door for Emma. It was a bit of an old-fashioned tradition, but he was raised to believe it was a common courtesy, especially on a date.

"This way, my dear," he invited

The Big Date

The pair walked hand in hand along the winding gravel trail. On the weekend this park would be filled with hikers and their dogs – an ironic fact for a place called Cat Rock. On a Thursday night, however, the couple encountered only a handful of other visitors as they walked through the quiet woods. Matthew led the way along the trail until they reached a small clearing just off the beaten path.

"What is all this?" Emma gasped.

The tiny meadow was encircled by small solar lights, staked into the ground. Even at dusk the lights created a romantic glow in the clearing. At the center of clearing a large blanket was laid out, topped with a wicker picnic basket, a bottle chilling in an ice bucket and a small Bluetooth speaker playing soft music.

"Guess that's my cue to leave," a voice chirped from the edge of the tree line. "Unless you kids want to invite me to stay?"

"Yeah, I don't think so," Emma chuckled.

"Thanks, Joel," Matthew said with a wide smile.

"No worries, mate," the man smiled back. Joel Carson patted his friend on the shoulder as he headed back out to the trail. Matthew had set the site up earlier that afternoon, but he needed someone to keep an eye on it while he went to pick up Emma. Fortunately, Joel owned and operated a couple of food trucks which allowed him to set his own schedule, for the most part. Given the importance of the night, he was more than happy to help out his old pal and stand guard for an hour or so. "Enjoy your evening, you two!"

"My, my," Emma grinned surveying that charming scene, "you've outdone yourself this time Mr. Sinclair."

"You're worth it, baby," Matthew smirked. Saying something humorously cheesy was Matthew's go-to move when he felt uneasy. He escorted his date to the picnic blanket and sat down next to her. "I just figured, with me taking over the McConnel account and you starting your residency in the fall, I know time will be at a premium. I wanted to make sure we had a nice night together before things got too crazy."

"That sounds like a wonderful idea," Emma agreed, grabbing onto his arm and leaning into him. "So, what do we do now?"

"We sit. We eat. We talk and relax and then if all goes well..."

"Yes?" she asked coyly.

"We gaze at the stars for a while," Matthew said with a sly grin. "There's a meteor shower tonight, and if the lights of the city don't ruin it we should have a front row seat."

"That sounds lovely," Emma chuckled.

"It does, doesn't it?" Matthew smirked in pseudo-self-adulation as he opened the picnic basket.

The Big Date

"Oh, brother," his girlfriend rolled her eyes, "I hope you brought something good. I'm starving."

* * *

After a lovely meal and some delightful conversation, the pair sat snuggled under a flannel blanket watching the impressive light show in the sky. Matthew leaned against the picnic basket and Emma leaned against him. It was the perfect date night for Emma. She was not fond of large crowds or noisy restaurants and there were very few activities she found more peaceful than star gazing. She assumed something must be up for Matthew to have gone to so much trouble. The couple had talked about their plans for the future many times, nonetheless, she had no inkling of what was about to happen next.

Matthew's hand nervously fumbled around in his pocket until it found a firm grasp on the velvet box. He was unspeakably anxious. He forced himself to focus all his attention on not shaking. His date would undoubtedly notice any significant jitters as she leaned against him. For a brief moment he questioned whether or not he could actually go through with it. Perhaps now wasn't the right time. Perhaps he should wait until they had dated a little longer.

Fortunately, the description of his co-worker's awkwardly delivered proposal came to Matthew's mind. The nervous young man relaxed slightly as he thought to himself, '*You can't do any worse than Phil did.*' He reviewed the often-rehearsed lines in his head one more time, and then once again, just to be sure. He had initially planned to say something flowery and poetic comparing the stars and her eyes to diamonds before revealing the ring. In the end, he decided neither one of them was the sappy type, so something much more plain and honest would work best. As he gently slid the ring box out of his pocket, Emma sat up abruptly.

"Matthew," she said in hushed tones as if someone was listening, "did you hear that?"

The engineer had heard nothing but the lines being recited in his head, and the pounding of his heart. "Hear what?"

"Someone's out there."

"What?" her bewildered boyfriend asked.

"I heard something, someone, out in there."

"Em, it's a public park. People have been walking by all night long."

"No," she insisted, still listening intently to the sounds around them. "It wasn't from the trail. It came from over there, in the middle of those trees. They both studied the tree line in the faint light of dusk, straining to see. "There it is again!"

"I heard it that time, too," Matthew stated. "Sounds like something rustling around in the bushes."

"Like what?"

The Big Date

"I'm not sure. It's too big for just a squirrel. Maybe a big dog or ..." His ponderings were interrupted by the sound of muffled voices off in the darkness. "It sounds like someone's in trouble!"

- 2 -
We're Not in Kansas Anymore

Matthew stood up and searched the dimly lit clearing. With a full dose of adrenaline flowing through his veins, he picked up a large branch off the ground to use for protection and started toward the tree line. Emma followed close behind as they both turned on the flashlight on their smartphones.

"Over there, I think," she whispered.

They were getting closer to the source of the noise. With each cautious step the sounds became louder and clearer until the pair could clearly identify human voices, at least one of which was female. Among the indiscernible words, there were grunts, moans, and thuds, suggesting the people were in some kind of struggle with one another. They unconsciously quickened their pace at the realization that someone might be in desperate need of their help.

They passed through a dense patch of foliage, catching a brief glimpse of two shadowy figures wrestling around on the ground. At the sight of the couple's lights, one of the figures delivered a hard blow to the other and scampered off. After a brief pause, the second person sprang up from the ground and chased after the first, disappearing once again into the darkness.

Matthew and Emma stood dumbfounded in the tiny clearing. Their senses remained on ultra-high alert, but they were uncertain what to make of what they had just witnessed, or what they should do next. Matthew flashed his light around the area looking for some sign that might indicate what the scuffle had been about.

"What's that over there?" Emma asked excitedly.

"Over where?"

"Back this way a bit," she said, directing the beam of his light, momentarily forgetting she had one of her own. "There!"

There was a slight glimmer in the grass as his light reflected off the surface of something metallic. Emma walked over and ran her fingers through the forest floor in search of the shimmer's source. It did not take long before she found the object she was searching for among the leaves and twigs. She picked up the item and held it out for her boyfriend to see.

"A key?"

"Yeah, it must have fallen out of one of their pockets while they were wrestling around."

"Looks like, maybe, a safety deposit key?" Matthew examined the item as he moved closer. "Or a skeleton key for an old door or something?"

"Maybe they dropped something else," his girlfriend suggested. "We should look around, just in case. It might help us figure out who was here and what on earth they were doing." The two scoured the small area looking for additional clues to the strange event but didn't find anything other than the key.

"I guess we should head back and pack up our stuff," Matthew suggested.

"Yeah, you're probably right," Emma reluctantly agreed. Not only was the mystery intriguing to her, but she was equally disappointed to see the night end.

The pair weaved their way through the dark bushes doing their best to trace their steps back to the picnic site. As he shuffled along, Matthew's thoughts were consumed with what he should do when they got back to the clearing. This was supposed to be their night. He had gone to all the work of orchestrating the perfect proposal moment, but the moment was past. He couldn't just get back to the picnic site and say, "Oh yeah, by the way, do you want to get married?" Not after what had just happened. At the same time, he couldn't imagine, nor did he want to let this opportunity pass.

With his mind preoccupied, he wasn't paying attention to his feet. He kicked something, stubbing his toe firmly. At first he assumed it was a large root or fallen log. After the initial throbbing subsided, he shone his light down at his feet.

"Wait a minute," he said curiously. "What is this?"

"What is what?"

Matthew bent down and began to brush the leaves off of a small object. Once cleared, he picked the item up and stood to show Emma what he had found. "This."

"It looks like some kind of jewelry box or something," she observed. "A pretty nice one too. Look at the detailed design carved into the lid. Do you think we should look inside it?"

"I betchya a dollar that whatever priceless gem is in here is what those folks were wrestling over."

"Does the key open it?" Emma asked eagerly.

"No...I don't think so," her boyfriend replied. "In fact, I don't see any kind of lock on it at all."

"Open it!"

Matthew handed his phone to his girlfriend and slowly eased open the lid of the small, wooden box. They both gingerly peered inside, but what they found was not what they had expected. The box held no jewelry or gems. No gold watches or diamond rings. To their shock, it held nothing. The interior of the box was solid wood. In the center sat a two-inch by three-inch brass plate with a small keyhole in the middle.

"That's odd," the engineer mused, examining the box closely from every possible angle. "It doesn't look like this thing opens up any other way. It's just solid wood."

"That can't be. It must open up somehow," Emma responded, pulling out the key she had found earlier. "Let's give this a shot."

Emma put her phone away and returned Matthew's to him. He shone the light on the brass plate in the center of the box. Emma placed one hand on her boyfriend's forearm and inserted the key with the other. It slid in and clicked in a way that was both satisfying and exhilarating. She took a nervous breath and slowly began to turn the key. There was no sign of any part of the box unlatching or popping open, so she turned the key a little further.

A faint glow appeared inside the keyhole as she turned the lock. Suddenly she felt a wave of nausea sweep over her with surprising intensity. Her face became flushed and her head started to spin uncontrollably. The glow in the keyhole intensified rapidly, growing steadily into a blinding bright light. The young woman squeezed her eyes shut, which only made her nausea and dizziness exponentially worse. She felt like she might faint at any moment, and then she did.

* * *

"Whoa, what was that?" Matthew exclaimed still feeling woozy and disoriented.

"What happened, Matthew?" Emma asked, her eyes still shut.

"I don't know," he replied, sounding thoroughly bewildered. "Perhaps we got mugged while we were ... the box is gone. Are you okay?"

He slowly opened his eyes and waited for them to adjust to the dim light. He had a wicked headache, and his limbs felt like dead weights. He lay flat on his back staring up into the air. It was very dark and there was no moon or stars to be seen – only strange looking clouds in the night sky.

"Yeah, just a little woozy. I'll be fine in a minute. Tell me what you see." Emma asked, with her eyes still squeezed tightly closed, partly because of her throbbing head and partly because of the weird feeling running through the rest of her.

"Not much" Matthew began as he gingerly sat up. It was then he realized not only had they been mysteriously knocked out, but they had woken up in a completely different place. "Oh, my!"

"What is it?" Emma inquired, finally getting the courage to open her own eyes. The dim light veiled most of her surroundings in shadow until her eyes had time to adjust from the box's blinding light earlier. As she waited, she felt the ground around her. It was not the soft moss and grass she remembered walking on in the forest. In fact, the ground was quite hard and cold as stone.

"Emma," Matthew spoke softly as he stood up, still rubbing his head. "I've got a bad feeling about this."

"Where are all the trees, Matthew? What happened to the trees?" She asked in a thoroughly confused, and somewhat uneasy tone.

The trees were gone, and it was clear the pair were no longer in the forest. They were inside a large room constructed primarily of carved stone. What Matthew had first thought to be strange clouds were, in reality, a stone carved ceiling. As the pair began to wander around they grew simultaneously more curious and more nervous.

"Check this place out," Matthew gasped, more impressed by his new surroundings than he was distressed about how they got there. The room was a large circle with a high vaulted ceiling, all of which was constructed out of dark gray stone – like granite. Along the outside wall there were ten archways carved out of stone, evenly spaced and identical. Inside each alcove was a wooden door with intricate designs carved into the surface. Matthew, feeling sturdier on his feet, walked to the closest archway. He attempted to open the door, but it was locked. He moved to the next door and the next. Having tested all ten doors, he found them all locked.

"That's strange," Matthew said.

"What's strange?"

"These doors," Matthew began as he studied one of the doorframes intently, "all appear to be locked from the other side. Actually," he said upon further inspection. "They almost look like they don't even open at all!"

"They have to open," Emma responded. "Otherwise, how'd we get in here?"

"And more importantly," he added, "how do we get out?" He turned around to look at his girlfriend, but she was no longer behind him. "Where did you go?"

"I'm over here," Emma shouted from across the room. The quarter section of the rotunda without arches and doors opened out into a rectangular work area.

"What did you find?"

"Somebody has a workbench set up here. Looks like a carpenter of some kind." Emma answered as she examined the large piece of wood laying on top of the bench. "Someone's carving up a new door here. Look at the symbols! I think they're some kind of writing, but it's no language I've ever seen."

"I think you might be right. It's all over these ones too," Matthew called back across the room. He continued to study the doors intently, looking for a way out.

"Hey, Matthew! You've got to see this!" she said in equal parts bewilderment and curiosity. "I found the box, and there's a whole rack full of keys over here too."

The young woman slipped the original key, which up until now she had been gripping tightly in her hand, into the lock of the door on the bench.

The key refused to turn. She set the key down on the workbench. There was a small metal rack stocked with numerous keys just like the one they had found in the park. She picked up a new key from the rack and examined it carefully. Again, she slipped the key into the door's lock and gave it a gentle twist. Even though the key turned in the lock, she did not see or hear any apparent effect. Overcome by curiosity, Emma picked up the box and opened the lid, revealing the brass plate and keyhole.

"Hey, you should come check this out," she called across the room.

Matthew took one last look at the door and then turned to face the desk. "Look at what?" he asked. "Emma?" Only silence answered him. "Emma? Where'd you go? Come on out Em, this isn't funny," Matthew yelled as he walked briskly toward the bench. "Where are you, Emma?" He called out again, this time sounding borderline panicked.

Emma was nowhere to be found. Her boyfriend looked over the contents of the workbench carefully, searching for some indication of where she may have gone. After examining the half-built door, he turned his attention to the box. He couldn't be sure, but he was fairly confident that the box he had found in the forest was a brownish color, whereas the one in front of him now was more of a midnight blue. Of course, the light in the forest had been dreadfully dim and his head was still quite fuzzy, so perhaps he was mistaken.

Matthew gently opened the lid of the small box and looked over the contents. The inside was solid wood, just like the first box, and it housed an identical looking brass plate. When he set the box down again, it snapped itself closed with a loud clap. The sound jogged his memory and he recalled hearing that exact same clap from across the room, just before he had turned around.

He would have pondered the sound, and Emma's untimely disappearance further had something else not caught his attention. He heard a strange noise and then a bluish light appeared in the center of the room. The light started as a glow no bigger than a quarter, floating in the middle of the room nearly three feet above the floor. It quickly grew larger and brighter. Matthew squinted as he stared, bewildered, at the radiant glow. The light slowly changed shape as if it were attempting to form something tangible. Matthew squeezed his eyes shut, hoping that when he opened them again the light would have evaporated, and he would be back in the forest with Emma.

When he opened his eyes, the light was indeed gone, but he had not returned to the forest. Matthew was still in the stone carved room standing behind the bench, but he was no longer alone. In the middle of the room stood a man, about six feet tall, who appeared to be in his early fifties. He had dark hair with hints of greying on the sides and a neatly cut beard. He wore a cream-colored sweater over a brown button-up shirt.

"What are you doing here?" the man spoke, sounding friendly but unmistakably upset. He examined Matthew from behind his thin wire-framed glasses.

"What did you do with Emma?" Matthew demanded, his mind racing and spinning. He felt as if he were on one of those episodes of the Twilight Zone that channel 37 always played after the late, late show.

"Who is Emma?" the man replied sounding genuinely confused.

"Who are you?" the engineer countered. "And why did you bring us here?"

"Hmm," the man said thoughtfully. "You mean to tell me you don't know how you got here?" The completely baffled look on Matthew's face was more than enough confirmation. "Where are you from, my friend?"

"Waltham."

"Waltham, as in Boston?" the man asked, his face flooded with recognition followed initially by relief and then by deep concern. "So, you are from earth, then. I'm not sure if that makes me feel better or worse."

"What do you mean, I'm from earth. Of course I'm from earth! What are you, nuts?" an exasperated Matthew retorted, sounding more than a little indignant. Then he paused and with great hesitation said, "Don't tell me this is some kind of alien ship or something."

"Oh no," the man replied calmly. "I assure you this is not an alien spaceship."

"Then who on earth are you, and where on earth are we?" the young man demanded.

"My name is Silas," the man replied. "But I'm afraid we are nowhere on earth, not exactly."

"What do you mean?" Matthew inquired, starting to regain his composure once again.

"You, my friend, are in my workshop. I have just returned myself and as you likely observed, I was quite shocked to find you here."

"But, if you didn't bring us here, then how did we get here?"

"How indeed?" Silas echoed thoughtfully. "You say you are from Boston. Where exactly were you, the last time you remember before you were here?"

"We were having a nice romantic evening out in Cat Rock Park," Matthew recalled slowly, his memory still a little jumbled. "We were having a picnic and I was just about to propose, when ...

"Yes, go on," Silas encouraged.

"When we heard some kind of scuffle going on in the trees. We went to see what it was. The people ran away, but Emma found a key." The man's interest was clearly piqued by the news of Emma's discovery. "Then I found a strange box," Matthew continued tentatively as if walking through a dense fog. He picked up the box on the workbench and displayed it for the man. "Just like this one. We opened it up, put the key in the keyhole and the next thing we knew we were in this room with a really wicked hangover."

"Hmm, it's just as I feared," Silas mused. "Well, let me see if I can make things a little clearer based on the few facts we have. You found a box and a key in a forest. Was the box exactly like that one?" Silas asked as he walked toward the bench and gently took the box away from Matthew. Something about the way Silas did it made him feel like the move was more one of caution rather than reprimand.

"I think so, but maybe a different color."

"Perhaps more of a caramel?"

"Yeah, I think so."

"And what about the key? Did you examine it closely?" It seemed as though the man had already put all the pieces together and was simply looking for confirmation of his suspicions.

"Well, no, not really," Matthew admitted. "Emma was the one who had the key."

Silas picked up the key Emma had left on the workbench and inspected it carefully. "It appears she left it behind. I imagine at some point the two of you put the key into the lock inside the box?"

"We did. You know, curiosity, right?"

The man paced around for a moment pondering the situation. "You seem to be a decent fellow, although I have recently discovered I am not always the best judge of character."

The young man wasn't exactly sure how to take that statement, but he assumed it was meant as affirmation. "Umm, thanks."

"It is imperative that we find your friend Emma, but I have other even more urgent matters to attend to, so," Silas paused briefly again to reconsider his plan once more. "So, I will need to rely on you for your assistance, which requires trusting you with the truth about this place."

"Whatever you need, just tell me how to find Emma."

"As I told you before, this is my workshop. You see, I have a very special gift."

"I can see you're a pretty talented carpenter."

"Yes, but there's more to it than you realize," Silas explained. "These are not ordinary doors. They are gateways to new worlds."

Matthew took a minute to process what he had just heard. "You mean like a wormhole or teleporter or something?"

"Nothing quite so outlandish," the man chuckled. "They are not passageways through time or space, per se. They take you to realms that exist outside of our normal reality."

"Alternate dimensions?"

"Not entirely, no. This is not a comic book. It's just that I have the ability to create worlds that exist outside of physical space."

"So, like, virtual reality."

"Something like that I suppose, except there is nothing virtual about them. They are 100 percent real. As real as this workshop in fact."

"I don't get it. How could some made up place be as real as this?" the engineer asked, knocking on the workbench with his fist.

Silas laughed softly. "I know it will be hard for you to believe, my friend, but this workshop was the first realm I created. This room exists nowhere. There is nothing outside these walls. But it is as real as either you or me."

"That's impossible."

"Perhaps, but it is also true."

"If this place doesn't exist in space, and there is nothing outside these walls, then how on earth did we get in here?!" the confused and exasperated young man demanded.

"You put the key into the box," Silas explained calmly. "Each key is linked to a door. When you insert the key into the box, it opens the door to that realm."

"Hmm," Matthew said thoughtfully. "Let's say I believe you." He was pretty sure that he didn't believe Silas' bizarre story, but he had no better explanation for what was going on. "How exactly do you create these realms?"

"The script carved into the doors. It is an ancient mystical dialect. The language has been preserved through the ages. Only one person in each generation is taught to read and write it. The words I carve into the door define all the basic parameters of the world it will lead to. Once the door is complete, however, the natural laws of the realm will take effect. Which means things can be changed and altered by anyone inside that world or by other circumstances therein."

"Okay," Matthew said, not thoroughly convinced but eager to move on to more pressing matters. "That still doesn't explain what happened to Emma."

"I'm afraid it does," Silas replied. "The key she left on the table is the one you found in the woods. Had she used it in the box it would have simply brought her right back here to the workshop."

"So where did she go?"

"Perhaps she took a new key and used it instead."

"And where would a new key take her?"

"Well, nowhere," Silas answered sounding a little puzzled. "A new key would not work at all. You see, before a key can open a gateway to a different realm, it must first…"

"It must first what?" Matthew asked impatiently.

"Oh dear," the man said quietly as he gazed at the door lying on the workbench. "Oh, I do hope she didn't…"

"Dude! You've got to finish your sentences! You're killing me here. You hope she didn't what?"

- 3 -
Incomplete

Silas held his hand momentarily over the brass plate inside the blue box. "Oh dear," he said again. "My guess is that your friend, Emma, inserted a new key into this door sitting on my workbench, encoding it for the realm to which it leads. After that, she put that key into this box."

"Okay, no problem. So, if we know where she is, why can't we just go get her?"

"You don't understand, my friend. This door is not finished, which means the realm it leads to is only partially completed as well. It could be a very confusing and chaotic place." Silas paused for a moment, considering the options available to them.

"That doesn't sound good!" Matthew fretted, filled with a deep sense of unease.

"For what it's worth," the carpenter said sympathetically, "it could have been much worse."

"How could this possibly get any worse?"

"She could have put the key in one of those doors over there." Silas motioned toward a couple doors leaning against the wall off to the side of the workshop. The doors were identical to all the others in size, shape, and material with one notable exception: they were completely void of any carved lettering.

"Where do those doors lead to?"

"Nowhere – literally nowhere. If your friend had used a key paired with one of those she would find herself in a dark and empty, infinite void."

"Okay," Matthew conceded. "That does sound worse. But I'm still not nuts about the current state of things."

"Nonetheless, you must go to this realm and find her."

"What do you mean *I* must go? You mean *we* must go, don't you? You *are* coming with me, right?"

"No, I have something much more pressing to attend to. I have already placed a box in this world. I will hide a key there which will lead back to Boston. Take a new key off that rack and insert it into the lock on that door over there."

Matthew grabbed a key off the rack and hurried to the door mounted in the archway furthest to the left. He placed the key in the door's lock and gently turned it to the right. Removing the key, he returned to the bench to find the carpenter chiseling out a new string of characters on the door.

"Excellent! Now, take another key and insert it into the lock on this door," the man instructed.

"Okay," Matthew agreed. He placed the first key into his pocket and took another from the rack. Once the key was linked to the workbench door he nervously asked, "Now what?"

"You will also need this," the carpenter said handing Matthew a small metal box about the size of a deck of cards. "Lay this over the brass plate in any box and the sensor on the bottom will tell you the destination of the last gateway."

"That way I will know if Emma has already found the box and gone home or if she is still wandering around somewhere in that world," Matthew surmised.

"Exactly," Silas confirmed. "The box I am leading Emma to is brand new, so if anyone has used it, it will have been her. When you get back home, be sure to keep the device somewhere safe. We don't want it falling into the wrong hands."

"I understand," Matthew agreed, wondering momentarily what *'the wrong hands'* meant.

"Now, put the key from the door on the workbench into the box and away you go!"

After receiving a few more instructions, Matthew opened up the box and inserted the key, "I'm not looking forward to this. The trip here was like going through a blender."

Silas chuckled. "Yes, it does take a little getting used to. Your body will adapt to the process eventually, but it might take some time."

"That's good to know, but I'm not planning on doing this that many times. Once to find Emma, once more to get home and that's it."

"Then this is farewell. Good luck."

"Thanks. You too." With that, Matthew turned the key and left the workshop.

* * *

Matthew felt a warm breeze blowing in his face as he arrived in the new realm. He still felt a little woozy, but as Silas had promised, the side effects of traveling through the portal were not nearly as severe as they were following his initial trip to the workshop.

"That wasn't so bad," he tried to convince himself. The young man began to take stock of his surroundings when he made a startling discovery. Silas had explained that the entry point for this realm was on the roof of an office tower. As a rule, the craftsman tried to place the gateway entry to each world someplace that would not draw a lot of attention. Matthew had expected to arrive on a gravel-covered tar roof next to an oversized HVAC unit. That was not where he found himself.

Silas had warned him that this world was incomplete, but Matthew was understandably caught off guard to discover the building he arrived at was still under construction. He found himself precariously balanced on an iron beam three stories above the highest completed level! Matthew gazed around nervously, trying to still the churning in his stomach. He was not a fan of heights.

After a few nervous moments, which felt like hours to the nervous engineer, Matthew spotted a ladder sticking up above the beams, about 20 feet from where he stood. "Come on, Sinclair. You can do this," he said, mustering his courage. "It's not that far."

"Hey! You!" a gruff voice yelled. The young man had been concentrating so hard on his route to the ladder that the voice came as a startling surprise to him. His foot slipped off the steel beam. In desperation he reached out to grasp a nearby post. With his heart still in his throat, he stepped back onto the beam and tried to breathe. "What are you doing up here?"

"Umm," Matthew said, still clinging to the post with all his might, "I'm looking for a way down."

"Well, how'd you get up here in the first place?" the man asked as he casually walked across the beams to where Matthew stood.

"It's kind of a long story," the engineer replied, relieved that he wouldn't have to find the way down on his own. The man sauntering toward him was well over six feet and barrel-chested. Matthew assumed that he must be one of the workers completing the building. He wore faded blue jeans, a flannel shirt, and a yellow hard hat. Just as Matthew was beginning to feel relieved to be back in a place where things made sense, he noticed something very odd about the man: he had no arms. *'How could a construction worker function with no arms?'* he asked himself. *'Especially up here!'*

"This way. Just follow me over to this ladder and climb down."

"Okay," Matthew agreed and began to walk cautiously across the beam.

"You know this is the second time we've had a civilian up on the beams today," the worker chatted casually as he walked. "You wouldn't believe it, but there was this young lady up here this morning, just wandering around, kinda like you," he chuckled as he looked back at Matthew who was inching his way along. "Although she wasn't nearly as scared as you are."

"Gee thanks," Matthew replied. On some level, his manhood objected to that comment, but right now he cared far more about not falling to his death than looking cool. He just wanted to get out of this place in one piece.

"Here you go," the worker stated. The ladder stood in front of them and stretched up about six feet above the beam. "Just grab the rails, swing your foot onto the rungs and climb down."

"Thanks," Matthew said as he cautiously mounted the ladder and began descending. After a few steps, he looked down to see how far he had to go. He had made a conscious effort to avoid looking down while standing on the beam, now he wished he had stuck with that plan. He looked back up, but the construction worker was already gone. Matthew looked below him once again, just to make sure. Nothing had changed – the ladder ended half way to the completed portion of the building. 'How is that even possible?' he thought to himself, gripping the ladder rungs a little tighter. The base of the ladder did not appear to be supported by anything. It was just suspended in midair.

Unable to find a better alternative, Matthew continued to slowly descend the ladder. As his feet approached the last rung he debated what to do next. He was still a good 15 feet from solid footing, but he was all out of ladder. "I hate heights."

Matthew wiped the sweat from his palms and secured his grasp on the ladder then slowly lifted his left foot off the bottom rung. Then he did the same with his right foot leaving the full weight of his body to be supported by his arms alone. Deep down he had hoped that the rest of the ladder existed but couldn't be seen. This was not the case. He carefully released the grip of his left hand and quickly moved it to a lower rung. He repeated the process, this time with his right hand. With each move, he felt a small jolt of pain in his arm as his body dropped one foot closer to the ground.

When he finally reached the last rung the young man realized he had gone as far as he could go. Both of his hands were clinging to the bottom rail with all their might as the rest of his body dangled below. Matthew looked down once more, his feet now hung about eight or nine feet above the floor below. He wasn't particularly excited about the drop, but at the same time his arms were getting quite tired, and he knew it wouldn't be long before his hands released their grip whether he wanted them to or not. Matthew reminded himself that the sooner he got off the roof, the sooner he could find Emma, and they could go home. "Bombs away!" he shouted forcing his fingers to let go.

The engineer hit the bottom with a thud. "That wasn't so bad," he commented as he stood up. "Now let's get out of here." He found a trap door with a ladder to the completed ninth floor. He climbed down and began wandering around the corridors. The hallway had the unmistakable look of an office building. The taupe colored walls and evenly spaced wooden doors with panes of frosted glass on the upper half reminded Matthew of many of the floors in his own office tower. Given the unfinished state of the building, none of the doors had names or even numbers printed on them. As he walked down a vacant hallway, Matthew recalled what Silas had told him about this realm.

"This world will be like your own, once it is completed," Silas explained. "But, don't forget that the door is only partially carved, which means the world will be incomplete. I cannot predict exactly how that will manifest itself, but I imagine you will see some rather bizarre things."

Matthew finally located and reached the elevator. He pressed the down button and waited. As he stood waiting for the elevator car to arrive, he reviewed the day's activities in his mind. What a day it had been. He had fully anticipated his date with Emma to be out of this world, just not quite so literally.

A few moments later the elevator doors opened, and Matthew casually walked in. He pressed the button marked G to take him down to the ground floor. It seemed odd to him that he was the only one in the elevator, and for that matter, the only person he had seen since he arrived was the armless construction worker. The elevator doors began to close in front of him, but just before they closed tight, Matthew stuck out his hand causing them to open again. He quickly hopped out of the elevator and back into the hallway. "What if the elevator is as complete as that ladder and I run out of cable by the fourth floor!" he questioned himself, staring into the empty elevator as though it were a pit of quicksand waiting to engulf him. "I think I'll take the stairs."

Matthew arrived on the main floor without incident and quickly made his way toward the front door. The only person in the lobby was a security guard who sat behind a large information desk. The guard looked at him and gave a friendly nod in his direction. Matthew nodded back and made his way out to the street. The street outside was as sparsely populated as the office building had been. The young man saw a taxi parked a few yards down the road. As he walked up to it, he noticed that there was no driver. He walked around to the driver's side and lifted the door latch. It was unlocked, and he could see through the window that the keys were in the ignition. He glanced around nonchalantly but saw no one.

"Sorry pal, but I don't have time to wait for you to finish your coffee break," he stated softly as he pulled the door open. There was a loud grinding sound as the door got stuck after opening only a few inches. A bewildered Matthew looked down to find that the door had become jammed on the asphalt. "What in the world!" Matthew exclaimed. The taxi was sitting flat on the ground. As he stepped back Matthew observed that the car had no tires. A quick examination of the other cars parked along the street revealed that they were all tireless.

"Don't move." a voice commanded from behind him.

"Hey, listen man," Matthew began to explain nervously. "I wasn't going to steal it. I just needed a ride that's all."

"I'm not interested in the car," the voice continued in the same strong tone. "It's you I'm concerned about. Now, turn around nice and slow."

Matthew complied, slowly turning to face his confronter. To his surprise it wasn't the cab driver who had come up behind him, it was a police officer. The man looked rather similar to the cops Matthew had seen in Waltham, with one significant difference. He wore black pleated pants and a navy shirt with a black tie, and a golden badge pinned on the chest. The only thing out of place was that he, like the construction worker, had no arms. Thinking back, Matthew realized it was possible the security guard in the lobby may have been armless as well.

"You're not from around here, are you?" the policeman inquired sternly.

"Well, no. Not exactly."

"What kind of freak are you anyways? I've never seen anyone with four legs. That's just unnatural."

"What? Four legs?" Matthew asked in confusion. "Oh, you mean my arms."

"Put those things down or I'll take you in right now, buster."

Matthew's initial response was to slowly lower his hands. Even without arms, the policeman was incredibly intimidating. That's when it hit him – no arms meant no hands, which meant no grabbing, punching or brandishing a weapon of any kind. He stood up a little straighter and looked the officer in the eyes. "Listen here, buster, I have more important things to do than stand here and listen to you make empty threats.

"Why you disrespectful little punk," the policeman fumed through a red face.

"Yeah, hold that thought, would you?"

Matthew sped across the street, scaled a six-foot chain-link fence and headed across the empty lot. The police officer ran after him shouting angrily. When the cop reached the fence, he was stopped short with no way to climb over, which seemed to both confuse and surprise him. Having safely evaded the police officer, Silas' words of instruction came back to Matthew.

"The people in this world will be sentient and you should be able to interact with them – to a degree," the carpenter explained.

"What you mean to a degree?"

"Because the realm is still being developed, it is important to give the people a limited consciousness. Living in a world where everything was in a constant state of change and flux, including your own body, would drive most people insane. Just imagine buildings popping up overnight, a forest or volcano appearing out of thin air, or one day to suddenly see, hear or speak when you previously didn't even know those things existed."

"I see what you mean. That would be a little freaky."

"Yes, indeed. Therefore, until the world is complete the only humane thing to do is to keep the inhabitants in a state of limited awareness. They are able to function and interact, but at the same time they are completely oblivious to much of what is going on around them."

As Matthew wandered the streets of the largely unpopulated city, he observed that Silas' description had been on the mark. Everything around him seemed like things were back home. Houses, streets, cars and shops - all looked like they could be from the neighborhood he lived in.

However, each one had a slight flaw – something was always incomplete. The windows had no glass panes, the manholes had no covers, the street signs had no names and trees had no leaves. The young man was fascinated by the strange world around him and even more fascinated with the mystical craft that had created it.

It was difficult for someone as practical as Matthew to accept that everything around him somehow existed outside of the normal physical dimension. It was even harder to swallow the idea that some meek-mannered man in a cardigan had created this entire world simply by carving some ancient script into a slab of wood. The fact that he had seemingly been magically transported from the forest to the workshop, and from the workshop to this realm, made it virtually impossible to deny.

The city was large and the odds of finding Emma seemed highly remote. According to Silas, he had added some signs that would help Emma head in the right direction and eventually find the key and box. Matthew couldn't imagine what it must be like for his girlfriend to navigate this world with none of the information he had. Without Silas' explanations and advice Matthew would not have gotten off the roof to the office building. As he thought about it further, he realized he likely would have gotten down about ten seconds after he arrived. Matthew was comfortable in predictable environments. He didn't function well with uncertainty. Emma, on the other hand, embraced new experiences with a zealous enthusiasm he couldn't even fathom or had any desire to experience.

"Alright, Matthew," he admonished himself glancing up and down the street, "look for a sign." He wasn't sure what he was looking for. Was it a glowing light? A trail of pixie dust? Or maybe he just blocked off all the roads except the one they needed to go down. "Oh," Matthew spotted something at the nearby corner, "the sign."

* * *

Emma's head was still reeling. Partly from the experience of being transported, or whatever it was that had happened to her, and partly from the disorientation of this new place. Arriving atop the office tower was unnerving, but the rest of this place was just downright bizarre. Every time her mind started to settle into thinking things were back to normal she would see something new that defied logic or reason. She was still trying to get the image of a furless dog out of her mind.

The young woman was walking down the street because she felt like she had to do something. Just sitting still and waiting was not her style. The complete uncertainty that permeated every aspect of her current situation left her highly uncomfortable. Determined not to let that stop her, Emma marched down the street searching for clues that would help her discern what was happening and how she could find her way home.

The city was sparsely populated so finding someone to ask for directions was proving more difficult than she anticipated. She eventually came across a small corner store and walked inside hoping to find someone who might be able to help her.

The confectionary was very similar to the one down the block from her apartment building, complete with a slushie machine churning blue and red ice. Emma glanced around the rest of the store and discovered that, other than the slushie machine, every shelf and cooler was completely empty.

"Hello there," a plump man greeted her from behind the cashier's counter. "Can I help you with anything?"

"Yeah," Emma smiled and walked over to the man, "can you tell me where I am?"

"You mean other than in my store?" the man laughed heartily.

"Yeah, other than that."

"Why sure, you're in the city."

"Yes, I got that. But exactly what city is it?"

The question seemed to baffle the man. "The city."

"Okay," she rethought her line of questioning. "Listen, my name is Emma, and I'm kind of lost."

"Emma, huh?" the stout man repeated thoughtfully. "Emma. I've heard that name before, somewhere. Where was that? Oh yeah! Right over there," he cheered attempting to point out the window behind him. The shopkeeper's assistance was limited, however, since he lacked arms – as everyone in this place appeared to – therefore he simply tilted his head in the general direction.

Emma glanced out the window and searched for whatever it was the man was pointing towards. "Umm, thanks!" She left the store and went back to the sidewalk. She located the object the man had pointed to.

She moved to the corner of the deserted street. Across the road a billboard loomed up in the air. The placement of the billboard seemed odd as it stood directly in front of a building blocking out most of the windows on the second and third floors. The strangest part of the sign, however, was what was written on it. In large red letters the sign said, "GO THIS WAY, EMMA," with an arrow pointing to the right. She glanced down the block to her right and then back at the billboard to confirm she had read it right. She slowly rounded the corner and began to wander down the street. A few moments later she spotted another sign in the distance. This time the words were on the side of a bus stop stall, but the message was the same. She continued down the street wondering if these signs would lead to her salvation or her demise.

Emma walked on for twenty minutes moving from sign to sign. She may have made the journey more quickly had she not missed the sign posted on the side of a parked bus. After circling around and getting herself back on track it was only a few minutes later until she found herself outside a quaint little two-story house. The white picket fence completed the picturesque vista. Planted in the front yard next to the brick sidewalk was a hanging sign. Surrounded by hand-painted flowers, the sign advertised the "Stay Here Emma Bed and Breakfast." She opened the small gate and walked up to the porch. She nervously knocked on the door and waited for a response.

The Heritage Key

- 4 -
Home, Sweet Home

Emma waited a minute and then knocked on the door again. A few moments later, she heard footsteps coming closer and a silhouette grew in the oval frosted pane of the door. She could hear someone fumbling around on the other side. Eventually, the sounds quieted, and an elderly woman's voice called out, "Come in."

Emma opened the door tentatively and stepped into the house. Once inside she saw the old woman wearing a faded, flower-patterned dress with an apron around her waist. The woman's silvery grey hair was neatly wrapped up in a bun and she wore a pair of horn-rimmed glasses. Of course, her most notable feature was her lack of arms, a strange trait that seemed to be shared by everyone else she had encountered in this place.

"How can I help you, my dear?" the old woman sweetly asked.

"Umm, I guess I'd like to stay here," Emma replied uncertainly.

"Oh, very good!" the woman beamed. "My name is Alice May. What is your name, sweetheart?"

"Ah, Emma. My name is Emma."

"Oh, how wonderful!" the B&B owner cheered. "I've been looking forward to your visit. Your room is all ready for you."

"How did you know I was coming?" the perplexed young woman asked.

"I really can't say, I just did, somehow. Are you traveling alone, dear?"

Emma's heart sank. She hadn't really stopped to think about it until now. She had kept herself focused on the task at hand – finding a way home. But the innocent question of this gentle old woman hit her like a Mack truck on the Interstate. She was traveling *alone*. She had assumed that if she could find her way home, somehow, that Matthew would be there waiting for her. She realized now that her assumption was faulty. Her mind raced with the possibilities. Matthew could still be stuck in the stone workshop – wherever that was. He may have relocated at the same time she had, only to a completely different place. Or maybe he was here, in the city somewhere, just as lost as she now felt. "Yes, ma'am. I'm very alone."

The woman's expression did not seem to noticeably change in response to Emma's emotional nosedive. "Very well, then. Follow me, your room is right this way."

The old lady led her to a narrow wooden staircase. Each step creaked as they ascended to the second floor. The old lady stopped next to the first door on the right. The door was closed prompting the woman to ask politely, "Would you mind dear?"

"Umm, sure. No problem," Emma reached out and turned the doorknob, opening the door.

Emma followed her host into the room which was small and furnished much like you would expect to find in any grandmother's house. Emma's attention was quickly drawn to the metal-framed bed covered with a patchwork quilt. On top of the quilt, in the center of the bed, sat a red wooden box with an intricately carved lid.

"Where did that come from?"

"Oh, I really can't say, my dear," the lady answered. "I know it arrived here specifically for you, but I can't remember who brought it or when. All I know is that when you arrived I was supposed to bring you to this room."

"I see," Emma replied, staring intently at the box.

Unlike her guest, Alice May did not seem the least bit curious or perplexed by the box's appearance. "The washroom is just down the hall and lunch will be served downstairs at noon. If you need anything else, just ask."

"Okay. Thank you," Emma said politely, closing the door behind her host as she left.

Emma returned her attention to the box on the bed. It looked virtually identical to the one Matthew had found in the woods, aside from the color. She gently opened the lid and found a similar brass plate with a keyhole inside. This time, however, there was a key inside the box as well. She picked up the key from the box and examined it. A small tag was attached to the handle with thin red ribbon. The tag had only one word printed on it, *HOME*.

When she first arrived in this world, she was still holding the key from the workshop. She had tucked it away in her pocket for fear of dropping it off the top of the building and losing it forever. For all she knew at the time, that key was her ticket home. Now she wasn't sure what to think. Emma retrieved the key from her pocket and compared it to the one from the box. They were identical as far as she could tell. She spent the next several minutes debating the wisdom of using either key in the box. The last two times she had done so it did not turn out well. She had no clue what was going on. All she knew was every time she used a key in one of these boxes she ended up in a strange place with a wicked headache.

It seemed clear to Emma that someone had set this all up. The signs on the street and the room at this house had obviously been designed to lead her to this box and key. The only questions were: who had set all of this up and would using the key take her to someplace better or worse. There was absolutely no way to know for sure, but undaunted the med student continued to try and reason her way through the problem. After nearly twenty minutes of debating with herself, she was no closer to a decision. A large yawn swept over her and her eyes began to feel heavy. She suddenly realized that although it appeared to be midafternoon where she currently was, it had been several hours since she and Matthew had watched the sunset in Cat Rock Park.

"Perhaps a quick nap will help," she said to herself as she laid down on the bed, holding the box on her stomach. "Maybe you should sleep on it, Emma. Who knows? When you wake up you might actually have a clue what to do." A grin swept over her face as her eyes slid shut. It had been an insanely crazy day. Part of her was genuinely stressed over how she would get home, but another part of her was thrilled by the adventure of it all. She gently rested her head on the pillow and within minutes was fast asleep.

* * *

It had taken him the better part of the day, but Matthew had finally followed Silas' breadcrumbs to the *Stay Here Emma B&B*. After being greeted by the ever-cheerful Alice May, he ascended the steps to the second floor of the quaint old house. He paused at the top of the stairs then opened the first door on the right. He anxiously walked into the room and looked around. The red box sat in the middle of the bed, right where Silas had said it would be. He ran over to the bed, opening the box's lid as fast as his nervous fingers would allow. Taking out the device the carpenter had given him he scanned the brass plate inside the box. A relieved smile swept over his face as the digital screen on the front of the device read: EARTH. He pulled a key out from his pocket and inserted it into the keyhole. "I'm right behind you, babe."

* * *

Emma opened her eyes and once again found herself in yet another strange and unfamiliar place. She was a little dizzy, but thankfully the severe nausea and disorientation that had initially accompanied these trips had begun to subside. Although the physical effects were diminishing, the med student was no closer to understanding what was going on. All she knew was every time she put a key into one of those boxes she wound up in some bizarre new place.

To her relief, this was the least odd place she'd been since the forest. A sense of calm washed over her as she realized she was in an apartment somewhat similar to her own. The young woman walked over to the window half expecting to see little green men running around outside. Much to her surprise, she saw nothing of the sort.

"That's the Southland Mall!" she exclaimed. "I'm home!"

Emma stared out the window for several more minutes, just to make sure nothing changed. She scrutinized every little detail looking for aberrations but found none. Being fully assured that she was indeed only a few minutes away from home, she turned her attention back to the rest of the apartment. The room was elegantly furnished and decorated, with evidence of a woman's touch. A pair of soft suede loveseats sat on two sides of what appeared to be a very expensive Persian rug. The room was devoid of electronics. Instead, the walls were lined with shelves stacked full of books. On the end table between the loveseats there were a couple of scented candles and a picture of an older man with a neatly trimmed beard. The man had his arm around a beautiful woman with long black hair.

"Enough sight-seeing Reilly," Emma scolded herself. "Let's get out of here before something else weird happens."

Jinxed by her own words, there was a strange sound behind her as she took the first few steps toward the apartment door. The young woman spun around to see a blue light growing over the center of the rug. The light intensified and expanded, slowly taking on the shape of a person. Emma wasn't sure if she should wait or run, but curiosity had glued her feet to the floor. The light dwindled revealing a red-haired woman with a startled expression.

"Who are you?" both women exclaimed in unison.

"What are you doing here?" the red-haired woman demanded.

"I'm sorry, I don't know how I got here. I just kinda showed up. But don't worry, if this is your place. I didn't touch anything and I was just leaving," Emma nervously explained.

"You! You must be the one who has it!" the woman's voice became increasingly angry. "You won't stand in my way! Give it to me now."

Fear had managed to unglue Emma's feet and she sprinted toward the door to make her escape. "I've had just about enough of this date," she muttered as she fumbled with the deadbolt. She could hear footsteps closing in behind her, which made her all the more frantic. Finally, the lock released and she flung the door wide open. She was about to leap out into the hallway when a sharp pain flooded across the back of her head and blackness began to cloud her vision.

As Emma was drifting off into unconsciousness she heard the woman's voice growl, "I don't know who you are, but nothing is going to stop me!"

* * *

Matthew's eyes opened and adjusted to his new environment. As they did he thought he heard the sound of heavy footsteps running away. He quickly scanned the small apartment room for any sign of Emma but saw none. "That's odd," the engineer mused walking toward the open door. He stepped out into the hallway, but the only indication of activity was an exit door at the end of the hall, closing slowly. Walking back into the room Matthew closed the door behind him and headed toward the window. "Ah, home, sweet home," he sighed happily. "At least that part worked."

His nostalgia was interrupted by a strange sound. The sound was vaguely familiar, but he couldn't quite place where he had previously heard it. As Matthew turned around he saw Silas emerging from the bluish light that was characteristic of traveling through a gateway and he suddenly recalled hearing the same sound when the carpenter had arrived in the workshop. "You made it!" Matthew greeted.

"As did you I see," Silas replied. "For that I am most glad. Did you find your friend?"

"No, but I am sure she found the red box and is back here already," the young man explained. "The door was open when I got here so I figure she had just left. I hate to be rude, but I'm going to take off and see if I can catch up with her." Matthew started toward the door, but then paused and turned back to Silas, "Thanks for .... an interesting time."

"Wait," Silas said calmly but in a tone that was rather forceful. "You can't leave yet, I need your help."

"Forget it, man. I've had enough of your crazy magic doors. I'm going to find my girlfriend."

"But I desperately need someone I can trust to help me." Silas' voice now sounded more grieved than strong. "It turns out that things are just as I feared, actually much worse. You see," the man picked up the photo from the end table. "This apartment belongs to my wife, Tara. That is why I made it the entry port back into this world. I figured it would be secret and secure."

"Good thinking, but…"

"She also had a wooden box that sat on the shelf, right here."

"That's great, but I…"

"It was a brown one," Silas patiently explained.

"Ahh, I see," Matthew said, no longer inching his way toward the door. "The one Emma and I found at the park."

"Indeed. But I now believe that someone was trying to take the box and the workshop key from her when the two of you stumbled across them in the woods."

"We found the key and the box, and traveled to your workshop," Matthew continued on Silas' train of thought.

"Precisely, for which I owe you a great debt of gratitude."

"I don't understand."

"Other than my wife, the key to my workshop is my most valuable possession. If someone were to get a hold of it, they would not only have access to all my supplies, but they could make their own set of keys for every realm I have ever created."

"And travel to all ten worlds freely."

Home, Sweet Home

"No," Silas said, his voice heavy with sorrow. "The doors you saw were just some of my most recent creations. There is a key in the workshop, which leads to the Great Vault where all the doors created by me and every other craftsmen of the past are stored."

"So, if someone got into your workshop they could visit any of those worlds."

"Yes, they could visit, or destroy, or plunder any or all of them."

"Ok, but Emma left the key she found in your workshop, so it is safe now."

"Indeed, it is, but I fear my wife is not," Silas said gravely. "While you were in the unfinished world I returned here and searched through her apartment. I then went looking for her at all of her favorite places around town. There was no sign of her anywhere."

"Perhaps she's just off visiting some other realm," Matthew suggested.

"I do not think so. Tara does not often visit any of my worlds on her own. Even when she does travel alone, she always leaves me a message to let me know where she is. No, I fear that whoever you saw her wrestling with in the park has captured her."

"Listen," Matthew said, sounding genuinely sympathetic. "I'm sorry, I really am, but I just don't think I'm cut out for all this adventure and mystical realms. I'm not a policeman or private eye. I can't help you. I have a nice life here, sure it might be a little vanilla at times, but it's a nice life. All I care about right now is finding Emma and going home." Matthew felt bad as he spoke the words, but it was the truth. He started toward the door, "I do hope you find your wife."

"So do I, my friend."

"Hang on!" Matthew cried as he stooped down to pick something up off the floor. "This is Emma's necklace!" he observed, his voice filled with shock. "What's it doing on the floor? I didn't see it here before."

"You said when you arrived the door was open?" Silas inquired. Again, his face held that thoughtful look that seemed to be quite common to him. "Perhaps the necklace was behind the door and that's why you didn't see it."

"But why would it be behind the door?"

"Yes, and why would the door be open, unless..."

"Unless what?" an overexcited Matthew demanded.

"Unless someone caught her here and then forced her to leave in a hurry," Silas hypothesized. "Perhaps because someone else was arriving through the gateway."

"That's right!" the engineer stated placing the last piece into a puzzle. "When I first got here I thought I heard footsteps running away, but when I got to the hall there was no one."

"I am truly sorry, but I fear that Emma has been taken against her will."

"By the same person who was after your wife, I bet." Matthew agreed.

"It seems our fates are meant to be intertwined after all."

"What do we do now?" Matthew inquired anxiously.

"I think the first thing we should do is recover the brown box from the woods. Once it is secure, we can contemplate our next steps."

* * *

Emma was startled awake by the sensation of cold water being splashed on her face. The red-haired woman dumped the remaining contents of a water bottle on the young woman to ensure she had come fully back to consciousness. The med student quickly observed that she was laying in the back seat of a car with her hands firmly tied together.

"Listen, lady," Emma pleaded. "I don't know who you are or what you're up to, but it has nothing to do with me. Just let me go and you can get on with whatever it is you're trying to do."

"Nice try, sweetheart," the woman responded dryly as she shuffled through the items from Emma's purse. "Where were you before you came to that apartment?"

"I don't know. Some weird place where everything was half missing."

"Strange," the woman replied, sounding genuinely confused. "And how did you get to this half-finished place?"

"You wouldn't believe me if I told you."

"Try me."

"I found a key and put it in the lock of a jewelry box."

"Of course, you did," the woman smiled with wicked satisfaction. "And where did you find this box?"

Emma considered explaining the whole story, but it all sounded too farfetched, even to her, so she just gave the short answer, "Cat Rock Park."

"Excellent. And did you happen to find the key there as well?"

"Yeah."

"I knew it. You will come with me and show me exactly where you found the key," the woman commanded.

Emma looked out the window of the car and could see the trees of the park nearby. She could also see that it was the middle of the night and the sky was dark. The woman opened the rear door and pulled her captive out of the car. The parking lot was virtually empty, aside from Matthew's car that still sat where he had parked it when they had arrived on their date. The park itself looked deserted as the pair marched down the trail and into the woods.

As they walked along the trail Emma inquired, "Who are you and why are you doing this to me?"

"My name is Morgan and you, my dear, are completely inconsequential. It is the key that I want. The key to the room with the doors. Once I have that you will be free to go."

"I don't have that key," Emma explained.

"Yes I know, but perhaps if you show me where you found your key, the key I desire will be close by."

Emma realized that the key her captor was looking for was not going to be in the woods. She clearly remembered leaving it on the workbench. She also realized that it was in her best interest not to mention that fact or that she had ever visited the *'room with the doors.'* She didn't know what this crazy woman was up to, but something told her the situation would only get worse if the woman thought Emma no longer had any value to her.

"It was just up here, I think," Emma said, wandering off the trail into the bush.

* * *

"It was somewhere in this area, I think," Matthew said scanning the ground with the light from his phone. "We had been sitting in that clearing and heard voices in this direction."

"Perhaps we are too late," Silas said dejectedly. "Perhaps whoever it is that attacked my wife and your girlfriend has already come back and found it."

"Yeah, I'm positive the box was right around here. Hang on," Matthew said as a sense of deja vu swept over him. "Do you hear voices?"

"Yes," the carpenter whispered. "They're coming from over this way."

The two men made their way through the trees as quietly as possible, moving toward the sound of the voices. As they drew closer they could see a dim light and two people up ahead.

"I'm pretty sure it was around here," Emma said, scouring the ground for the key she knew wasn't there.

"Keep looking, and make it quick," Morgan demanded.

"You there!" Silas shouted. "What's the meaning of all this?"

Morgan took one quick glance down at Emma and then sprinted off through the woods with Silas in pursuit. Matthew ran to where Emma was kneeling on the ground and flopped down next to her.

"Are you okay?" he asked.

"Yeah, I'm fine," she said with a relieved smile. "What in the world is going on!"

"It's a long and very bizarre story," the young man answered with a slight chuckle. "I'm not sure I completely understand or believe it myself. All I care about right now though is that you're okay."

– 5 –
Where Do We Start?

After spending several minutes simply hugging one another Emma and Matthew eventually began to compare stories and put together the pieces of what had been going on. Matthew did his best to explain all about Silas, the doors, and keys, and she told him what she could about Morgan and her obsession with the workshop. Eventually, Silas returned and informed them that Morgan got away.

"If she appeared in the apartment through a gateway, then she must have the brown box and at least some of Tara's keys," Matthew surmised

"Yes, which more than likely means she has Tara as well," Silas confirmed.

"Who is this crazy woman, anyway?" Emma asked.

"Morgan is, or should I say was, one of my wife's dearest friends. They became very close and eventually I offered to show her one of my realms. It's not something I usually do, but I felt certain we could trust her."

"Apparently not," Matthew said flatly.

"Yes, apparently not," the carpenter sadly agreed. "We took her to a nice little world, full of fields and wildlife – very idyllic. Of course she loved it. After our return, Morgan kept talking about going back to that world again. Then she started asking about what other realms existed and if she could visit them someday as well. I began to feel like she was becoming overly enamored with it all, so I started to pull back from her a little. Tara still spent time with Morgan, but my wife refused to talk about my work or any of the realms I had created. Not long ago, my wife told me the two of them had had a falling out. She didn't say over what exactly, but it wasn't hard to surmise. I had thought Morgan would just give us the cold shoulder for a while. At worst she'd try and tell others about the things I can do, but who in their right mind would believe her?"

"Apparently she wasn't content to just let it go," Matthew observed.

"Indeed."

"So, what do we do now?" Emma inquired.

"You mean besides go home and forget all this ever happened?" Matthew asked. His girlfriend shot him an icy look which clearly communicated *that* was not an option. "Just kidding. Of course, we're not going to do that."

"I will return to my workshop," Silas proposed. "I will make a new set of keys to match the ones Tara had with her, which we assume Morgan now has."

"What should we do?"

The carpenter pulled out a purple box from his satchel and handed it to Emma. "Once I am gone, take this box and hide it somewhere. Somewhere safe. Morgan knows who you are, so it can't be any place she'd think to look for it. We can ill afford for her to have more than one box at her disposal."

"I think I know a place," Matthew offered.

"Very well. Once the box is hidden go to the Red Robin near the Southland Mall and wait for me to return."

With that, Silas pulled out a key and inserted it into the keyhole of the purple box. The now-familiar light enveloped him and a moment later he was gone. Matthew put his arms around Emma and the two of them walked back toward the path to the parking lot.

"Well, you can't say I don't know how to show a girl a good time," the young man joked.

"Oh, brother!"

"Hey, by the way, there was something I wanted to ask you," he said, his voice taking on a more serious tone.

"Yes, what is it," she replied sounding a tinge nervous.

"Do you mind driving home? I've kinda had a long day," he smirked.

"Oh, *you've* had a long day?" Emma feigned indignation. "Get in the car, Romeo."

* * *

"Yeah, just a minute," a voice shouted from behind the apartment door.

"Are you sure this is a good idea," Emma asked.

"It's perfect," Matthew insisted. "We need somewhere safe and secure that is not directly linked to either one of us. Your place is out. My place is out. My office is out. The med lab is out."

"I suppose, but..."

"Plus, I already have a spare key, and it's only a couple blocks from Tara's apartment and the re-entry gateway."

The latch inside clicked as it was undone and then the apartment door swung open. They were greeted by a young man with a wide smile. He combed his wavy blonde hair away from his eyes and greeted them enthusiastically, "Hey! How are you guys doing? How did the big date go, huh?"

"Umm, unexpectedly," Matthew replied, trying to discretely signal that the topic was out of bounds. "Can we come in for a second, Joel?"

"Yeah, sure, you bet," Matthew's friend said sounding both concerned and confused. He could tell from their demeanor that things had not gone as planned at the park and a quick glance at Emma's hand revealed it was still ringless. "What's up, guys?"

The three friends sat down in Joel's surprisingly spacious living room. Although food truck vendor doesn't sound like a very prestigious occupation, Joel was a qualified and well-respected chef in the area. He had built his business up to include four separate trucks offering food of a quality which rivaled some of the city's best restaurants.

Where Do We Start?

Matthew took a minute to ponder where to start and how much he should actually reveal to his old friend. As he was thinking something caught his eye that made him chuckle. "Is Jules here, by chance?"

"Yeah, she's just in the washroom," Joel answered sounding surprised. "How'd you know?"

"You've got a little something here," Matthew replied pointing to his bottom lip.

"Oh," the chef giggled sheepishly. He wiped the lipstick off the corner of his mouth and then shrugged his shoulders. "Thanks, Matt. You know how it is."

"Ah-hem," Emma elbowed her boyfriend in the ribs trying to get the conversation back on topic.

"Right, um, I need a favor."

"You name it, buddy. What's up?"

"You see, the thing is, the other night at the park…"

"Hi, everyone," a young woman with sleek features greeted them as she walked into the room.

"Hey, babe. Matt and Emma just stopped by to, well, I don't know why they're here. They just stopped by."

"Do you guys want a drink or something?" Joel's girlfriend offered.

"No, thanks, Jules, we're good," Matthew said politely, trying to get back to the matter at hand. "Here's the thing – long story short, we found this box and we need a safe place to store it for a while."

"Oh, I get it," Joel smiled broadly. He assumed that something had gone wrong at the park and this was Matt's Plan B. No doubt the ring was inside this jewelry box and his friend needed a safe place to keep it where Emma wouldn't accidentally stumble across it. "Sure, not a problem."

"Thanks, buddy," Matthew said handing over the box.

"How 'bout I just put it over here on the bookshelf?"

"Okay, but not too high," Emma interjected. "I want to be able to reach it too."

"Sure, no problem," Joel replied with a devilish grin. Then, stretching his lanky arms upward, he slid the box onto the very top shelf. "How's this?"

"You're such a pest," Juliette chided. "Bring it back down."

Joel immediately complied to his girlfriends' request, as he always did. Juliette was about to complete her Master of Business degree and was a regional manager at a local bank, both of which were extremely impressive accomplishments at her age. She was bright, beautiful and charming, and the chef was convinced that on every possible level he was insanely lucky to be hooked up with a girl like her – and he treated her accordingly.

"So, Joel told me all about your big date. How'd it go?"

* * *

Silas entered Tara's apartment through the gateway and quickly looked around to make sure he was alone. He made one last quick but thorough search for any sign of Tara's keys or any clue as to where Morgan may have taken his wife. The carpenter knew that searching the apartment again was redundant. He had already scoured the place twice and found nothing. Nonetheless, he couldn't convince himself to abandon the faint hope that things weren't as bad as they seemed. After finding nothing new, he made the short walk from the apartment to the mall to meet up with his new friends. As he entered the Red Robin Matthew called out to him from a corner of the restaurant, but much to Silas' surprise he was not alone.

"Hey, Silas, good to see you," Matthew greeted. "Guys this is the man I told you about. Silas, this is Joel and Juliette."

"Hello," the man said politely, but with unmistakable apprehension. "I didn't realize you were bringing guests."

"It's fine, really," the young man explained. "Joel is a good friend and I'd trust him with my life."

"We just got to thinking about it," Emma added. "And we figured maybe we could use a little extra help."

"But all we've told them so far is that we met a really decent guy who urgently needed some help,"

Matthew reassured. "So, if you don't want to share your private stuff with strangers, that's fine."

"Totally, man," Joel jumped into the conversation. "We don't mean to butt into your business. Just say the word and we'll take our burgers and split."

Silas pondered the situation carefully for several minutes. His craft had always been a closely guarded secret, and what had transpired with Morgan was a poignant example of why. He had only dared to reveal as much as he did to Matthew and Emma out of sheer desperation and because they had already found their way into his workshop. Extending the circle any further seemed like a terrible risk – one that could have dire consequences. On the other hand, time was of the essence and as Emma had pointed out, he really could use all the help he could get. Knowing that Morgan was in possession of Tara's key and a box filled him with enough dread to consider Matthew's proposal. "Very well," he reluctantly agreed, "if you trust them Matthew, so shall I."

"Cool, so what's the sitch?" Joel eagerly asked.

Silas spent the next 20 minutes doing his best to explain the situation to the two newcomers. As he told the story of what he did in his workshop and what had happened to his wife, Matthew and Emma confirmed the facts with their own experiences. Not surprisingly, Joel was all in right from the start. His girlfriend, however, needed a little more convincing.

"So, you're telling me that the box you left at Joel's place is some kind of trans-dimensional teleportation device?"

"No, that's not how it works," Silas corrected.

"But basically, yeah," Emma chimed in. "I had a hard time coming to grips with it too, but I have no other explanation for what happened to us. In the end, I decided to just accept it, even if I didn't understand it."

"Hmm, okay," Juliette mused.

"You don't have to be totally convinced now," Matthew suggested. "You just have to be willing to turn the key once and see what happens. After that, the rest will take care of itself."

"Well then, if we are all on board, let's continue," Silas stated.

"What did you find out?" Emma asked.

"Tara had several keys with her at the time Morgan captured her. I now believe that she purposefully separated the key to the workshop when she realized she might not get away. We must assume, however, that Morgan now has all the other keys that were in my wife's possession."

"Exactly how many keys is that?" the engineer inquired apprehensively.

"About a dozen, I believe."

"Holy falafel!" Joel blurted out. "A dozen keys for a dozen worlds? That's wild!"

"It is also a lot of ground for us to cover," Silas stated solemnly.

"And Morgan could be heading to any one of those realms at any time," Matthew added.

"So, what's the plan?" Emma asked.

"I will take half the keys and the four of you will take the other half," the carpenter proposed.

"Classic divide and conquer," Joel cheered, "I like it."

"Shouldn't one of us come with you?" Emma inquired.

"No, I don't think so," the carpenter replied. "I know my way around these realms and will be able to cover ground quite quickly on my own. It would be best if the four of you stuck together I think."

"What are the odds we're actually going to catch this Morgan person anyways," Joel questioned. "I mean, she could be anywhere in any of those dozen places you talked about. How are we supposed to track her down? And what's to keep her from just hopping from one place to the next? We could be chasing our tails for years."

"You must remember that Morgan is looking for the key to the workshop," Silas explained. "This will drive all of her actions, which gives us somewhat of an advantage."

"But Joel's right," Matthew objected. "She could stay one world ahead of us the whole time."

"Or enter a world right after we leave," Emma added.

"That is why I made these," the carpenter said, grimly pulling out a pair of black keys.

"What are those?" Juliette asked.

"They are nullification keys. Once you have used this key in a box the lock is valid for one more turn only. After that it can no longer open any gateway to anywhere."

"Which means anyone trying to use the box after that point would be stuck in that realm," the engineer surmised.

"Yeah, so what you're saying is don't screw it up," Joel chuckled nervously.

"Indeed," Silas affirmed. "After you have searched a realm use the nullification key and then open a gateway and leave."

"That way," Emma picked up the train of thought. "If Morgan enters that realm after we've left, there will be no way for her to get out!"

"That is correct. If we do not capture Morgan during our initial search of all twelve realms, we can return to each world one by one, knowing that she will not be able to escape."

"Wouldn't we be stuck there too?" Juliette inquired.

"Not if we bring a new, unlocked box with us."

"Too bad we couldn't just find Tara's box and use one of these keys in it," Matthew hypothesized. "That way she would be cut off from accessing any of your realms, including the workshop."

"Very true," the carpenter agreed, "but since we have no idea where she's hidden it, tracking her through the other worlds is currently our best option."

"Okay then, where do we start?" Joel said eagerly.

Silas handed Matthew a set of six keys on a ring with a tag that read: Mr. Spiffy's Car Wash. He also gave him one of the nullification keys, which Matthew immediately added to the key ring as well. They agreed that they should have some way to update each other on what progress had been made. At the same time, they did not want to waste time waiting for each other to return before they could move on to the next realm. In the end, they decided that Joel's apartment would make the ideal rendezvous point. The purple box was already there and they could use the whiteboard on the fridge to update each other on their progress.

"One question," Emma said, "how do we know which key is which?"

"Yeah, they all look identical to me," Juliette agreed.

"Oh, well, I never thought of that," Silas admitted. "I can tell the difference just by holding them. It's hard to explain, but I can just, kind of, hear what realm a key is for when it is in my hand. Tara was starting to master this skill as well, but it took her a very long time to do so."

"Something tells me we don't have that kind of time," Joel quipped.

"Indeed not. Matthew, do you still have the device I gave you to scan the boxes?"

"Yeah, it's right here."

"Excellent. If you look at the bottom you will see a clithridiate opening."

"A what?" the engineer asked, examining the device. "Oh, you mean a key-shaped hole!"

"Yes, that is what I said," Silas replied matter-of-factly. "The device will scan any key you insert and tell you which realm it is linked to."

"Does Morgan have one of these devices, too?" Emma asked.

"No, she does not, which is another great advantage for us. She will be traveling blindly from one world to the next."

"I guess that's it then," Matthew said. "Good luck everyone."

"Thank you, my friends," Silas added. "I do not think I could do this all on my own."

"Don't worry," the med student said in a soft and kind voice. "You'll get your wife back."

"I truly hope so, I would be lost without her."

After making their way back to Joel's place, Silas gave a few last-minute instructions on where Morgan might be searching for a workshop key. Juliette gave Silas her key to the apartment so he could come and go as he pleased. Joel grabbed the purple box off the shelf and set it on his coffee table. He opened the lid and saw, for the first time, the brass plate with the keyhole in it.

"Wow, you guys weren't kidding, were you? I mean, I didn't really think you were lying, but man, there it is. We're really going to do this, aren't we?"

"Man up, Carson," Matthew demanded. "You're looking wussy in front of the girls." Everyone burst into laughter, which was the tension breaker they all desperately needed. "Okay, who's first?"

"I believe you four should go first," the carpenter suggested. "To be honest, I've never sent four people simultaneously through a gateway before. I have heard of it being done many years ago though. So, it *should* be fine."

"And with that rousing vote of confidence, here we go!" Joel chimed.

"Make sure you are all touching each other when the key is turned, or somebody will get left behind."

"That's not a huge deal right now, but we certainly don't want it to happen on the return trip," Emma theorized.

The four friends held hands as Matthew inserted the key into the brass plate. "The first time's a little rough, but it will pass," he informed them. "See you on the other side." The engineer turned the key and the four young people were enveloped in light, then they were gone.

"Hmm, it actually worked," Silas grinned, with the slightest tinge of surprise in his voice. He once again opened the box, which had automatically shut after the gateway closed, and inserted one of his keys. A moment later the apartment was filled with the bright bluish light of the gateway.

* * *

As the bright light faded, Silas found himself in a dark and desolate place. The terrain was harsh and uneven. Jagged black rocks burst out of the ground at random and odd angles. There were no signs of life, no plants or animals to be seen. The sky was overcast and dark, with heavy black clouds that muted the sun's light leaving this realm very dim and depressing. There was no path or road to speak of, nonetheless, the carpenter seemed to know where he was going. He made his way carefully around and over the dark stones moving steadily, although the uneven terrain slowed his progress.

After some time, Silas came to an area where the tall jagged rocks gave way to smaller ones and his view opened up. Ahead he could see what appeared to be a series of dark caves carved out of the ebony stone. As he drew nearer, the thin metal bars sealing the cave entrances also became visible. His pace slowed even further as he approached cautiously.

"Hello?" he called out softly. "Hello? Is anyone there?"

At first there was no response, so he continued to move forward slowly. Of all the realms Tara had keys for this was the last one he wanted to encounter Morgan in. The carpenter took a few more cautious steps and then called out again. "Hello? Anyone?"

There was a quiet shuffling within one of the caves. Silas stopped dead in his tracks and waited. Even though the prisoners were locked in their cells he remained on guard. After another moment, he called out one more time, "Hello?"

"Silas! Is that you?" a woman's voice cried out from the darkness of one of the caves.

"Tara!" he shouted, running toward the cave. He reached the entrance, which had the number VII carved into the stone above it but was stopped short by the bars that blocked the way. "Tara is that you, my love?"

"Oh Silas," a woman with long dark hair moved out of the shadows and up against the bars. "You won't believe what has happened!"

"I know, my dear. Morgan has betrayed us."

"She has my box and my keys. Oh, I'm so sorry, I should have listened to you."

"You have nothing to be sorry for. This treachery belongs solely to Morgan."

"What are you doing here? You need to go and protect the workshop," Tara said frantically.

"The workshop is safe for the time being," the carpenter assured his wife. "Morgan did not find that key, and it is now safely stored inside the workshop itself."

"Oh, thank goodness! But there is more you need to know."

"I have some friends who are helping me secure the other worlds as we speak. We will track Morgan down and make her pay for her betrayal. Now, let's get you out of there shall we?"

"That's just it," Tara explained sadly. "I don't think you can."

"What do you mean?" her husband asked, as he strode away from the cave.

Silas moved quickly toward a stone pillar with a large rectangular panel sitting on top. There was a three-foot square wooden plate on the ground in front of the pillar. He moved around to the back side of the stone column and examined the controls on the panel. On the left side of the panel was a large dial surrounded by 25 numbered circles. The carpenter urgently turned the dial to point at the circle marked VII, then shifted his gaze to the right side of the board. His hand reached for something but grasped only air

"What the blazes?" Silas exclaimed. He stared down in disbelief at the panel, seeing only an empty keyhole. "Where is the key?"

"That's what I was trying to tell you," his wife shouted from her cell. "She took it."

"But ... but that was the only key for these cells. If she has taken it, I have no way to get you out."

"Yes, I think that was her plan. I think she believes that you would trade the key to your workshop for the key to open my cell."

"And how could I not?" Suddenly a mortified look swept over his face. "If she used the panel to put you into a cell, that means she could have ..." Silas bolted away and began to check the numerous other cave cells contained in the rock structure. With each cell he investigated he became more and more distraught. Several minutes later he returned to Tara's cave looking utterly dejected. "They're gone. They are all gone!"

– 6 –
To the Trees

"Is everyone okay?" Matthew asked.

"I'm gonna hurl!" Joel exclaimed.

"Jules, are you alright?" Emma asked, putting her arm around the woozy traveler. "It will start to wear off in a few minutes, I promise."

Matthew surveyed the area, trying to get his bearings on where they were and, more importantly where they needed to go. The realm they had entered was a large forest with tall sturdy trees, similar in size to the redwoods he had seen in California as a kid. A quick scan of the immediate area showed no sign of Morgan or any other inhabitants. Silas had explained that almost all worlds he had created were inhabited. Most realms had sentient beings of one kind or another. Some were similar to the people of earth and others were quite different. He also told them they would come across many forms of wildlife, both familiar and strange. Most of the beasts were friendly, however, there were a few species one would be wise to avoid.

"Well," Joel stated boldly, wiping his mouth on his sleeve. "The good news is I don't have to hurl, anymore."

"How's Jules doing, Em?"

"I think she's getting there. Give us another minute or two."

"Dude, you really weren't kidding," the chef said, looking at his new surroundings. "That was some trip and *this* is a trip too!"

"I know," his friend agreed. "It's simultaneously hard to believe and hard to deny." Matthew instantly realized how corny, albeit accurate his statement sounded. "Let's check things out a bit while we're waiting for the girls to recover. You go that way and I'll go over here, but don't go far. We'll meet back here in five minutes."

"Sounds good, chief." Joel chirped heading off to investigate the area. The size of the trees made it difficult to see for any significant distance. The timbers were not only of immense diameter, but they rose high into the air creating an almost solid canopy of leaves. As he weaved his way through the forest he felt the smooth bark of each tree he passed. The tree trunks, a light tan in color, had deep vertical grooves winding their way upward, causing the chef to have a sudden craving for Twizzlers.

Joel did not want to wander off too far or heaven forbid lose his way back to his friends. He was about to turn around and head back when his hand discovered something on the surface of one of the trees. He examined the trunk momentarily and then said aloud, "Yep, I'm done."

* * *

"It does get better, I promise," the med student comforted her friend. "The first time it happened to me I just laid on the floor for I don't know how long. Every time I tried to open my eyes everything was spinning uncontrollably. Things kept spinning even with my eyes closed, but at least I couldn't see it all twirling by."

Juliette gave an uneasy chuckle. "I know what you mean. I feel like I got hit by a truck."

"Take your time. The boys are having a quick look around. They'll be back in a minute."

"Thanks, I think I'm okay now," the bank manager said, slowly sitting up and leaning against a tree. Juliette had always been one of those people who liked to be in control, which made pretty much everything about this experience highly unsettling.

"For what it's worth, I hardly felt anything this time."

"I'm looking forward to that, I'm just not looking forward to the three or four more times I have to do this to get there."

"Everything okay here, Em?" Matthew asked, returning a few moments later.

"Yup, I think we're all good."

"What did you boys find?" Juliette asked, rising to her feet with a little help from Matthew.

"Nada," Joel declared, rejoining the group. "Nada in every direction as far as I could see."

"Yeah, me to," the engineer confirmed.

"Except for this," Joel said pulling out his phone and displaying a recently snapped photo.

"What is that?" his girlfriend asked.

"Claw marks. Freaking huge claw marks!"

"Whoa," Matthew gasped, zooming in on the photo for a better look.

"Yeah, and that's not all. They go further up the tree than I can reach. Which means somewhere out there is one big, sharp-clawed hombre roaming about."

"Who says there's only one?" Matthew pointed out.

"Whatever they are, or however many there are out there, I don't want to be around next time they stroll by," Emma declared.

"So, what do we do now, Matt?" Juliette asked.

"I'm not sure. Silas said that the entry point would be in or near civilization, as would the box. So, I guess if we want to find the box we need to find some people."

"What do we do," Joel pondered. "Just pick a direction and go?"

"No," Juliette interjected. "Our best move is to walk in a spiral out from this point. It might take a little longer, but if we just start heading out we could be going the exact opposite direction of where we need to be."

"Makes sense to me, Jules," Matthew agreed. "I hereby nominate you to be in charge of navigation. Lead the way!"

"The sooner the better, babe," Joel quipped, helping her to her feet.

* * *

The group had been walking through the dense forest for two hours. Although it was difficult to be certain, they believed they were now several hundred yards out from the original entry point. At no point in their hike had they seen any indication of people or villages nearby.

"I don't think this is working, guys," Emma sighed.

"Oh, thank goodness!" Joel exclaimed. "I totally agree, I just didn't want to be the one to say it. I mean, it was a great plan, Jules. It's just that there is nothing here."

"You're right," Juliette conceded. "If there were anything around here we should have seen some sign of it by now."

"Back to square one, I guess," Matthew said dejectedly. "Hey! What was that? Something just hit me in the head."

"Probably just an acorn or pinecone or something, bro."

"Did you guys see that?" the engineer asked, looking up into the treetops.

"See what, Matthew?"

"Dude, give me a boost," Matthew instructed.

"What are you up to Matt?" Joel asked as he interlocked his hands.

"There!" Matthew cheered. "Hey! You up there. Come down here and talk to us, please!" The others in the group looked up into the dense foliage but did not see anything. "I swear I saw someone up there."

"Hey, we just want to be your friends!" Emma called out to the unseen visitor.

After a few moments of silence the leaves began to ruffle, and then the face of a man appeared, peeking upside down through the branches. The man stared at the four companions for a minute, sizing them up. Then, with surprising speed and agility, he made his way down one of the large trees, landing on the ground several feet away from where they stood. The man leaned out from behind a tree and continued to look them over. For a man who climbed trees and apparently lived in the woods, he was surprisingly well groomed – clean shaven with his hair neatly combed to one side. He wore a light-weight shirt, with a drawstring in the lower hem and something that resembled a pair of snug fitting sweatpants. The most notable part of his wardrobe however, was his bare feet.

"Hi, my name is Matthew."

"Matthew," the man repeated.

"Maybe he doesn't speak English," Joel suggested.

"Yes, Matthew. What is your name?"

There was a long pause. It was uncertain whether the man was going to respond or scamper back up the tree. Finally, the man spoke, "My name is Winston Charles. It is a pleasure to meet you, Mr. Matthew."

"Ahh, thanks," the dumbfounded visitor sputtered. "Umm, these, these are my friends, Emma, Joel, and Juliette."

"Very nice to meet you all," Winston replied politely. He stepped out from behind the tree cautiously and then squatted down on the ground. "You are not from around here, are you?"

"Is it that obvious?" Juliette laughed.

"I'm afraid so, Ms. Juliette," Winston answered with a grin. "Our people do not spend so much time on the ground. I have been watching you wander in circles for quite some time and I am not sure what to make of it all."

"What do you mean?"

"What I mean, Ms. Emma, is simply, since you have come to this world I assume you are friends with Mr. Silas and Ms. Tara. And yet, you are alone and seem to know nothing of our ways. Tell me, Mr. Matthew, what is your purpose here."

"Silas did send us here," Matthew explained.

"He was just a little sketchy on the details," Joel chimed in. "Sorry Matt, you've got this."

"Silas told us that when we arrived we should seek out the people who lived here, which is what we have been trying to do, but clearly we have not been doing a very good job of it."

"Intriguing," the man said thoughtfully. "And what would you do, Mr. Matthew, if you found these people you are looking for?"

Matthew looked at his companions as he tried to decide what to say next. Winston seemed like a decent fellow, someone he could trust. Perhaps telling him the truth could fast track their mission. On the other hand, it would be wise to conceal the fact that they possessed several gateway keys and especially the nullification key.

"Tell him, Matthew," Emma encouraged.

"We are your friends Winston, but someone is coming who is not. Someone who has betrayed Silas and Tara and is looking for unfettered access to all their realms. We need to find the people who live here, so we can stop her."

Winston stared at each of the four visitors carefully for a very long time, without uttering a word. The friends stood nervously awaiting his judgment. Then, without warning, he turned and raced back up the tree, disappearing into the canopy.

"Wow, did you see that guy move!" Joel gawked. "He flew up that tree like it was nothing."

"What do we do now?" Juliette asked. "Should we wait, or did we just blow our one chance?"

"I don't know," Matthew admitted.

Suddenly, one end of a heavy rope burst through the leaves and fell to the ground. Winston appeared once again, climbing down the tree as quickly as he had gone up. When he reached the ground, he scampered over to the rope hanging down from the tree top and gave it a strong tug to ensure it was secure.

"Alright, come this way," the man instructed. "Our people stay off the ground to avoid predators, especially after dark. Our town is built on the top of the trees. As you can see, we have become quite adept at climbing up and down. However, strangers like yourselves would not likely make it to the top. So, please, come take hold of this rope and my friends will pull you up."

"All of us at once?" Juliette asked.

"Haha," Winston laughed. "You can't climb trees without strong arms, Ms. Juliette. You will be fine."

The rope had several loops at the bottom for each of them to put one foot into. They gathered around closely and positioned themselves to get a strong grip. When they were ready Winston called out and the rope began to ascend into the treetops. The four friends nervously held on as the rope's slack began to disappear.

"ARPAGE! ARPAGE!" Winston shouted in a panicked voice. "Hang on."

The rope began to raise the off-worlders from the ground quickly and in a rather jerking motion. They were about to question what was happening when a blood-curdling growl echoed through the wood behind them.

"ARPAGE!" Joel shouted out. He did not know the precise translation of the word, but assumed it meant *'pull faster'*.

They were raised higher and higher into the air. Once their feet were off the ground the rope began to twirl. As they spun around each one got a brief look at the beast that was producing the spine-chilling cries. It appeared to be something akin to a sabretooth tiger, though much larger than one would have suspected. The animal sped towards the dangling off-worlders, propelled at an impressive velocity by its six muscular legs. The bottom of the rope was nearly 20 feet off the ground when the beast arrived. It lunged up into the air, swiping at the visitors with its front paws. One of the animal's razor-sharp claws came just close enough to nick the heel of Emma's left shoe, sending it tumbling down through the air. The creature circled around, preparing to take another run at the off-worlders.

"Hey! Hey! Hey!" shouted Winston, who was still on the ground below. His calls drew the attention of the beast who turned to pursue its new prey. Winston ducked behind a nearby tree and began scampering upward.

Before they could see if their new friend managed to escape, the visitors entered the tree's canopy. It took several minutes to pass through a thick layer of branches and leaves, but eventually, they emerged back into the clear air. When they reached the top they saw two men similar in appearance to Winston holding the rope which ran through a pulley on the end of a hoist arm. The men kept the rope steady as the four visitors nervously stepped onto a wooden platform.

"I told you it would be fine," Winston greeted casually, despite breathing heavily.

"Winston, are you okay?" Emma asked, feeling great affection for the man who had just saved their lives.

"Oh yes, Ms. Emma," he replied, chest still heaving, "I'm just fine. That was a rather close call, I must say."

"A little too close," Matthew clarified.

"It certainly did get the old heart pumping."

"What was that thing?" Juliette asked.

"We call it a kuleta-kifo."

"Yeah, and it calls *us* lunch," Joel smirked.

"Well no need to fear, Mr. Joel. They can't get up here. Now, my new friends," Winston said motioning for them to turn around and look the opposite direction, "welcome to Arbolada!"

"Dude, check this place out!" the chef gasped.

"What is it, Mr. Joel?"

"I don't know, man. I guess I just expected to see little huts or treehouses or something."

"This is amazing," Emma said.

The four friends looked around in wonder. What they saw was not the primitive dwellings they had all anticipated. Instead, they were surrounded by a city. Buildings, one or two stories tall, stretched as far as the eye could see. Though constructed entirely of wood, Arbolada looked surprisingly similar to the suburbs of Boston.

"How?" the engineer began. "How is this possible? There's no way these trees could support the weight of all this. No way."

"Perhaps not in your world, Mr. Matthew," Winston, who was once again squatting down, grinned. "But Mr. Silas designed these to be stronger than – what is it he called it – oh yes, stronger than steel. In fact, we have to go to a different part of the forest to harvest trees to build with because we have no tools that will cut through these ones."

"Fascinating."

"Would you like to look around?"

"I think it's safe to say that we all certainly would," Matthew replied.

"Very well, follow me." Winston led the travelers through the town showing them various buildings, shops, and homes, including his own. Much of it seemed very familiar and normal, but other parts were undeniably out of place. After a while, they halted the tour to stop for drinks at a local restaurant. Surprisingly, there were no chairs in the establishment and the tables were at half their normal height.

"Just sit anywhere you like, Mr. Winston," the restaurant owner called out as the group walked in.

Winston led his guests to a round table off to one side and squatted down next to it. The visitors all tried to squat as well, but most of them couldn't do it comfortably or didn't last long before their muscles gave out and they switched to kneeling instead. Joel just sat cross-legged on the floor, which left the table at a comically tall height compared to his body.

"Winston," Emma began gently. "I don't mean to be rude, but why do you guys always sit like that?"

"Yeah," Matthew chimed in. "And you walk quite differently too. Kind of squatty and you use your hands on the ground, almost like a second set of feet. Although, I suppose here *we're* the ones who walk differently."

"Ha ha, very true Mr. Matthew. Not many of us have seen people walk around so straight up before! Mr. Silas has shown me how he walks in your world, but when he's here he usually walks as we do."

"It makes sense," Juliette suggested, "for people who are so adept at climbing trees."

"I suppose so, Ms. Juliette. I've never really thought much about it. It's the way everyone has always done it and it works very well for us. It is just natural for us I suppose. Now, what would you like to drink?"

"I don't know, what's good here?" Matthew asked.

"Oh, just about everything. Mr. Alistair is quite the cook."

"Say," Joel said, his eye's gleaming, "do you think I could go back into the kitchen with him and see how he does his thing? I'm almost certain you guys have some pretty unique dishes here. Well, unique for us anyways."

"I'm sure that can be arranged, Mr. Joel. Mr. Alistair is a good friend of mine and a very agreeable chap."

A few minutes later Alistair came over to their table and took their order, which Winston made on behalf of everyone. Joel followed Alistair back to the kitchen, doing his best to imitate the walking posture of the locals, which was hysterically entertaining for everyone. As they waited for their drinks to be prepared they discussed other similarities and differences between their two worlds. Both sides seemed to be fascinated by the conversation.

"Mr. Winston!" a young man shouted as he burst into the restaurant. "There you are. Thank goodness."

"What is it, Mr. Callum?"

"More off-worlders, on the north end of town," the young man panted.

"Mr. Matthew, are you expecting any others?"

"No," Matthew answered and then looked at the young man. "Is it a woman?"

"I do not know."

"Maybe Silas has come to tell us he has already caught her," Juliette suggested hopefully.

"It is not Mr. Silas," Callum stated. "We all know Mr. Silas and his arrival would not have generated concern."

"If it is Morgan, she will be looking for the key," Matthew declared.

"There are no keys here," Winston said. "Mr. Silas is very clear about that rule."

"This place is much bigger than I expected," Emma said. "How are we going to track her down?"

"We don't have to," Matthew explained. "Eventually she will head for the box. That's where we'll be waiting."

"What should we do, Mr. Matthew?"

"Just stay out of her way, Winston. She's dangerous. Don't give her any cause to hurt someone."

"Mr. Callum go spread the word. How can I help, Mr. Matthew?"

"Can you take us to the gateway box? Do you know where it is?"

"Certainly."

"Morgan is mean, but the five of us should be able to easily subdue her," Emma said. "So, just keep the rest of your people out of harm's way. We don't want anyone else to get hurt."

"Or used as hostages," Juliette added.

"Very well. Mr. Callum will get the word out. My people will give her a wide berth. In the meantime, let's get you to the gateway box. It's not far from here, but if she is coming from the north, we should move quickly."

"Your order is up!" Joel declared proudly, carrying a tray full of cups out from the kitchen with Mr. Alistair trailing behind. He slid the tray gently on to the table with a broad smile. "What? Did I miss something?"

– 7 –
Crank & Lug

"Quickly, this way," Winston instructed.

The group made its way through town, running along the plank sidewalks which lined the wooden streets. As much as Matthew would have liked to continue to admire the architecture of this strange place, he had more urgent matters to deal with. The further they went the more he could feel a sense of agitation and apprehension at their presence. It could simply have been that Callum's message was spreading and onlookers were wondering if these were the off-worlders they were supposed to be cautious of. On the other hand, it was possible that the people of Arbolada held Matthew and his friends responsible for bringing the others here and putting their community at risk.

"It is not far from here," Winston explained. "The box is inside a house of thankfulness."

"A what?" Joel asked.

"I believe, Mr. Joel, in your world you would call it a, um, church?"

"How far is it?" Matthew asked as he continued to jog to keep up with Winston's scampering pace.

"Just around the corner, Mr. Matthew."

As they rounded the corner, they could see a sizable building with a steeple. They entered through the ornate wooden doors to find a large open space with nothing in it but a small covered table at the front.

"This way," Winston directed. "The box is under the table."

"Okay, we need some kind of plan here," Matthew said.

"This room is pretty wide open," Joel observed, "not too many places to hide."

"Winston, are there any other exits?" Matthew asked.

"Yes, there is one up here to the left."

"And there is an office or something up there on the right too," Emma noted.

"Okay," the engineer thought for a moment. "Joel, you and Jules wait up in the balcony. When Morgan comes in, you guys come down the stairs at the back and block off that exit."

"Got it."

"Okay."

"I'll take the front exit with Emma," Matthew said. "And Winston, you can camp out in that room over there. Nobody moves until she is in the middle of the room. We don't want her slipping out."

"Right," Emma agreed. "But we have to make sure we stop her before she gets to the box and slips away."

"Why don't we just use the nullification key and trap her here?" Juliette asked.

"We could," Matthew pondered. "Unless she happened to bring a spare box with her."

"And who knows what kind of a mess she could make here before we return with Silas," Emma added.

"You're right," Juliette agreed, "we have a chance to put an end to all this right now."

"How long do you think we'll have to wait?" Joel asked.

"Depends how long she searches around for the key, I suppose," his girlfriend answered.

"And how long it takes her to figure out that this is where the box is kept," Emma added.

"However long it takes," Matthew stated. "We'll be here waiting for her when she arrives. No matter what, she's not getting away from the five of us."

"You got that right!" Joel declared confidently.

"Okay, let's get to our spots and lie low, before she sees us and knows something's up," Juliette suggested.

"Good idea," Matthew agreed. "Good luck everyone."

* * *

Three hours had passed since the group had split up and retreated to their various hiding places. Thankfully, Allister had delivered their lunch to them shortly after they had arrived. Dusk was starting to settle in and, according to Winston, sunset occurred very quickly on top of the trees. Thankfully, he had come out of the room at one point to turn on all the lights inside the house of thanksgiving. Their task would have been exponentially more difficult to accomplish in the dark.

Joel and Juliette heard the muffled sound of the door latch being turned. Unfortunately, since they had no way to communicate with the others, they could only hope that everyone else was able to see what was going on inside the large room from their vantage point.

A solitary figure walked into the room, moving cautiously but determinedly. Morgan looked back and forth and even behind her several times as she slid through the room towards the table. Clearly, she knew exactly where she needed to go to find the box. When she was three-quarters of the way through the room, Winston sauntered through the office door.

"Oh, hello," he said calmly. "I didn't realize anyone was here. I was just putting the final touches on my thanksgiving homily for tomorrow. Is there something I can help you with?"

"Um, yes, thank you," Morgan answered in tones that were unexpectedly sweet. "I am a dear friend of Mr. Silas. He invited me to visit this beautiful place, but it is, sadly, time for me to return to my own realm."

"I see."

"Yes," Morgan smiled and continued to move toward the front of the room. "Anyway, he, that is Mr. Silas, told me that he placed the gateway box underneath that table right there. So, if you'll pardon me, I'll just grab it and be on my way."

"Certainly, Ms.?"

"Morgan, my name is Morgan."

"Certainly Ms. Morgan. It was a pleasure to have you in our world."

"Thank you, I had a lovely time," Morgan walked up to the table and moved around to the back side. She knelt down and looked under the table, searching the shelf for the gateway box. After shuffling around some papers and other things stored under the table she looked up again and said to Winston, "I can't seem to find it here. Do you happen to know where ..."

"It's not there," Matthew boldly pronounced.

"It's over, Morgan," Emma proudly added.

Morgan rose to her feet and stared down Emma with an icy glare. "YOU! I should have dealt with you when I had the chance. I will not make that mistake again."

"Give it up, Morgan," Matthew commanded. "We've got the box and we've got you surrounded."

"Yeah," Joel shouted from the back of the room. "Nowhere to run to, nowhere to hide, baby!"

Juliette rolled her eyes at her boyfriend and then added, "It's over."

"Is that what you think?" Morgan asked defiantly. "You think *you* can stop *me*? You think you have the upper hand? You think you have me outnumbered? CRANK! LUG!"

The back door burst open, almost breaking off of its hinges. A large and burly man stomped into the house of thanksgiving, nearly hitting his head on the top of the doorframe. His face had Neanderthal-like features and his chest and arms bulged with muscles so large it appeared as though his skin could barely contain them.

A second thug kicked open the side door behind Matthew and Emma. Although slightly smaller in proportions than the first he was still an intimidating form, with a shaggy beard and hair, and two overgrown incisors sticking up out of his lower jaw.

"Um, Matt?" Joel said nervously, putting his arm around his girlfriend and moving toward the middle of the room, backing away from the behemoth who had entered behind them. "Now what?"

Matthew and Emma also moved toward the middle of the room, putting some distance between them and Morgan's goon. He tried to think of a viable Plan B, but his mind was preoccupied with the size of their new adversaries.

"You still don't have the box," Emma shouted.

"Oh, I don't have the box?" Morgan taunted. "Please, I will find the box and be off to the next realm long before my boys are done with you delicate flowers."

"Don't worry about the box for now guys," Matthew whispered. "These guys are big..."

"They're huge!" Joel corrected.

"These guys are huge, but they're bound to be slow. As soon as an exit opens up, we get there as fast as we can and regroup outside, agreed?"

"Sounds good to me," Juliette said.

"Yep."

"Me too."

"Out of my way!" Morgan demanded, moving toward Winston and the office door.

"No," he said defiantly.

"Lug. Move him."

The brute from the side door lumbered toward Winston, cracking his knuckles and dawning a sadistic smile. When he was halfway across the room the four friends sprinted toward the recently vacated doorway.

"Come on, Winston," Matthew shouted as he exited the building through the now unguarded side door. "Get out of there! It's not worth it." Winston took the young man's advice and quickly maneuvered around the thug and out the door.

"Let them go," Morgan instructed. "They're not important." She opened the door to the office and after a short period of searching discovered the gateway box. She carried it back out to the main room and set it on the table. "Once I'm gone, this world is yours to do what you wish. Just make sure no one gets access to this box. No one."

"Got it," Crank growled punching his fist into his open hand.

"I'll be back later to see if you've found the workshop key and reward you accordingly. In the meantime, enjoy yourselves boys," Morgan said with a devilish smile. "See ya!" She flipped open the lid to the box and inserted one of several keys she had on a ring. The room was filled with light and a moment later she was gone.

* * *

"What do we do now?" Joel exclaimed between breaths.

"I'm not sure," Matthew answered.

"Winston! You're hurt," Emma cried.

"I will be fine, Ms. Emma, although that giant lump did get a pretty good punch in as I ran past."

"We need somewhere safe to think and plan out our next move," Matthew suggested.

"My home is not far from here, Mr. Matthew. We will be safe there."

A few minutes later the off-worlders were inside Winston's home being introduced to his wife, Isabella. For a long time the discussion revolved around the size and strength of Morgan's hired muscle. They were all frustrated by how easily they had been outwitted and felt embarrassed by the overconfidence that had left them so easily exposed.

"None of that matters now," Emma finally said. "What matters now is the box."

"Emma's right," her boyfriend concurred. "If we can get to the box we can find out where Morgan has gone and go after her."

"Exactly," Joel chimed in. "Crank and Lug were still shouting threats at us long after the gateway light had faded. That means she left those two oversized bozos behind. Wherever she is, she will be on her own."

"Not necessarily," Matthew cautioned.

"What do you mean?"

"Matt is right," Juliette agreed. "We have no idea whether or not the beefcake brothers are the only thugs Morgan has enlisted. Actually, the fact that she left them behind would suggest she's got at least a couple more on standby."

"And now she knows Silas has help on his side too," Emma added.

"We'll have to worry about all that later," her boyfriend said. "At the moment we just have to get to the box."

"Pardon me, Mr. Matthew, but what happens when you find the box and leave? Will those two giant men follow you?"

"Umm, well, no, Winston," Matthew tried to explain, suddenly feeling an overwhelming sense of guilt about the answer. "You see, once we pass through the gateway, the box will be locked. No one, including Crank and Lug, will be able to leave Arbolada."

"But we are a completely peaceful people. We have no weapons or trained fighters. Those two brutes would easily dominate us. You can't leave us here defenseless."

The room was silent for several minutes. The four friends hated the idea of leaving Winston and his people at the mercy of the overgrown bullies, but the truth was, none of them were fighters either. They had done well to get out of the house of thanksgiving in one piece as they were no match for Crank and Lug. The very best they could do is attempt to drag the two goons with them when they passed through the gateway, but they all knew that would just inflict their brutality on a different world and all its inhabitants.

"Whadda we do, Matt?" Joel finally asked.

"Listen, Winston," Emma said gently. "We love your home, and we love your people. If we could do something to help them we would, but we just can't. Not right now anyway. If we can get to the box we can follow Morgan's trail and hopefully stop whatever maniacal plan she's cooked up in that twisted little brain of hers."

"Easy there, Em."

"Sorry. I really don't like that woman.

"Emma is right," Matthew agreed. "Once Morgan has been taken care of we will talk to Silas and personally come back here with whatever it takes to deal with those two oafs, once and for all. But to do that, we have to get to the box and get out of here."

"That's for sure," Juliette added. "In the meantime, just tell your people to stay clear of those guys. Give them what they want to keep them happy and make sure they don't go on some kind of rampage. Just pacify them until we come back."

Winston considered their words carefully. It was clear that he did not like what they were suggesting, but he also seemed to recognize that it might be the best of the bad options they had available to them at the moment.

"They are right, Winston," Isabella called from the next room.

"I know, Izzy," the man reluctantly conceded. "I know."

"It is very kind of you to promise to return to assist us," Winston's wife said, entering the room.

"It's the least we could do," Juliette replied.

"Yeah, what kind of jerks would we be if we just ditched you and never came back," Joel smiled.

"Very well," Winston said confidently. "How are we going to get you folks to that box?"

"Does that office have any exterior windows?" the engineer inquired.

"Unfortunately, no."

"Seems to me we need some kind of distraction," Joel suggested.

"What do you mean?" Isabella inquired.

"We don't have to defeat those two bozos, we just need something to draw them outside or at least get them away from the front of the room."

"How much time do we need in the office," Juliette asked.

"Not long," Matthew replied. "A minute, maybe. Two tops."

"Any ideas, Winston?" the med student asked.

A sly smile crept on to the man's face. "I could round up some of the guys for a little game of nutclang."

"Huh?"

"Nutclang. Izzy, go find Callum, Auggy, Hugh and whoever else you can round up and tell them to meet me at the deli across from the house of thanksgiving right away. Make sure they bring their gear."

"Again, I say, huh?" Joel chuckled.

"Nutclang is a local pastime, Mr. Joel. What you folks would call a sport, I believe. Two teams face off against each other on a course or field. Everyone wears a helmet, a vest, and," Winston leaned closer to Matthew and Joel, and whispered, "and other protective gear."

"Got it," Matthew smiled knowingly.

"Each vest has a thin metal plate on the front and back and every player is armed with a slingshot and a bag full of applecorn nuts. The goal is to reach the other team's base without getting hit. If an opposing player hits the plate in your vest you must return to your base and wait out a three-minute penalty."

"I get it," the chef cheered. "It's just like laser tag or paintball."

"But far more dangerous and painful from the sounds of it," Matthew added.

"I've come home with some mighty fine welts, indeed, Mr. Matthew. I am certain that if we get enough guys targeting those brutes Morgan left behind, we'll eventually draw them out."

"But, Winston," Emma said, her voice laced with concern, "if you provoke them like that aren't you risking getting hurt yourself?"

"We will clear everyone from the area first, Ms. Emma. The chaps on my team are more than fast enough to outrun those fools. I'll make sure everyone stays a safe distance away until they've calmed down again. Maybe we'll even send in some food or something. It'll be fine. Besides, you were right. The best way for us to get rid of those two is for the four of you to get out of here and come back with help."

"I promise we will," the young woman declared.

"I don't doubt it at all, Ms. Emma. Not at all."

* * *

Crank lay lazily in the middle of the floor, looking even larger sprawled out than when he was standing. Suddenly he felt a sharp pain in his rib.

A moment later another pain struck, this time on the bottom of his foot.

"Buzz off, Lug," the oversized brute grunted "I didn't do nuttin'."

Another pain erupted on Crank's thigh causing him to jerk upright and spin around to glare at his partner. "I said cut it out!"

"And I said, I didn't do nuttin'!" Lug retorted as he leaned against the office door.

Another applecorn nut came rocketing through the air and nailed Crank square in the back of his head. He gave an angry shout and lumbered to his feet. His dopey eyes scanned the room. Lug took a projectile to the gut and moaned woefully. Another nut shattered the window in the office door, raining shards of glass down on his head.

"Up there!" Crank moaned, pointing to the left side of the balcony. Another nut whistled through the air and struck his pointing hand. "And over there!"

Both thugs were now on their feet and sauntering toward the back of the room. Callum and Jepson leapt over the balcony rail and gently landed on the floor below. As they ran for the rear exit, Auggy and Hugh appeared in the doorway, firing their sling shots over their fleeing companions. As they ducked for cover, Winston and another man stepped out and fired their shots.

Crank and Lug slowly moved toward the back of the building, trying to shield themselves from the continual volley of shots being fired at them. The applecorn nuts were clearly not doing any damage of consequence, but they certainly caused a significant amount of pain, not to mention a great deal of annoyance. As the two goons reached the back doors all six men scampered away, quickly disappearing down the block. Crank let out an angry shout as he watched them vanish and then followed his partner back into the building.

"They're coming back," Joel whispered, standing watch at the office door. "This would be easier if this window was still here."

"How much time do we have?" Matthew asked.

"Thirty seconds at the speed they're moving, less if they notice we're in here."

"Okay, I've scanned the lock to see where Morgan went."

"Shouldn't we go back and update Silas?" Emma suggested.

"Sounds good to me," her boyfriend agreed inserting the nullification key into the box and turning it. "Come on guys, we only get one shot at this now."

"Everyone hold hands," Juliette reminded. "We don't want to leave anyone behind."

"You can say that again," Joel quipped.

"Alright, here we go," Matthew said, turning the key and filling the room with light.

Lug threw open the door and looked into the office, just in time to see the lid on the gateway box flip closed.

"Oh, that can't be good."

− 8 −
Good News & Bad News

The four friends arrived in Tara's apartment, made their way hastily back to Joel's place, and collapsed on the couch. They all felt physically and emotionally exhausted from their experience.

"Man, that was one crazy ride," Joel eventually broke the silence.

"Tell me about it," his friend agreed. "It's been a wild couple of days."

"That's for sure," Emma affirmed.

"Well, at least my head didn't feel like it had been inside a dryer set on Perma Press when we got back this time!" the Juliette said with relief.

After another brief moment of silence, Joel spoke up again. "Don't you guys think, maybe, we're in a bit over our heads here? I mean, Silas seems like a decent fella, but I'm used to driving my trucks around, not tangling with freaks like Crank and Lug!"

"No doubt," Matthew agreed. "Arbolada is a long way from my office cubicle, that's for sure."

"But we can't leave Silas to do this all on his own," Emma insisted. "And what about his wife? How can we abandon her? Trust me, I've spent some quality time with this Morgan chick, and if she gets the key to the workshop I can guarantee she will go from world to world, collecting all the baddies she can find – guys who make Crank and Lug look like puppy dogs – and eventually she's gonna end up bringing them here. I'm certain of it."

"Even if she doesn't," Juliette added. "Think of all the innocent people like Winston who would be hurt if we don't stop her somehow."

"Winston," Joel chuckled. "That dude was all kinds of alright!"

"He sure was," the engineer said. "I certainly hope we run into more folks like him along the way. So, what do you guys think we should do next?"

"Well," Emma began thoughtfully. "You know where Morgan went to from Arbolada, right?"

"Yeah, according to the device Silas gave me it was some place called Bhal."

"Okay, so that's our next destination. The question is, when?"

"I don't know guys," Juliette spoke reluctantly. "I'm not sure I'm ready, just yet, to throw myself back into another situation where my neck is on the line."

"I know what you mean," Matthew sympathized. "It would kind of be nice to not have to deal with evil henchmen or some psychotic woman."

"Don't say it," Juliette warned her boyfriend, who sat tight-lipped but had a twinkle in his eye born out of the witty remark he had on the tip of his tongue.

"The thing is," Emma explained. "Morgan is still out there wreaking havoc on more worlds like Arbolada. For all we know she has more goons at her disposal too."

"Emma's right," Joel concurred. "Even if we're not in those worlds, fighting those baddies, seeing those folks suffer, the truth is, now we know. We know they're there. We know it's happening. I couldn't live with myself if I just stayed on the sidelines."

"Me neither," Matthew admitted. "But I think it's safe to say we all need a moment or two to regain our bearings and psych ourselves up for what's to come."

"Agreed," his girlfriend affirmed. "But not too long. We can't let Morgan get too far ahead of us."

"I say we chill for the night and head out first thing in the morning," Joel suggested.

"Sounds good," Matthew declared. "We should assume Emma's place is not safe because Morgan knows who she is and where she lives. She probably has enough info to figure out who I am too."

"Emma can come back to my place and you boys can camp out here for the night."

"Fine by me. I should also make some calls and get someone to drive my truck for me the next couple of days."

"I guess I should develop a bad case of mono or something. Sayid's not going to be happy about that."

"Don't worry, sweetie, I'll write you a doctor's note."

"Gee thanks."

"Classes are on break this week. Dr. Stevens is wrapped up in a project with some guys from the physics department, which means I have no T.A. duties right now, so I'm good."

"I have some vacation time I need to use up. I just need to call the bank and let them know."

"Great, sounds like we've got it all covered," Matthew sighed. "A night off would be nice. We'll meet back here in the morning."

"Not too early," the chef quipped.

"If Silas hasn't shown up by then we'll leave him a note on the fridge, as planned, and head out."

The friends lounged around for several more hours, relaxing and trying their best to feel normal. Of course, they all realized that normal was a thing of the past. Even once this was all over they would still live with the knowledge that all these different realms were out there, somewhere. Their view of the world, and life in general, would never quite be the same. But for tonight they did their best to pretend.

* * *

"Mornin' boys!" Juliette greeted cheerfully as she walked in the door.

"Morning, babe! You ladies want an omelet?"

"No thanks, we stopped on the way over and picked up our lattes and scones."

"Your loss," the chef chuckled.

"Did you guys leave a message for..." Emma began, closing the apartment door behind her. "Oh, hello, Silas. When did you get here?"

"Good morning, Emma. Delightful to see you again. Good morning to you too, Juliette. I arrived about an hour ago, I suppose."

"As I was saying," Matthew picked up where they had left off, "there's good news and bad news."

"I see. Well, let's have the good news first."

"The good news is we went to Arbolada and met Winston. Morgan showed up also, and we were able to track her to Bhal, which is where we're heading today. After she left we used the nullification key and returned here last night."

"Haha," Silas chuckled. "I'm sure she'll enjoy that world! That is all good news indeed."

"Don't get used to it," Joel shouted from the kitchen.

"And what is the bad news, Matthew?"

"The bad news is Morgan was not working alone. She had two thugs with her named Crank and Lug. Big and nasty guys. Unfortunately, they were still in Arbolada when we left, and now that the box is locked there is no way for them to leave."

"Which means Winston and all his friends are left to deal with them," Emma added sadly.

"The people of Arborlada are very strong in spirit," Silas said quietly. "They will endure until we are able to return and deal with those two cretins."

"I hope so," the med student replied. "How did you make out?"

"I too have good and bad news."

"What's the good news?" Juliette asked. "We need all of that we can get."

"I went to Garda. It is a dreary and dreadful place."

"This is the good news, right?" Joel chimed in again.

"Yes, Joel, it is," Silas smiled gently, but with a noticeable hint of sadness. "I went to that realm because I thought Morgan might have left my wife there. Sure enough, she was there." All four of his companions cheered loudly at the news. "Or I should say is."

"What! She's still there?" Emma asked. "Why?"

"Tara is being held in a prison cell that has only one key."

"Who has the key?" Matthew inquired, but the look on Silas' face revealed the answer. "Oh."

"Until I retrieve the key from Morgan there is no possible way to free my wife. Tara suspects that Morgan will only give up the key to her cell in exchange for the key to my workshop."

"But you can't!" Juliette gasped, and then added, "But how can you not?"

"Exactly," the carpenter said. "But I have taken precautions to ensure that never happens. Now we must focus our attention on apprehending Morgan. Which brings me to the bad news."

"What? Wait, that wasn't the bad news?" Joel asked walking into the room with two plates of omelet.

"Unfortunately, not. It's about the two brutes you encountered on Arbolada. Morgan released them from cells on Garda, similar to the one my wife is being held in."

"How many cells did she open?" Matthew asked, suddenly realizing the gravity of this revelation.

"Too many," Silas answered solemnly. "Garda was created by the ancient craftsmen. They discovered that even in the most well-constructed worlds there are occasionally bad apples. To protect their realms craftsmen through the ages have taken these troublemakers out of their realms and incarcerated them in Garda."

"Which leaves you with a whole barrel full of bad apples," Joel stated.

"Indeed. As a safety precaution, there was only one key for the cells and it was kept safely on Garda itself. Tara and I are the only ones with a key to Garda, so we never imagined the cell key was in any danger of being stolen. Aside from the two of us, the only ones who even knew of the key's location were locked behind bars and unable to get to it."

"But, when the right evil person snuck in," Emma hypothesized.

"The prisoners struck a deal," the carpenter confirmed. "Their freedom for their allegiance."

"So, you're saying that Morgan will have more guys like Crank and Lug out there helping her," Juliette said.

"Many more, and some far worse than those two, I'm afraid."

"Well, you definitely win the Bad News Award," Joel concluded, setting down his plate.

"By the way," Emma began tentatively following a long lull in the conversation. "I've been wanting to ask you…"

"Yes, Emma, what is it?" Silas replied in an inviting tone.

"Exactly how did you learn to do, you know, what you do?"

"I was chosen, by the previous craftsman. You see, at a certain stage in his life, each one of us must seek out someone with the necessary traits to learn the craft. These traits are known as the Heritage. When the time comes, each of us must find a new apprentice who possesses the Heritage and train them to take our place."

"But how?"

"And why you?"

"Is it, like, a family thing, passed down from generation to generation?"

Silas chuckled softly, "Apparently Emma wasn't the only one pondering this question. It is quite simple actually."

"That seems unlikely," Joel quipped.

"The Heritage is not necessarily passed through bloodlines, though it is true that the child whose parent is a craftsman is more likely to be qualified to learn the craft themselves."

"So how do you find someone ... qualified?" Juliette asked.

"We carve a special door using the script the ancients gave us. That door opens a portal that leads us to an eligible candidate."

"But how do you know who it's leading you to," Matthew inquired. "What if there is more than one person standing there when you arrive?"

"There usually is," Silas explained. "In fact, it often takes numerous journeys through the portal to even identify who the candidate is."

"The one who's *always* there, right?" Emma deduced.

"Exactly."

"Don't people get suspicious when you keep materializing in front of them all the time?" Matthew questioned.

"Of course they would," the carpenter conceded. "The gateway of this particular door, however, is unique in that instead of a bright flash of light you kind of fade in so that no one particularly notices your arrival."

"So, once you figure out who the portal is leading you to you train them to carve the doors like you do?" Emma asked.

"Oh no," Silas replied. "After identifying the individual, the craftsman observes them for a period of time."

"Like a few hours?" Joel suggested.

"More like a few months, sometimes as much as a year. Wielding the craft is not a power to be handed out lightly. Often a craftsman will go through multiple candidates before selecting an apprentice."

"Silas," Matthew began nervously. "Was Morgan your apprentice?"

There was a long and anxious pause as the four friends waited for the carpenter to answer. "No. She was not. However, the candidate door did lead me to her more than once. At first, it seemed ideal as she and Tara were already close friends. Showing her that first world was a sort of litmus test to see if she might actually be the one. But I soon grew uncomfortable with her appetite for the realms and decided to look for another candidate."

"Did she know?" Juliette probed. "Did she know that you had rejected her as a candidate?"

"No, there was no possible way for her to know because I never hinted that she was a potential candidate in the first place." His voice took on a clear tone of sadness as he added, "I never even told Tara."

"Well, whatever the reason, she's certainly got a super-sized bee in her bonnet now," Joel observed. "So, what do we do about it?"

"The plan hasn't changed," Matthew stated confidently. "We still have an advantage."

"What advantage is that?" Emma asked.

"First, now we know what to expect, so we won't be caught off guard like we were last time."

"And second?" Juliette prompted.

"Second, based on our experience in Arbolada Morgan is only taking a couple of these thugs to each world, which means we should only have to deal with a few of them at a time."

"And," Joel added, "every time we use the nullification key in a box that safely exiles those baddies in that world!"

"That's helpful for us, but not so great for the locals," Emma reminded.

"True, but one problem at a time. We'll go back and deal with those guys later, I promise, Em."

"Indeed we will Matthew. You have my word on that, Emma," Silas promised.

"That's a pretty thin silver lining on a pretty dark cloud if you ask me," Joel said. "But at this point, I'll take whatever I can get."

* * *

It was almost noon by the time the four friends returned to Joel's apartment. Prior to opening the gateway to his next world, Silas had strongly recommended they get themselves wetsuits before traveling to Bhal. He assured them they would not regret it. They likely could have come back sooner, but they all found it difficult to step away from the normalcy of being out and about town. Now that they had returned, however, there was no reason for delay.

"Are you sure we are supposed to put these things on now," Joel asked. "Not just take them with us?"

"Silas specifically said, 'You'll want to wear wetsuits when you go,' so I'm wearing a wetsuit when I go," his friend responded. "All set ladies?"

Juliette and Emma had purchased black suits with pink and green stripes up the sides, respectively. Matthew's suit was solid black and Joel's had a large, red splatter pattern across the front and back. All four suits came down to just above the knee and had either short sleeves or none at all.

"What are you doing with the keys Matt?" Joel inquired.

"Well, I figured I would try to keep them in some sort of order," Mathew explained. "Just in case the device Silas gave us ever got lost or broken."

"That's a brilliant idea."

"Yeah, it would be bad if we didn't know which key brought us back to earth," Emma agreed.

"Or worse," Juliette added. "What if we accidentally used a key that took us back to a world we had already been to?"

"A realm where we had already used the nullification key," her boyfriend followed her train of thought to its conclusion. "We would be trapped."

"Exactly. So I started with the nullification key next to the Mr. Spiffy's tag. Then earth and Arbolada," Matthew explained. Then, repositioning another key to sit fourth from the tag he concluded, "and now Bhal."

"Okay, is everyone set?" Emma asked.

"Ready as I'll ever be," Juliette answered, summing up the sentiments of the entire group.

The four friends clasped hands as Matthew inserted and turned the key. Light filled the room as the gateway opened and the group departed for Bhal.

* * *

"What in the blue blazes?" Joel cried out.

"Is everyone here?" Emma inquired. "Is everyone okay?"

"I'm a little woozy, but fine," Juliette answered.

"I'm fine too."

"What in the blue blazes?" the chef repeated his question having received no response the first time. "It's like we've been dropped into the middle of a typhoon or hurricane or something!"

The group had landed on a sandy beach, but rain was coming down in torrents. Drops of water fell from the sky with enough force to sting slightly as they hit the new arrivals' skin. Although they had been in the realm for less than a minute they were all thoroughly drenched.

"I don't think it's a hurricane," Juliette said over the sound of pounding rain. "It's pouring buckets, but there's not really any wind."

"Well, I guess we know why Silas recommended the wetsuits," Matthew quipped as he surveyed the area. "It's hard to see much from here. Maybe we should split up and look around a bit."

"I can't even tell what time of day it is," his girlfriend commented. "The sky is just a solid mass of grey clouds."

"Looks like there's water in front of us and forest behind us," Joel observed. "Why don't we scope out the beach first? Jules and I will go this way. Matt, you and Emma head that way."

"Sounds good," the engineer said loudly over the sound of the pounding rain. "Let's say, walk for about fifteen minutes and then turn around and meet back here."

Joel gave Matthew the thumbs up signal, then put his arm around Juliette and headed off down the shoreline. The waves were crashing into the beach with force, although not at any great height. The sand was cool to their feet and saturated with water, suggesting that it had been raining for a while.

"The drop off must be quite steep for those waves to crash into the shore like that," Joel suggested.

"Maybe," Juliette replied huddling close to him as they walked. "I'm sure glad we wore these suits. I'm chilly as it is, I can't imagine what it would be like walking around in regular soaked clothes."

"It would weigh a ton for one thing," her boyfriend agreed.

"I hope the sun comes out soon."

"You know what they always tell divers to do when they get too cold?"

"Not a chance!"

"I'm just saying, it feels kinda nice," Joel laughed.

"You are a gross little boy!" Juliette chuckled, playfully pushing him away, but quickly pulling him back to take advantage of his body heat.

The pair walked along for about ten minutes, although neither one could be sure exactly. Given the recommended attire, they assumed they would end up in the water at some point. So, no one brought watches, phones or anything else that might be damaged. Besides, as Joel pointed out, the wetsuits were kind of short on pockets. Matthew had purchased a waterproof waist pack to hold the keys and the scanning device, but those were the only items they had brought with them to this realm.

"Hey, Jules. I think I see someone up there."

"Maybe. It's hard to make out through the rain, but maybe."

"Do you think we should head back or go ahead and meet these folks."

"Silas would have warned us if the locals were hostile, right?"

"I suppose," Joel replied. "But then again, he's not much with the details, that guy. I mean, how hard would it have been to say, 'By the way, you're walking into a monsoon'?"

"Did you hear that?"

"What?"

"I think I heard voices," Juliette said. "But it's hard to tell over the rain."

After walking several steps further, the couple could clearly make out the voice ahead saying, "Hello."

"Sounds friendly enough," Joel stated. They quickened their pace slightly moving toward the oncoming individuals. "Looks like there's at least two of them, maybe more," he said squinting through the rain and dim light.

"Hello," the voice shouted again, this time much clearer and louder.

"Hey there!" the chef shouted back as loud as he could.

There was a brief pause and the oncoming people appeared to stop moving for a moment, then the voice called back once more, "Joel?" The couple both recognized the voice and hurried to meet up with their friends.

"Well," Matthew began. "I guess it's safe to say we're on an island."

"Yep," Joel agreed. "And not a super big one either. There might be something in the middle of that forest, but it can't be very much."

"But if there's nothing on this island," Emma pondered aloud. "Where are all the people?"

"And buildings?" Matthew added.

"And the box?" Joel asked. "Maybe on another island?"

"Well, how on earth are we supposed to get *there*?"

"That's a very good question, Jules."

The Heritage Key

– 9 –
Up in the Air

Silas' feet landed gently and slowly sunk several inches into the ground. Every time he returned to Cumulus he was awestruck by its beauty. The billowy white cloud he currently stood on was one of thousands that filled the sky of this realm. The arrival gateway cloud was relatively small, no more than 30 or 40 feet in diameter, however, some of the clouds stretched out for hundreds of yards.

Silas soaked in his surroundings for a moment and then pulled a tan colored shirt out of his satchel and slipped it on. The shirt had long sleeves and a drawstring at the bottom, which he synched up as tight as he could. Along each side hung a flap of bright red fabric. He slid his arms through the loops that hung midway down the flaps and then poked his thumbs through holes in the bottom corners of the red fabric. As the carpenter raised his arms out to the side, the flaps stretched taut. Without any sign of hesitation, Silas leaned forward and fell off the cloud. The red fabric flapped aggressively but provided enough wind resistance to allow him to glide through the air. The synthetic wings were not sturdy enough to permit actual flight, however, the carpenter skillfully coasted through the sky on the air currents.

Silas could see several others soaring around on the air currents, all wearing shirts similar to his. In fact, everyone in this realm wore this type of apparel virtually all the time. Gliding shirts, which were typically a white or tan with brightly colored flaps, were the only way to get from one cloud to another, and they also served as insurance, just in case someone accidentally stumbled off the edge. The carpenter leaned to his right and coasted over toward a column of pink tinted air. When he first crafted this world, he designed the updraft columns with a light rose hue. Updraft columns were the only way to climb to higher altitudes, therefore it was essential for them to be easy to identify. As he climbed rapidly upwards he passed another glider diving down to a lower cloud somewhere. The passerby waved politely as the two met.

Silas exited the updraft column near the top and glided across to a large cloud. The cloud held three houses built from narrow logs with thatched roofs. Three were of modest size and appearance. He landed gently on the soft ground and slipped his arms out of the loops, allowing the flaps to fall limp at his sides.

"Well, hello there!" a cheerful voice greeted as a woman walked around the corner of the first house.

"Hello, Kaww! It is wonderful to see you again."

"Nice to see you too," the woman smiled. Her form was distinctly female, but she was clearly not entirely human. Her copper hair looked almost feather-like and her nose was hard and hooked much like a hawk's beak. "It's been a while since you visited our neck of the woods."

"Indeed, it has," Silas agreed. "Too long I think. Unfortunately, this must be a very quick visit."

"Is something wrong?" Kaww asked, sounding genuinely concerned.

"Yes, something is very wrong."

"What, pray tell, is it?"

"My wife, Tara, has been captured and her keys have been stolen," the carpenter gravely explained.

"Oh, my stars!"

"I have come to warn all the people of Cumulus to be on the lookout for a woman with bright red hair."

"I'm afraid your warning comes too late, my old friend," a man said as he glided gracefully onto the cloud next to Silas.

"Talon!" the carpenter greeted. "Just the man I was looking for. Tell me what has happened."

"I just heard the story myself," the man explained. "It appears the woman you are looking for has already come and gone."

"What do you mean?" the carpenter inquired.

"She arrived nearly an hour ago and flagged down Jimmy Fletcher's kid, who just happened to be flying by. Word is she took Jimmy Jr.'s gliding shirt and left him stranded down below."

"Where did she go?" Kaww asked.

"We're still trying to piece it together, but she was spotted on several different clouds," her husband explained. "Eventually she made her way to the sunflower field, which is where Larry Crow saw her leave through the gateway."

"It appears I have come too late," Silas affirmed. "I must continue on my pursuit. Be sure to spread the word across the clouds that if she or anyone else should enter this realm, everyone must steer clear of them. They should be considered most dangerous."

"We already have some of the fledglings going from cloud to cloud with that very message," Talon explained.

"What was she doing here? Why would she come back again?" Kaww asked, deeply concerned.

"She was looking for a very special key," Silas explained.

"Are you sure about that?" the man asked, "cause she didn't really hang around very long. It seems like the only thing she was looking for here was the gateway to leave."

"Intriguing," the carpenter pondered the suggestion. "It is also odd that she showed up in this realm alone."

"Why is that?" Kaww asked.

"When we have crossed paths with her in other worlds she has had some hired muscle along with her."

"Oh, that's not good," Talon blurted out.

"What?" the other two said in unison.

"The only thing she did while she was here was bust into the house of the Bomber twins and take a couple of their gliding shirts."

"It would seem she plans to come back, and bring some friends with her!" Silas deduced.

"Big friends too," the woman added. "Those Bomber twins are some pretty hefty boys!"

"Perhaps we should post some guards at the entry gateway," the man suggested.

"No," Silas said cautiously. "Whoever she brings back will be too dangerous for any of you to confront. Post someone nearby to keep an eye on things and sound the warning should someone arrive, but under no circumstances should they confront the off-worlders."

"I'll get to it right away," Talon agreed.

"And I will go down to stand watch on the gateway until your sentries arrive," the carpenter stated.

The man quickly dove off the cloud, attaching his arms to the flaps on his glide shirt as he sailed downward. Silas, much more cautiously, slid his arms through the loops and securely grasped the bottom corner of the flaps with his thumbs before stepping off the edge. He circled around, passing several other clouds as he spiraled his way back down toward the arrival gateway.

He landed a few minutes later on a cloud that was nearby and slightly higher up than the one he had first appeared on. It didn't take long for him to spot the three large men standing on the cloud below. They wore metal body armor and each one had something strapped to their back. After a moment Silas recognized the men and knew that the items on their backs were almost certainly jetpacks or flamethrowers – neither of which was good news for the inhabitants of Cumulus.

"What's going on down here?" Talon asked quietly as he glided in for a smooth landing.

"Not too much," Silas answered in similar hushed tones. "You see those three big louts down there?"

"Tough to miss them."

"The one closest to us is called Mazcar, the guy next to him is Meftor and that big fellow at the back is Clobaz."

"Who are they?" Talon asked apprehensively.

"They are all members of a gang called The Death Rivets. They come from a mech realm, and are notorious for inflicting cruelty without remorse, with the aid of their machinery."

The pair watched the three men shuffle around on the small cloud below, until the carpenter made a surprising discovery, "You know who I don't see?"

"The red-haired woman?"

"Indeed. At first I assumed she was merely hidden from view by the bulky frame of those three behemoths, but now I'm not so sure."

"But if she's not there, where is she? Is she still on her way?"

"No, that's not possible," Silas explained. "Morgan has only one key for Cumulus. If she did not pass through the gateway with those three brutes, she would have no other way of getting here later."

"Then she must have moved on already, but where?"

"And why didn't the three stooges go with her?"

Talon pondered the situation for a moment and then suggested, "Perhaps she wanted to avoid drawing attention to herself, but where could she be headed?"

"The gateway," Silas deduced.

"The gateway is right below us, my friend, and as you said, she is clearly not there."

"No, the exit gateway. She's going to sneak out of here and leave her thugs behind to do her dirty work for her."

"That's a clever plan."

"Yes. It seems she has learned from her run-in with my friends in Arbolada and adjusted her strategy accordingly." Silas considered his next move momentarily and then instructed his friend, "You stay here and keep an eye on these three lugs. Just watch them. Do NOT engage with them, promise me."

"I have no intention of taking those beasts on myself, don't worry. What are you going to do?"

"Morgan is on her way to the box. If I'm lucky I might be able to get there first, in which case I can trap her in this realm just long enough to force her to relinquish the rest of Tara's keys."

"Go," Talon encouraged.

"If she gets to the box before me, I will need to follow her, if possible," Silas explained.

"I understand."

"But I promise I'll return to deal with these three oafs as soon as I can."

"You don't have to explain yourself to me, old friend. Go save your wife."

Silas jumped off the cloud and glided toward the nearest updraft column. He rose as high and as fast as he could, then, leaning out of the pink air, he soared above houses, shops, and playgrounds, headed toward the exit gateway's location. About halfway there he had lost too much altitude and had to circle back to catch another updraft stream. It wasn't a long detour, but every second counted. He had no idea how much of a head start Morgan already had on him. Having been to Cumulus once already, she would have a general idea of where she was going, but the carpenter knew first-hand how confusing it could be to navigate your way through the clouds.

Silas spotted the large cloud covered with sunflowers and glided down toward it. Unfortunately, the small garden shed that housed the box was on the far side of the field. From 40 yards away he could see the figure of a woman step around the corner of the shed and open the door.

"MORGAN!" he shouted at the top of his lungs.

The red-haired woman shot an icy glare across the field as she calculated how much time she had before her foe's arrival. "Stop right there," she commanded.

Silas coasted to the ground in the middle of a field of what looked similar to four-foot-tall sunflowers. "Why are you doing this?" he pleaded.

"Don't play coy with me, *craftsman*," she spat. The way she said the word divulged a knowledge of the Heritage that ran far deeper than Silas had expected. "You should know exactly why I am doing all this. If you don't, you soon will."

"Please, Morgan! Tara is your friend. How can you be so cold and treat her with such cruelty?"

"Am I the one being cruel?" she looked at him incredulously. "You could put an end to all this right now. You could free your wife in an instant – just give me the workshop key."

"You know I can't do that."

"You can't or you won't?" Morgan asked shaking her head in mock disappointment. "Not even for your wife? I guess we all know what you really value, don't we?"

"That's not fair. I love Tara."

"Since when do you care about fair?"

"I will stop you!" the carpenter declared pacing towards the shed.

"Not today, you won't," she stated flatly. "Better luck next time, old man!" she sneered and stepped into the shed.

Silas was no more than 10 or 20 feet away when light momentarily poured out of the shed. He landed on the edge of the sunflower field and ran into the now empty shed. He opened the box and briefly placed his hand on the brass plate, listening to its most recent destination.

The craftsman paused, momentarily considering his next move. Mazcar, Meftor, and Clobaz were still in Cumulus. The three criminals had been prisoners in Garda since long before Silas' time. He had heard of the offenses for which they had been incarcerated and he knew that if left free in Cumulus they would terrorize the entire land and all of its people. He also knew he was only one small step behind Morgan. To stay and help the people of this realm would risk Tara's fate, which he was simply unwilling to do.

As difficult of a decision as it was to make Silas used his nullification key and then opened the gateway to Earth. Fifteen minutes later Silas was back inside Joel's apartment, frantically scribbling a note on the fridge's whiteboard. It was imperative that the others knew what he had discovered. He wrote:

Friends, be aware: Morgan first travels to a realm alone, seeking nothing but the box. Once she has found it, she leaves, only to return with the criminals best suited to dominate that world. I believe she leaves them in that world to search for the key, while she moves on to the next realm. Knowing this may prove to be to our advantage. Be cautious. Good luck. Silas

He hoped that the others would return here and find the message before they traveled to their next world, but he could not afford to wait and deliver the information in person. The carpenter walked resolutely out of the kitchen, into the living room and opened up the box on the coffee table. He pulled out a gold key from his satchel and inserted it into the brass plate. Morgan was one step ahead of him, but she would not stay there for long if he had anything to say about it.

* * *

Silas emerged from the light of the gateway into a dim and dingy world named Rend. The narrow alley he stood in was lined with boxes and cans, stacked against the metal walls of the buildings. There was a constant hum and buzz of machinery working all around, creating a symphony of clicks, ticks and grinding sounds. Billows of steam and smoke wafted out of the numerous pipes and chimneys, then drifted slowly down the alley.

"Outta the way buddy," a gruff voice commanded.

Silas shifted over to the side of the alley to allow the hefty man carrying a crate full of mechanical parts to pass by. The man barged ahead, pressing the carpenter into the iron wall beside him. "Pardon me," Silas sarcastically called after the man, who didn't seem to notice or care. "Now where to?" he asked himself.

Although Silas had been to this realm many times he still found it confusing to navigate. Perhaps it was because all the streets were so narrow and closed in limiting the view in all directions. Or perhaps it was because Rend had been crafted by someone else. Following a few moments thought he started out down the alley in one direction. A few steps down the road, however, he turned around and headed back the other way.

After nearly an hour meandering through the streets and alleys of Rend, Silas came across a small shop selling steam boilers of various sizes.

"Whatever you need ma'am," the owner of the store lobbied a potential customer. "We've got it. You need a small steamer for your iron or your coffee maker, presto, the MWS 500. Have a bigger job? The MWS 1000 simply can't be beat. It's relatively compact, but with enough PSI to run any major household appliance. Or perhaps you're in the market for something super compact. I just got this in this week, that's right, a Hughes 2.0. I guarantee you I'm the only shop in this quadrant of the city with one of these."

"That's lovely, young man," the woman replied. "But all I want is a one-inch rubber washer and half a dozen copper springs."

"Very well," the obviously disappointed salesman agreed. "Here you go, ma'am."

"Thank you so much, Nicky. You're a good boy," the woman smiled, taking her purchases and heading out into the street.

"You're still as smooth as ever, Nicolas," Silas chuckled.

"Silas!" the shop owner cheered. "What the devil are you doing here? I haven't seen you since that time with the ... well in a long time."

"Yes, you still owe me for cleaning that up."

"Right, of course."

"And I've come to collect."

"No problem," Nicolas grinned. "I just got this in, it's a Hu…"

"I don't want any of your spare parts Nicolas," the carpenter interrupted. "I need information."

"What kind of information?"

"Have you heard of any strange visitors to the realm in the last day or so?"

"Nope, I can't say I have. No one out of the ordinary. Same old same old here."

"Uh-huh," Silas replied skeptically. "On second thought I will take the Hughes 2.0."

"Excellent! That'll be 20 credits. You won't regret it. This is a quality little machine. I promise you."

"Nicolas. How about now? Do you recall any strange visitors?"

"Well, now that I think about it," the shop owner replied. "There was this one red-head lady who stopped by yesterday."

"And?"

"And what?"

"Can't you tell me anything more about her?"

"Oh sure," Nicolas beamed, "I can tell you *a lot* more. But first, are you sure you don't want some micro-piping for that steamer?"

– 10 –
All Wet

A search of the interior of the island had come up empty. Other than trees and soggy moss-covered ground there was nothing to be found. The dismal, weather in conjunction with the futility of their search, left the four friends rather despondent.

"No one saw anything?" Matthew asked again, consciously overlooking the fact that everyone had already clearly stipulated as much.

"Nope. Nada. Nothing. Zero. Zip. Zilch," Joel definitively announced.

"Nothing but rain and water," Juliette added.

"Same here," Matthew agreed sadly.

"What about ..." Emma began tentatively.

"What is it Em?"

"It's probably nothing."

"Nothing is what we have now," Joel clarified. "What are you thinking?"

"What about that pole we saw in the water, Matthew?"

"Right, I forgot about that."

"What pole?" Joel and Juliette asked in unison.

"When we were first walking around the island we saw a pole sticking out of the water about ten feet offshore," Matthew explained. "It looked like it might have had a rope or cord of some kind hanging off of it, but it was hard to see it clearly through the rain."

"Speaking of the rain," Juliette said. "Do you think it's ever going to stop?"

"I don't know," her boyfriend answered. "We've been here an hour or two and it certainly hasn't let up so far. What do you say we go check out that pole, shall we?"

"We've got nothing better to do," Matthew noted.

* * *

It took the group a while to locate the pole through the dim light and heavy rain, but Emma eventually spotted it. "There it is!" she shouted.

Matthew and Joel waded cautiously into the water, slowly making their way out to the partially submerged pole.

"Are you guys okay?" Emma shouted over the thunderous sound of the rain pelting the water's surface.

"So far so good," Matthew shouted back.

"The water is not as cold as I expected," Joel added. "Don't get me wrong, it's no Jacuzzi, but with the wetsuit it's bearable, at least for a while."

The two young men stood next to the pole, waves splashing against their chests at regular intervals. The pair examined the wooden post projecting out of the water. Matthew discovered a thick rope knotted around the top of the pole. The rope angled steeply down into the water.

"Maybe it's an anchor line or something," Joel suggested with a shoulder shrug. "Wait, that's dumb! Who would tie an anchor to a post? What purpose could that possibly serve?"

"Beats me," his friend said, reaching down into the water as far as his hand could stretch. "I think there is something down there. It may not be an anchor, but there's definitely something."

"Let's check it out!" Joel cheered with all the glee of a young boy and then dove under the surface of the water. A few moments later he resurfaced and drew a deep breath. "There's a boat down there!"

"What?"

"Yeah, a little wooden rowboat. It's not far below the surface, just a couple feet out from the post. The rope goes down and runs through a couple pulleys on the bow and stern."

"Where does the other end of the rope go?"

"I can't tell, it just kind of runs out into the water somewhere."

"Did you see the hole that caused the boat to sink? Can we fix it?"

"I didn't get a chance to look at every inch of it, but I don't think there is a hole."

"But how..."

"I think it just sat out in the rain long enough that it filled up with water and sank."

"I suppose it wouldn't take long when it's coming down like this," Matthew observed. So, do you think if we could empty it out it would float?"

"I don't see why not. And my hunch is that this rope is supposed to help guide the boat over to the next island or whatever else is out there."

"Sounds like we have a plan then. Emma! Juliette! We're going to need your help out here," Matthew called back to shore.

* * *

The four friends managed, with a fair amount of time and a lot of effort, to tilt and lift the sunken rowboat just enough to raise one of the gunnels six inches above the surface of the water. As soon as they released their grip the boat quickly found its equilibrium and once again sat level. Thanks to their work, the very top of the boat now rose slightly above the surface.

"That's progress," Matthew huffed. "Let's take a one-minute breather and then get back at it."

"Not too long," Emma said between deep breaths. "We don't want it to ... to fill up again.

Following a short break, the friends got back to work. Matthew and Joel lifted one side of the boat as high as they could, while Emma and Juliette held up the other side, preventing it from dipping back under the water's surface and refilling the boat. Each time they performed this maneuver more water flowed out of the boat. Less water meant less weight, which allowed the boys to lift higher, displacing even more water. After another twenty minutes of repeating this procedure, the boat sat predominantly on top of the water with only a small pool of water remaining inside.

"That should do it," Matthew declared

"Yeah, but for how long?" Juliette asked. "The rain's coming down as hard as ever. Look, it's already accumulating in the bottom of the boat."

"How do we know the boat won't sink again before we reach the next island, or whatever is at the other end of this rope?" Emma pondered.

"And with the weight of all four of us in the boat it will be riding that much lower in the water to begin with," Joel added.

"No one saw anything we could use to bail with, did they?" Matthew questioned. No one had. He considered the situation for a moment and then suggested, "Maybe I should go on my own."

"Why would you do that?" Juliette inquired.

"Only one person in the boat is less weight. And, like Joel said, less weight means the boat rides higher and stays afloat longer."

"By that logic, I should be the one to go," Emma stated resolutely. "I weigh a lot less than you or Joel."

"Are you calling me fat?" Joel pretended to be offended while bulging out his stomach as far as his wetsuit would allow.

"And what happens when you make it to the other side?" Juliette asked.

"That's assuming there is another side and you actually make it there," Joel chimed.

"When I get to the other side, hopefully there are folks over there who can help me come back and get you guys," Matthew replied.

"Or, we could just wait for the rain to stop," Emma offered.

"That could be a long wait," Joel responded.

"And we don't have that kind of time. Every minute we sit here Morgan gets further ahead of us."

"Fine," Emma conceded. "But either we all go, or I go."

"What do you guys think?"

"I say we all go," Juliette stated.

"Ditto," her boyfriend agreed.

"Well, I'm not letting you go alone, Em, so I guess we're all going."

The guys hoisted Emma and Juliette into the boat. Then Joel, the taller of the two men, boosted Matthew over the gunnel as well. Finally, the girls leaned to the opposite side, offsetting the weight, as Matthew pulled his friend up into the boat as well. Joel's prediction was on the mark. The boat was sitting noticeably lower in the water now that they were all aboard. Also, the unrelenting rain had already filled the water in the bottom of the boat to their ankles.

"Ok, if we're going to do this, we better get to it," Matthew suggested. "Emma and I will start pulling on the rope, which should move us off in that direction. You two do what you can to bail out the water with your hands. When we start to run out of steam we can switch."

"Sounds good."

"Ok."

"On it."

"Remember, the faster we get this tub moving, the sooner we can, hopefully, get back on dry ground."

"We may find ground," Joel quipped. "But something tells me it ain't gonna be dry."

After only a few minutes the gateway island disappeared behind the sheets of rain that continued to pour down. With the shore out of sight it became very difficult to judge how fast they were moving, or how much ground they had covered. The two couples switched roles several times, attempting to keep the freshest arms pulling on the rope. As time wore on, however, the task of bailing water by hand was nearly as tiring as moving the boat. They could all sense that they were fighting a losing battle as the boat was filling with water faster than they could bail it out.

"If we don't reach shore soon, we're going to be swimming," Joel observed.

"At some point that may not be a bad idea," Emma suggested.

"How so?" her boyfriend asked.

"Well, our bodies are already half submerged in the water and eventually the drag on the boat will be greater than if we just dove in and pulled ourselves along."

"Perhaps," Matthew considered the idea. "Then again, since the boat is connected to the rope it can only sink so far into the water. If we go it alone, what happens when we run out of energy?"

"And who knows what else is swimming in this water," Juliette cautioned.

"I say we stick with the boat as long as it stays afloat," Matthew stated.

The words were no sooner out of his mouth than he saw a glimmer of something metallic streaking through the air. There was a loud bang followed by the sound of splintering wood.

"Is that a..." Joel gawked.

"A trident," Matthew stated examining the three metal prongs that had punctured the hull of the boat. Water began gushing in through the ragged holes created by the projectile.

"Where did that come from?" Emma cried out.

"I saw it fly through the air from over there," Matthew explained, pointing toward the front of the boat.

"What do we do now?" Juliette asked.

"We could make a swim for it," Joel suggested. "If that's where the trident came from there must be land ahead."

"If another one of those things comes flying our way, I'd rather it hit the boat than me," Emma noted.

"Hello!" Matthew shouted.

"What are you doing?" his friend questioned. "You'll give away our position!"

"Dude, we're in a boat, connected to a rope, and judging by the accuracy of that first shot I don't think our location is a mystery."

"Good point."

"Hello!" he shouted again. "We come in peace! We are friends of Silas!" There was no response for a moment and then the boat lurched.

"Are we sinking?" Joel asked.

"No, we're moving forward!" Emma cheered.

"How is that possible?"

Matthew leaned over the bow and discovered a second rope secured to the nose of the boat, which was now taut. "Looks like someone is towing us in."

"Hopefully someone friendly," Juliette quipped.

"Towing us is far more friendly than hurling another trident, that's for sure!" Joel observed.

Ten minutes later the boat slowed to a stop as it ran aground. The visitors were unsure what the best course of action was. Should they get out and greet whoever it was that had pulled them in, or should they just stay put and wait to be invited ashore? The four friends sat nervously in the boat for several minutes, waiting for some sign of welcome. Finally Joel stood to climb out of the boat.

Suddenly the tip of a trident appeared, like the one that had punctured their boat. Joel quickly sat back down as the weapon moved towards them. As the spear emerged through the curtain of the dense rain its bearer was finally revealed.

"Who are you?" a brusk voice inquired. The voice was surprisingly strong coming from a tall slender man. "Why are you here?"

"We are friends of Silas," Matthew explained. "He sent us here."

"Why should I believe you?" the man demanded.

It was an excellent question and one none of the travelers had previously generated a satisfactory answer to. There was nothing they could offer as definitive proof of their intentions or their relationship with Silas. The people of Arbolada had welcomed them warmly, but it seemed folks here were not so trusting.

"We are here to capture Morgan," Emma explained. She was playing a hunch, but she knew it was a risky one. According to the device, Morgan had traveled to this realm, but she was clearly no longer on the gateway island. That meant she more than likely ended up on this island at some point. If the inhabitants had recognized her for the evil woman she was then the four friends' arrival would be a welcomed development. That is assuming they weren't suspected of being her allies, in which case this not-so-warm-welcome would make sense. On the other hand, if the person holding the trident was not a local, but rather one of Morgan's henchmen, then revealing their true purpose in coming to Bhal could be a fatal mistake.

The man on shore stared at the boat's passengers long and hard, for an uncomfortably long time. His expression did not flinch, and his weapon did not waiver.

"Get out of the boat," he commanded. "Slowly. One at a time." Matthew got out of the boat first, sliding down into the nearly waist deep water. "Move to shore."

Matthew cautiously moved past the tall, thin man and made his way out of the water to the sandy beach. Once he was out of the water he glanced back at the boat but could scarcely see his friends through the driving rain. When he turned back around he was startled to be facing two more men holding tridents, both of which were pointed directly at him.

"This way," one of the men instructed, motioning inland with his weapon.

These men were similar in stature to the one who had greeted them at the boat. Up close, Matthew could see their facial features looked like a person from earth, although their skin tone was noticeably pale, with a grayish tint. He also noticed subtle gill-like slits on either side of their necks, however, he fought hard not to stare at this oddity lest he offended his captors.

"Where are we going?" Matthew asked.

"This way," the man repeated, nudging him gently, but firmly, with the face of his trident.

The men led Matthew off the beach and into the trees. A few yards in they told him to stop. They securely bound his hands with a woven seaweed rope, which they also tied around a nearby tree. Then they walked back towards the beach and out of sight. Matthew stood next to the tree, alone for quite some time, wondering what would come next. The only comfort he had was that being held tight against the tree provided some shelter from the pouring rain, reducing it to heavy drizzle. He could not see or hear anyone else. He had no way of knowing if his friends were being held together at the boat or individually in the forest. After what seemed like a very long time, the man who had first met them on the shore reappeared. At least Matthew *thought* it was the same man, but in truth, all three men looked quite alike to him.

"Who are you?" the man asked again in a cordial, but firm tone.

"My name is Matthew. I am a friend of Silas."

"What is your intention here?"

"Morgan has kidnapped Tara and stolen her keys. We are here to stop her."

"What makes you think she's here?"

"We caught up with her in Arbolada, but she escaped. The gateway she passed through brought her here."

"Hmm," the man said thoughtfully. "I'm inclined to think you might be telling the truth. After all, Morgan's other companions are far more formidable than any of you."

"Um, thanks, I think," Matthew replied. "That means she is here then? Do you know where? We need to catch her as soon as possible."

"I'm afraid you're too late for that," the Bhallian stated sadly. "She was here but has already moved on. She took advantage of our kindness and hospitality when she first arrived. At that point we had no reason to be suspect of her intentions. She clearly knew Silas and Tara quite well and was extremely cordial to all of us. Then she returned, this time with four others who proved to be especially cruel and violent."

"But they are gone now?"

"No. Morgan is gone. The others remain. They have been terrorizing the islands: destroying property, ransacking homes and attacking anyone who stands in their way. Last we heard they were on Oncoryhn Island, but they may have moved on from there by now."

"The men you speak of are criminals that Morgan released from prison," Matthew explained. "It could be that free reign of your world is their reward for assisting her in her vendetta against Silas."

"Perhaps, but as erratic as their behavior initially seemed, they are being rather methodical about it as well. They tear through every inch of one island, leaving no rock unturned, before moving on to the next. Almost as if ..."

"They are looking for something. Morgan is searching for a very special key which she believes is hidden in one of the realms. That's undoubtedly what these mercenaries are hunting for."

"Wait here," the man instructed.

Matthew raised his hands as much as he could, displaying the seaweed ropes still fastened around his wrists. "Exactly where do you think I'm going to go?"

The man smirked slightly, the most noticeable sign of friendliness he had displayed so far. He marched off into the trees and quickly disappeared in the foliage and rain.

– 11 –
Being Bait

Ten or fifteen minutes passed before the man returned. He smiled at Matthew softly and began to loosen the knots in the seaweed rope.

"This seems promising," Matthew grinned back.

"My friends and I have questioned each of your group separately and you have all given us the same answers, which makes us inclined to believe you are being honest."

"Or we just did a good job of getting our stories straight," Joel joked, appearing through the trees. As soon as the words left his lips he immediately regretted speaking them. "Which is totally not at all what we did."

"We also agreed that Morgan's other companions are extremely strong," the man explained further, "but not so clever."

"Neither are some of us," Juliette cracked, walking up behind her boyfriend, with Emma and the other two locals close behind.

"My name is Koho. These are my friends Salmo and Huchen."

"Nice to meet you," Matthew replied cordially, rubbing his now freed wrists. "Where exactly are we, if you don't mind my asking?"

"You are in Bhal," Koho replied cheerfully, "but of course you already knew that. This island is called Trutta. We were sent here to keep watch for anyone else trying to come through the gateway on Fario to further oppress us."

"You're pretty wicked with that trident," Joel admired. "Are you, like, the local ninjas or navy seals or something?"

"Elite soldiers," Juliette translated for her overly enthusiastic boyfriend.

"No," the Bhallian chuckled. "We are the local fishermen. Bhal has no military to speak of so our skills with a trident are our world's best hope of defending itself."

"Sweet," Joel nodded. "Hey, would it be okay if I got a closer look at one of those things?" The two Bhallians chuckled softly and one of them handed his trident over to Joel, who became enthralled as he examined it.

"Speaking of fish," Matthew began tentatively, "do you mind if I ask you what these are all about?" he asked, motioning to the sides of Koho's neck.

"They are exactly what you suspect they are, gills. The only way for us to travel from island to island is to swim, so they are somewhat of a necessity."

"What about the boat?" Emma asked.

A fourth Bhallian joined the group. He was shorter than the others and appeared younger, although the age of the people of this realm was quite difficult for the off-worlders to gauge. "All clear on the beach," he reported.

"Thank you, Slake," Koho acknowledged, then returned his attention to the new arrivals. "That boat was a special provision for Silas to allow him to get here from the gateway island. Once on Trutta my people would assist him in getting from place to place."

"Now that you shish-kabobbed it with your trident I don't think it will be doing anybody any good," Joel noted, returning the spear and tuning back into the conversation.

"Quite true. I'm afraid our young friend, Slake, got a little over anxious when he thought another group of Morgan's thugs were on their way."

"Pretty decent shot though," Joel admired. "He totally nailed the hull perfectly!" The three older Bhallians snickered. "What?"

"I'm guessing he wasn't actually aiming at the boat, hun," Juliette explained, patting her boyfriend gently on the back.

"No harm, no foul," Matthew said, trying to not sound as troubled as he felt by the recent revelation. "So, where to now?"

"There is a village not far from here," Koho stated. "Salmo and Huchen will take you there. It is not much, but you will be able to find some food, a warm fire, and shelter from the rain."

"Now that you mention it," Emma began, "does it ever stop raining here?"

"Of course it does," Koho chuckled. "Every now and then we have a dry day or at least a dry afternoon. The rain is especially hard right now, but during the dry season it is typically more of a drizzle most of the time."

"The dry season, huh?" Joel chuckled.

"A warm fire sounds delightful," Juliette said, urging the group to get on its way.

"Very well. My friends will take care of you. I will come and find you later and we can talk some more."

* * *

After getting fed, dried off and warmed up, the four friends began discussing their current situation, and more importantly their next move. They sat huddled around a small fire inside a quaint little hut made out of a bamboo-like material.

"What do we do now?" Emma asked.

"Morgan's gone, so we need to find the box and continue to chase her down," Matthew stated.

"But we can't just leave these poor people to be terrorized by Morgan's henchmen," Juliette objected.

"Jules is right," Joel affirmed. "Winston convinced us that bailing on him and everyone else in Arbolada was the right thing to do, and it seemed like it was. But that decision has not sat well with me from the minute we made it."

"Agreed," Matthew said. "But what can we do to help these people other than catch Morgan and put an end to all of this? I don't like leaving these folks to fend for themselves any more than you do, I just don't know what the better alternative is."

"I don't know either," Emma conceded. "But we have to find one. I won't be able to live with myself if we keep abandoning people."

"The problem is we're not fighters," Joel observed. "Koho and his trident chucking fisherman are more of a threat than we are. Even if Slake's aim is a little off."

"What can we do that they can't?" his girlfriend agreed.

After a few moments of thoughtful silence, Matthew spoke up with a gleam in his eye, "We can be bait!"

"What are you talking about, Matt?"

"Morgan's thugs are looking for the key to the workshop, right?"

"Yeah, but we don't have it."

"No, we don't. But they don't know we don't. If we can convince them that Silas gave us the key, not only for this world, but the workshop as well, they are sure to come after us to get it."

"That's great and all," Joel interjected, "but then what?"

"I might be able to help with that," Koho offered. "I didn't mean to eavesdrop on your conversation. I just came to check in on you and see how you were doing, when I overheard your plan."

"It's more of a theory than a plan at this point," Joel corrected, "but go on."

"We are fishermen, as you know. We use our tridents to spear large fish or ward off attackers while we're in the water, but most of the time we fish with nets."

"Nets strong enough to hold one of Morgan's goons?" Emma asked.

"I believe so," Koho smiled, "but likely only one."

"Which means we'll have to get them to split up," Matthew postulated.

"How are we going to do that?" Juliette asked.

"I have no clue," Matthew answered.

"Let's not forget, they're all on some other island too," Joel added.

"My people can take you over to Oncoryhn Island, assuming Morgan's men are still there."

"That reminds me," Matthew began, "how is it that these guys can travel from island to island without a boat? Do they have gills like you?"

"You have?!" Joel exclaimed. "Well, I'll be jiggered," he concluded after spotting Koho's gills.

"Dude, you were standing right there when I asked him about that at the beach!" Matthew said in bewilderment.

"Hey, it's been a crazy couple of days," Joel defended himself.

"No," the Bhallian chuckled as he answered Matthew's question. "They arrived here wearing clothes similar to what you have, but they also had removable feet fins and portable breathers. With these, they can swim almost as well as we can."

The mention of flippers prompted Matthew to glance at Koho's feet for the first time. He was fascinated to see they were significantly larger than a normal man's foot would be and his extra long toes appeared to be webbed together. "Sounds like Morgan knew exactly what kind of world they would be coming into."

"Perhaps her first visit was simply a scouting mission," Emma surmised.

"That's smart," Joel agreed. "Then she could return with thugs perfectly equipped to run roughshod over the entire realm."

"So, luring them into the water isn't of any advantage to us," Juliette observed. "How else do we split them up?"

"I hate to say it, but I think we have to split up," Matthew suggested.

"That sounds like an incredibly bad idea," Joel objected.

"I agree," Emma added.

"I don't like it either," Matthew confessed, "but if they don't know which one of us has the key they will be forced to split up if we all scatter in different directions."

"I agree with your logic, Matt, but I don't like it."

"It will be fine, Joel. Koho will get his people to set up four different traps in four different areas. All we have to do is run to our designated locations and the Bhallians will do the rest."

"Is that all?" Joel said facetiously

"We also have to get to those locations before we get caught," Emma said unenthusiastically.

"And not get lost along the way," Juliette noted.

"I didn't say it was a flawless plan," Matthew conceded. "But unless anyone can come up with something better, it's all we've got."

"Wow, you really know how to sell it, buddy," Joel joked. "Okay, I'm in."

"Me too."

"And me."

"I am very grateful to all of you," Koho smiled. "I will go talk to some of my people. We will prepare the nets and plan the location of the traps. I will return shortly."

After their host left, Matthew spoke to his friends again, "Guys, I know this isn't an ideal situation, but..."

"It's the right thing to do," Emma interjected gently. "We all know it, Matthew."

* * *

The visitors had enjoyed a good night's sleep thanks to the warm fire and the hospitality of their hosts. They rose to the new day and devoured a hearty breakfast before venturing outside. The torrential downpour of the previous day had relented a little and was now only a heavy rain. Koho had visited their hut earlier that morning and informed them that preparations were nearly complete. He also explained that he had sent scouts ahead to Oncoryhn Island to confirm that Morgan's henchmen were still there. The report had come back positive and so it seemed everything was in place to move forward with Matthew's plan.

"I have recruited three others, along with myself," Koho stated. "We will accompany you in this mission and ensure that you find your way to the designated areas. And should you not be able to outrun Morgan's men, we will defend you with all our might."

"Thank you Koho," all four of the friends said in unison.

"Now what?" Emma asked.

"It is a short swim to Salveli Island and then a slightly longer one to Oncoryhn. If we leave soon we should be able to make it there by midday, easily."

"How do you know it's midday when you can never see the sun?" Joel smirked.

"High tide is at midday and midnight," the Bhallian explained. "In between we just more or less guess."

"Great work, Koho," Matthew replied. "I think we're ready to go."

"I also took the liberty of sending some people ahead to start circulating rumors of off-worlders traveling through Bhal with a key to the workshop."

"Good thinking," Joel chimed. "By the time we arrive, those thugs will be just itching to chase us down."

"Alright then," Matthew encouraged, "let's get on our way then."

Koho led the visitors to the shore on the far side of the island, opposite to where they had landed in the boat the previous day. At the beach they waded into the water, each with a Bhallian partner. As the water rose above waist-deep, the four friends each stood behind their companions and locked their arms around the Bhallian's neck. Once the off-worlder's grip was secure, the locals dove forward into the water and began to swim toward the next island, doing their best to keep the off-worlders' heads above water.

The Bhallians' stamina in the water was truly impressive and after twenty minutes of swimming, they reached the next island, which was small and mostly uninhabited save for a handful of wild rice farmers. The group traveled quickly around the shore until they reached their next launch point. Before proceeding, Koho gave them their final instructions.

"Our plan is to arrive on the south shore of Oncoryhn Island. At last report, Morgan's men were

Being Bait

on the east coast, but that may have changed, especially if they've heard news of your arrival."

"Okay, everyone ready?" Matthew asked. His three friends all nodded affirmatively. "Alright. See you on the flipside."

The group waded back into the water and the Bhallians began to swim towards Oncoryhn Island. When they arrived, they were met by a young woman who was nervously pacing the shore.

"They're in town," the woman said.

"Very good," Koho replied. "That *is* good, right? Of course it is. Everything is going according to plan," he reassured himself and then confidently added, "Follow me, everyone."

Koho led the group cautiously from the beach into the tall, palm-like trees as the other Bhallians dove back into the water and returned home. A few minutes later they stood on the outskirts of a small town, filled with huts similar to what they had seen on Trutta. Three other men met up with them just outside of town.

"These men will be our guides," Koho introduced. "Matthew, you will stay with me. Emma, this is Masu."

"Hello," Emma said politely.

"Arripis will go with Juliette and my brother Kisutch will go with you, Joel."

The off-worlders briefly greeted their new friends and then turned their attention back to the task at hand. It didn't take long for them to spot the four

Garda escapees. The men were oversized, though not quite as large as Crank and Lug. Their bodies bore numerous scars, which appeared to be caused intentionally by ritual rather than wounds from battle, or possibly a mixture of both. Their faces displayed heavy-set brows and deeply inset eyes with amber irises. The four men were moving from hut to hut, leaving a wake of townspeople scattering in fear.

"Okay guys," Matthew said nervously, "moment of truth."

"Be careful everyone," Emma pleaded.

"No one be a hero," Joel instructed, squeezing his girlfriend's hand as he spoke. "Just stick with your guide and keep running."

"Everyone ready?" Matthew asked.

"I guess so,"

"Yep."

"As ready as I'll ever be."

"Okay, then," Matthew paused and waited.

"Do it, Matthew, we'll be fine," Emma prompted.

Matthew reluctantly led his friends out of the trees and stood in plain sight of the town. It only took a few moments for one of the large men to notice the off-worlders. Upon seeing them he quickly alerted his fellow goons.

"Get 'em!" the man shouted in a gravelly voice.

"Whatever happens," Matthew yelled loudly, even though his friends stood nearby. "We can't let them get the key to the workshop!"

Being Bait

The four thugs began moving toward the edge of town, gradually picking up speed. "Move it, you worthless slogs," the man in the lead jeered. "Don't let them escape! Those piddly little people are our ticket outta here!"

The Heritage Key

- 12 -
Pursued

"That's our cue!" Joel gave Juliette's hand one last affectionate squeeze.

The four friends ran off into the trees. Each one followed their Bhallian guide in a different direction, constantly looking back to gauge the proximity of their pursuer. It was imperative they did not get caught. However, they also did not want to get too far ahead and risk losing the man chasing them.

"This way," Kisutch called out.

Joel wove his way through the trees, doing his best to keep pace with his guide. At one point he glanced back to see how much of a lead he had on his pursuer. The large man behind him lumbered on with surprising speed. Danmok was the largest of the Farine brothers. He stood over seven feet tall, but it was his substantial girth that made him such an intimidating figure. His mouth snarled in between heavy breaths as he trampled through the trees. The look in his eyes quickly convinced Joel that Danmok would tear him apart with his bare hands, if need be, to find the workshop key.

Joel turned his attention forward again, just in time to lunge to the side and avoid a head-on collision with a sizable tree. Danmok was closing in on his prey, but Joel felt confident in his ability to stay ahead of the brute.

"Almost there," Kisutch called out again.

Joel slowed his stride slightly to draw the man chasing him in a little closer. As he ran between two large trees his peripheral vision caught sight of a Bhallian man concealed behind the tree on his left. Joel fought the impulse to turn and look at the man lest he give away his location, but from that momentary glimpse he saw what he believed to be a thin-bladed filleting knife held against a rope that stretched up into the treetops.

Moments after Joel had sped past the man with the knife, he heard a commotion behind him, followed by loud and angry shouting. He turned to see Morgan's goon suspended in midair. The man dangled above the ground as the Bhallian with the knife slowly lowered the net.

"Got him," the guide announced proudly, walking back toward the captured man. "Great work, Keta!"

Kisutch pulled the man's hands through a single hole in the netting and tied his wrists together tightly with seaweed rope. The other man handed Kisutch a trident and then lowered the net down fully to the ground. The captured man lay helplessly on the ground, hands tied, and the tip of the trident pressed uncomfortably against his chest. Keta tied the thug's ankles together, leaving just enough slack for the man to shuffle along, then he began to search the man's pack for weapons or anything else of interest.

"You can take these," Keta smiled, handing Joel the man's flippers and breathing device. "He won't be needing them anymore."

"Thanks," Joel said, taking the equipment. "I wonder how the others are making out."

* * *

Juliette ran through the forest doing her best to keep up with Arripis and not think too much about the man trailing behind her. As she wove through the trees she thought to herself how much easier this would be if she were wearing a tracksuit, not a wetsuit. Neoprene was great for swimming, but not nearly as comfortable for sprinting.

The large man chasing behind her was Finkar, the youngest of the Farine brothers. He bore a painful looking scar across his right cheek and was missing several teeth. Although he was smaller than his other siblings, Finkar still boasted a physique that was disturbingly impressive in size and power, especially to someone he was determined to hunt down.

Arripis sped through the trees ahead of her, occasionally calling back to urge her to *'come on'* or *'keep up'*. Juliette took a quick glance back to see how much time she had before the man behind her caught up. When she spotted him through the trees, the distance was not nearly as great as she had hoped. As she turned her attention forward, her foot snagged on a protruding root and she tumbled to the ground.

Juliette scrambled to her feet as quickly as she could and started off again. A quick self-diagnostic revealed no major injuries from the fall, simply a few scrapes. She sped forward with all the haste she could muster, but soon realized that Arripis had vanished from sight. Juliette wasn't certain if she had gotten turned around when she fell or if those few seconds lost in her wipe out were enough for the Bhallian to run out of sight.

Warding off the panic that pressed hard to overcome her mind, Juliette resolved to continue on in the direction she *thought* she was moving prior to tripping on the root. Hopefully she was headed more or less toward the trap, or perhaps Arripis would eventually notice she was no longer behind him and circle back to find her. Neither option instilled her with a lot of confidence, but that was all she had to hang on to. She could hear Finkar behind her, closing in quickly. Most of the lead she had on him had been lost in her fall.

Juliette was certain this was the end. She could feel Morgan's henchman right behind her, reaching out to grab her. She was also running out of gas. Perhaps she shouldn't have quit going to spin class two months ago, she thought to herself as she pushed her body for every last ounce of energy it had in it.

Suddenly she was jolted by a heavy impact from the side. She felt a pair of long arms wrap around her as she flew sideways and tumbled to the ground. She stopped rolling just in time to look back and see a hefty net fall from the trees above and land squarely on Finkar's head. The large mesh, weighted with heavy stones around the edges, pulled the brute to the ground and held him there, helplessly trapped.

"Are you alright?" Arripis asked, releasing his grip from her. "One minute you were right behind me and the next you were gone. I was terrified that I might have lost you."

"I'm fine," Juliette smiled gently, easing herself back on to her knees. "I'm just glad that's over with."

* * *

Emma's legs burned as she ran through the trees, doing her best to keep pace with Masu. The man behind her, named Molway, was the fastest of the four brothers and gained ground on her with every stride. She wasn't sure how much longer she could stay ahead of him. Her pursuer taunted Emma as they ran. She could not decipher what he was saying, but she could tell, without a doubt, her speed wasn't living up to his expectation.

"This way," Masu called, veering hard to the left.

By the time she processed the instructions, there was a large tree directly in front of her. Emma swerved to the right to avoid the collision and then made a much wider turn to the left. Once her turn was complete, she spotted Masu off in the distance but was blindsided by a freight-train of a man flying around the opposite side of the tree.

The two crashed to the ground and struggled with one another for a few moments, however, it did not take long for the large man to get the upper hand and pin his prey to the ground.

"Now, where is that stinkin' key?" he asked in a gruff voice as he began to fumble around Emma's body looking for where the key might be hidden. Of course, since she was wearing a skin-tight wetsuit, there were very few hiding places. If these guys had been smarter they would have realized that from the start and focussed their efforts on Matthew who was the only one of the four wearing a waist pack. "I knows you've got it somewheres, girly. And I'm going find it, even if I have to…"

The lout's words were interrupted by an attack from behind. Masu wrapped his long, skinny arms around the man's neck and attempted to pull him off of Emma. It took a minute but the man eventually broke Masu's grip and tossed him to the ground. Having momentarily forgotten about Emma the oversized thug turned his attention to the Bhallian. He straddled Masu and began flailing away at him with heavy punches. Masu did his best to fend off the blows, but his wiry frame was no match for the brute's hefty arms.

Suddenly the punches stopped. Molway just sat still, looking stunned. His eyes rolled back in his head and he toppled over onto the ground like a giant sack of flour. As the man fell, Masu saw Emma standing behind him holding a large tree branch with an angry look on her face.

"Take that, girly," she said defiantly. "Are you okay Masu?"

"Yes, thanks to you. We should tie him up quickly before he comes to."

"I have a long list of things I'd like to do to this jerk," she said with obvious spite, "But tying him up will do to start."

* * *

The large man rumbled through the trees in eager pursuit of his quarry. Morgan had promised him and his companions their freedom, but not until they found the workshop key. Thus far they had turned three islands upside down and hadn't found the slightest hint of the key's location. If these off-worlders had a workshop key of their own, it would put an end to the search and buy the criminals their full independence.

Karlok had been imprisoned on Garda for a very long time. The nature of the realm dramatically reduced aging, allowing some of the captives to be held there for centuries. Karlok and his three brothers were among the most recent prisoners, despite the fact they had all been taken to Garda decades before Silas had learned the craft. Even though he was out of his cell and able to do as he pleased in Bhal, he would not feel truly free until his debt to Morgan had been expunged. Catching Matthew and gaining access to the workshop was, both literally and figuratively, the key to making that happen.

The last glimpse Karlok had caught of Matthew saw him running for the beach. The oversized man burst through the treeline and then slowed to a stop as he stepped onto the sand. He stood still for a moment puzzled by what he saw. Matthew stood 15 feet out from shore with water almost up to his waist.

"Ha! Where you gonna go now, boy?" the thug scoffed.

"You just ... you stay right there," Matthew stammered nervously. His legs wobbled as the waves crashed into him.

"You're mine," Karlok scowled. The brute stomped through the water, stopping five feet in front of Matthew. Being a much larger man, the water only rose mid-thigh on him. "Gimme the key."

"No," Matthew replied weakly, "I'm not going to give it to you. It's my job to keep it safe."

"Fine. I'll just come take it from you then," Karlok scowled. Anger swelled inside him at the insolence of this runt. He lunged forward with two large strides. He reached out to grab Matthew's neck. Suddenly the ground vanished from under his feet and he plummeted under the water. Moments later Karlok resurfaced, coughing and spewing out water. His hands slapped at the water frantically, but he was he was still barely keeping his head above the surface.

A Bhallian rose up behind the man and grinned. "His feet are secured," the man reported. He wrapped one arm around Karlok's chest, pulling him back toward shore. Very soon the goon's feet found solid ground again. The slender man quickly tied the other's hands together while he still gasped for air.

"Oh, by the way," Matthew smiled, "Watch out for the drop-off – it's pretty steep."

Karlok, glared in rage as the Bhallian dragged him back to shore. Matthew took a step forward and fell into the water. After a few moments of doggy paddling, he passed the drop-off and found sure footing again. He turned just in time to see Koho surface where Matthew had been standing moments earlier. The Bhallian's hands were still raised high above his head.

"I was getting worried," Matthew chuckled. "I wasn't sure how long you could stay down there."

"I can breathe underwater indefinitely," Koho explained, "but I'll be honest, you were getting a little heavy." A broad smiled spread across his face.

By the time they got back to shore, the other Bhallian had dragged Karlok onto the beach and laid him face down in the sand. He searched the man's pack and handed Matthew the captive's flippers and breather. "What are we going to do with these guys now?"

"Assuming we've caught all four, our men will transport them to Sevan Island. It is not far from here, but farther than they would be able to swim unaided. The island is barren and uninhabited. We will exile them there until Silas returns."

"Sounds like a plan," Matthew said. "*Assuming* we've caught all four."

"We got ours!" Emma cheered as she walked up the beach with Masu leading their prisoner behind them.

"Emma!" Matthew cried out and ran to greet his girlfriend. "I'm so glad you're okay."

"So am I – I mean I'm glad you're okay too," Emma laughed. "Actually, I'm glad for both."

"We caught ours too," Juliette called out, coming down the beach from the other direction.

"Way to go, Jules!" Matthew congratulated.

"Thanks. You too. But where is Joel?"

"I'm right here, sweetheart," Joel said, emerging from the trees. "And I brought my plus one."

"Excellent work, all of you!" Koho beamed. "My people will be forever grateful to you."

"Don't mention it," Joel grinned.

"We should take these men to Sevan before they find a way to escape their bonds," the Masu stated.

"Of course," Matthew replied, "and we need to continue on with our business too."

"With these guys captured and Morgan already gone, as interesting as it would be to stay and look around a bit more, we need to find the box and move on to the next world as soon as possible," Emma observed.

"Koho, do you know where Silas keeps the gateway box?" Juliette asked.

"Of course, it is on the island of Ohrid," the Bhalllian explained. "It is not far from here. If you use the feet fins and breathers you took from these men, you should be able to make it there easily. Keta can lead you there if you like."

"Sounds good to me," Joel said. "I've got to get out of this rain before my whole body turns into one giant prune!"

"Thanks again to all of you," Koho smiled warmly. "I hope to see you again, soon."

The off-worlders said goodbye to all their new friends and watched with deep satisfaction as the four thugs were led away toward exile. Once Koho and his men had gone the visitors began putting on the flippers they had seized from Morgan's men. Keta couldn't help but giggle as the four friends waddled around on the beach trying desperately not to stumble, thanks to their newly augmented feet.

"This way everyone!" the Bhallian called out and then dove gracefully into the water. Ten minutes later they were all back on semi-dry ground, this time on the Island of Ohrid. "The box is in a house in the village just ahead. Follow me."

"It sure felt good to help these people," Matthew stated.

"No doubt," Joel agreed.

"Yeah it did," Emma began reluctantly, "but at the same time, it makes me feel all the worse that we abandoned Winston and everyone else on Arbolada. I thought we were doing the right thing, but now I'm not so sure. Maybe we could have helped them after all."

"Instead they're stuck dealing with Crank and Lug on their own," Juliette added.

"I know how you feel," Matthew sympathized, "but there's nothing we can do about it now. If we went back we would be trapped there ourselves."

"You're right, but..."

"The best thing we can do now is capture Morgan so we can go back to Arbolada with Silas and take care of Crank and Lug once and for all," Joel declared.

"We are here," Keta said, motioning them toward the door of a small hut. "This is where I leave you. Good luck."

The four friends walked inside and found the gateway box sitting on a shelf. Matthew pulled the device out of his waist pack. After opening the wooden box, he scanned the brass plate.

"Looks like Morgan went to a realm called Rend," he revealed.

"Alright," Joel said. "Let's go! Rend, here we come."

"Not so fast," his friend cautioned. "I don't have a Rend key."

"That must be one of the keys Silas has," Emma surmised.

"And based on what the Bhallians have told us, she likely traveled to that world at least a day or two ago," Matthew added.

"So, what do we do now?" Juliette inquired.

"Well, we either go home or on to a different realm," Matthew replied.

"A visit home would be nice," Emma said. "However, the sooner we get to the next realm, the sooner we can track down Morgan."

"True, but I wouldn't mind a change of clothes before we head to the next world," Joel suggested. "This wetsuit is starting to chafe."

"Fine," Matthew agreed. "We'll make a short pit stop at home, do a quick wardrobe change and maybe some food, and then on to the next realm."

"Which one?" Joel asked. Do we just randomly choose a world?"

"Yeah," his girlfriend added. "How are we supposed to guess where she will show up next?"

"We don't."

"Matthew's right," Emma agreed. "We just pick a new world and go there. If Morgan is already there, we deal with it. If she hasn't arrived in that realm yet, we use the nullification key and move on, so when she does arrive she will be stuck."

"Makes sense to me," Joel affirmed.

Matthew pulled out the black key, inserted it into the box and gave it a turn. "Okay, guys. Make sure we're all touching. We don't want to leave anyone behind. Ready?" he asked inserting the Earth key into the brass plate. "Here we go!"

– 13 –
Apples and Oranges

"Enough is enough," an exasperated Silas implored. "I'm not going to buy everything in your shop, Nicolas! If you know where Morgan is, tell me now. If not, just say so and I'll be on my way."

"I don't know where she is ... exactly," the shopkeeper said, with clear resignation in his voice. "But, give me some time to ask around, and I'm sure I can find her."

"For a price, no doubt."

"Hey, it's only fair I get compensated for my efforts isn't it?"

"Just like it's fair that I should actually get something of value before paying a nickel, right?" Silas asked, raising one eyebrow incredulously.

"I suppose so," Nicolas reluctantly agreed.

"We seem to have an understanding then. Exactly how long will this asking around take?"

"Well, it's difficult to say..."

"NICOLAS!"

"Come back in the morning and I should have something for you by then ... probably."

"Very well, I will see you first thing in the morning."

"Not first thing. I'm a late riser." Silas gave the shopkeeper an icy stare. "But not tomorrow, of course. Tomorrow I'll be up bright and early checking in with all my contacts."

"I'll see you first thing tomorrow, then."

Silas left the shop and wandered through the narrow streets of Rend. Even as evening drew nigh, the buzz of machinery remained constant. A haze of smog wafted high above the ground, further dimming the light of the setting sun.

He entered a small building, which from the outside looked much like a tiny factory. Inside he was greeted by a pleasant man dressed in an old-fashioned suit and wearing a copper bowler hat. As the man smiled at Silas his handlebar mustache wiggled gently.

"Welcome to the Common Inn," the man greeted.

"Thank you," Silas replied politely.

"You're not from around here," the man observed looking the visitor over through his welding goggles. "You have absolutely no enhancements that I can see. How do you manage?"

"Oh, I get by," Silas chuckled gently. "Might I reserve a room for the night?

"Certainly, that will be thirty credits."

Silas handed the man some coins to pay for the room. When he was first creating realms, he gave each one a unique monetary system that was tailor-made for that specific culture. He soon realized however, it would be much easier for him to move from realm to realm if he only needed to carry one form of currency.

Apples & Oranges

"Do you need any help with your luggage, sir? I've just had an upgrade. This puppy can lift 200 pounds without even trying," the man boasted, proudly displaying the gears, pistons and other machinery integrated into his right arm.

"No, no luggage. Sorry."

"Very well," the man replied sounding clearly disappointed, "follow me."

* * *

The next morning Silas woke early to the sound of machinery grinding away. The sound was constant in Rend, but it seemed like mornings were always much louder than any other time of the day. He enjoyed a custom-made omelet for breakfast, in the hotel restaurant, prepared by a chef with a gas burner implement embedded into his arm at the wrist, then set out.

It took him some time to wind his way back through the town to Nicolas' shop. The streets were packed full of people going in all directions. At this time of day no one set their own pace. The best you could do was jump into the mass of bodies and go with the flow of traffic as people streamed through the streets of Rend like a gentle river. Eventually, he did reach the shop and managed to work his way over to the edge of the street in time to hop out of the current and into Nicolas' doorway.

Silas was not entirely surprised to find the door was still locked with the "Sorry, We're Closed" sign hanging in the window. He also wasn't pleased. Every minute he delayed was a minute further ahead of him Morgan got. The further ahead she got the more worlds she would take control of and the more desperate Tara's situation became.

Silas pounded on the door but there was no answer and no sound of movement inside. He had no choice but to wait for the shop owner to arrive, whenever that may be. As the morning wore on he became more and more impatient. He resolved to wait until midday. If Nicolas had not shown up by then he would move on and search for other leads on Morgan's location. The reality was, even by now, it was quite likely that Morgan had already left this realm. If her pattern remained consistent, shortly after her first visit she would return with some hired thugs to scour this world for the workshop key. This meant there might still be time to catch up with her, but that time was quickly evaporating.

"Top of the morning to you!" Nicolas cheerfully greeted.

"Hardly the *top* of the morning. I've been waiting here for hours," Silas replied dryly.

"Oh, I'm terribly sorry about that, old friend," the shopkeeper said, unlocking the door and leading the way inside, "but it was all for a good cause. I promise."

"And what is that?"

"Come in and I'll tell you all about it. Would you like some tea?"

"No, Nicolas. I would like some information. Some useful information."

"No reason we can't have both," Nicolas grinned turning on a kettle. "I talked to one of my contacts this morning and he told me he heard from a friend of his that your red-haired vixen was holed up in a factory in the Theta Quadrant."

"Where in the Theta Quadrant?" Silas asked, excitement in his voice.

"On Boffin Street, on the outskirts of town."

"That's about as far from here as you could possibly get," Silas observed. Rend was divided into four quadrants; Beta, Aeta, Zeta, and Theta. Each quadrant was essentially a city in and of itself, separated only by a narrow road paved with bright red bricks as opposed to the muted colors of the cobblestone on all the other streets in the realm.

"I'm afraid so, and at this time of day it will take you forever to get down there. You might as well wait until later in the day when the crowds are not so heavy."

"No. We are leaving now. I've waited long enough."

"What do you mean *we're* leaving? I have my shop to attend to."

"Yes, you have customers lining up by the dozens," Silas sarcastically replied, looking around the empty store. "You are coming with me and you're going to show me the quickest way to get to this factory."

"I can give you excellent directions," Nicolas offered.

"Wonderful, you can give them to me on the way," Silas said, grabbing the shopkeeper gently but firmly by the arm and pulling him toward the door.

"But, the tea!"

* * *

"Ahhh, that feels better!" Joel beamed, once again clad in his usual garb of blue jeans and a t-shirt. "Any longer in that wetsuit and my body would have had more wrinkles on it than a Shar-Pei."

"Boy, you can say that again," Matthew agreed.

"Any longer in that wetsuit..."

"Don't," Juliette interrupted. "Matt, you should know better than to set him up like that. He can't resist."

"Everyone ready to go?" Emma asked.

"Hopefully we don't have to deal with any more water worlds, but it might not be a bad idea to pack a few extra supplies, just in case," Matthew suggested. "You never know what we might run into out there."

"That sounds like a good plan," Juliette concurred. "Joel and I can raid his pantry a bit too and see if we can dig up some granola bars or trail mix or something."

"Speaking of which," Matthew added, "is anyone else here a little hungry?" The rest of the group agreed that the breakfast they had eaten in Bhal had long since worn off.

"I was kinda thinking that too," Joel said. "So I took the liberty of ordering us a little something. I know this great food truck in the area. They don't usually deliver, but for the right customer I think they'll make an exception." Everyone chuckled. "It should be here any..."

Joel's facetious commentary was interrupted by the doorbell. He went to the door and opened it wide. A young man with shaggy hair and a bushy mustache stood in the hallway holding a large paper bag.

"Here you go, boss," the young man smiled.

"Thanks, Jeremy," Joel replied taking the bag. He passed the food to Juliette and then handed the young man some money. "Keep the change."

As Joel continued to talk to the young man about how business had been going the last several days without the proprietor around to oversee things, the other three friends divvied out the food and began to eagerly devour it. A few minutes later Joel closed and locked the door and rejoined his friends. Despite being the last to start, he was, as usual, the first to finish eating. Once everyone had eaten their fill and the extra supplies had been gathered the group was ready to move on to their next adventure.

"I added a note to the white board to let Silas know we had come to the same conclusion about Morgan's strategy as he did," Juliette explained. "At least from what we've seen so far."

"Where to now?" Emma asked.

"Well," Matthew replied, "this key is the next one on the ring, so I guess we're off to..." Matthew scanned the key with the device Silas had given him. The screen displayed the word: SERENITY.

"Sounds horrible," Joel scoffed mockingly.

"Let's just hope it's not one of those ironic names," Emma interjected. "Like an oversized mob enforcer named Tiny."

"I guess it's time to find out," Matthew said resolutely. "Once more into the breach."

"Seriously, Matt?" Joel questioned. "You're quoting Shakespeare? You do know how all his plays turn out, don't you?"

"Fair enough," Matthew laughed, "what wise words would you have us depart on?"

"When you've gotta go, you've gotta go," Joel smirked as Matthew turned the key.

* * *

The four friends arrived in Serenity and quickly discovered the realm more than lived up to its name. Tranquil fields filled with flowers were periodically interrupted by the calm waters of lakes and ponds or the bright green foliage of groves of fruit trees and the occasional vineyard. It was all a most welcome contrast to their time in Bhal. The visitors were greeted by the warmth of the sun, which seemed to be set at just the perfect temperature, leaving them feeling toasty warm, but not sweaty hot. As much as they would have enjoyed wandering the fields and soaking in the beauty of this realm, they had a job to do. The sooner they could finish and move on to the next world the better.

Matthew thought back to the first world Silas had described taking Morgan to. From what he saw around him, it seemed quite likely that the realm they had visited was Serenity. If he was remembering the details of the story correctly, the box should be located a couple kilometers south of the entry portal in a small olive grove.

What Silas had failed to mention in his recounting was that the sun in Serenity did not rise in the east and set in the west. In fact, it did not rise and set at all. Instead, the sun remained in its position directly above the center of the realm, which also happened to be directly above the entry portal. As the time for evening approached, the light of the sun would simply dim from a bright white to a pale yellow, allowing night to fall upon the land. Not only did this astrological anomaly make getting their bearings extremely difficult, but, if they remained here long enough, the off-worlders would certainly be caught off guard as the light faded from high noon to midnight in a matter of thirty minutes.

"The sun's not moving," Matthew finally concluded, after observing it for quite some time.

"So, how on earth are we supposed to figure out which direction is south?" an exasperated Joel asked.

"My guess is that waiting until it's night and looking at the stars isn't going to do us any good either," Juliette replied.

"So what do we do?" Emma inquired. "I don't see any locals nearby, so asking for directions is out."

"I say we go this way," Joel declared as he started to march off.

"Why that way?" his friend questioned.

"Because," the chef explained. "We have to go some direction and this seems as good as any. Besides, this way is slightly downhill, and you always go down south and up north."

"That makes absolutely no sense," his girlfriend objected.

"Yeah, I'm pretty sure that's just a figure of speech," Matthew countered, "but I don't have any better ideas."

"Silas said the olive grove was only a couple kilometers from here," Emma recalled. "So, if we don't find it in the next 30 to 40 minutes we should come back here and try a different direction.

"Agreed," Matthew said. He pulled a red ball cap out of the small backpack he was carrying and hung it on the protruding branch of a nearby tree to mark the area where the entry portal had originally delivered them. "Hey! Wait up!" he called out as he jogged slightly to catch up with the others who had already started out.

For the first time in what seemed like a very long time, the two couples allowed themselves to *be* couples. The idyllic world through which they strolled created a sense of romance equal to that of walking the streets of Paris or a gondola ride down the canals of Venice. With no one immediately present for them to chase or to run from they could simply relax and revel in being with one another. As the couples, not entirely subconsciously, drifted off in their own directions they also moved in closer to their partner.

They made a point not to get separated by too much distance, yet they were all pleased to take full advantage of the tranquility of this realm. It wouldn't last long but, at least for a brief time, everything was good.

They hardly spoke at all. This wasn't a time for words. Just being close to one another was enough to fill their hearts with calm and warmth. The beautiful world around them added to the tenderness of the moment. Occasionally someone would make note of a particularly interesting or stunning part of the scenery, but for the most part their full attention was on each other. Eyes locked, arms wrapped, breathing synchronized. They needed this moment, perhaps more than they had realized.

As the friends walked along through the luscious fields, they passed a number of tree bluffs, many of a variety they had never encountered before. Although no one said it out loud they were all thinking how good it felt to be in a world that was calm and serene. It felt good to not be running for their lives or dodging blows from oversized goons or spears from well-intentioned, albeit misguided locals. The blissfulness of their environment was almost enough to fill them with a sense of peace, if it were not for the fact that they all knew it likely wouldn't be long before that tranquility was shattered in one way or another. Eventually Joel and Juliette caught up again with their friends and all four of them walked along together.

"This place is amazing," Joel beamed. "Did you see that apple orchard back there? The apples were absolutely fantastic!"

"I can't believe you ate those!" Matthew exclaimed. "Those things could have been severely poisonous!"

"Hmm, I didn't really think of that."

"You could have totally died!" a mortified Emma added. "But, now that you mention it, did you try the oranges?" she snickered, "They were delicious!"

"They sure were," Matthew agreed.

"Oh, come on!" Joel shouted in mock objection.

"Seriously, they were really cool," Emma continued. "They looked like normal oranges, except the rind was as thin as the skin of an apple or pear. You didn't even have to peel them, just bite into it and enjoy!"

"Hey," Matthew interjected, pointing to stacks of pointy leaves sticking out of a number of dirt mounds nearby. "What do you think those things are over there?"

"Looks like pineapple to me," Joel replied nonchalantly.

"No, seriously."

"I am serious."

"Yeah, Matt, they look like pineapples," Juliette agreed.

"That's so weird," Matthew gasped. "Why would pineapples grow in the dirt here?"

"Where do you think they should grow, sweetie?" Emma asked trying desperately to control her impending giggle.

"On pineapple trees, of course."

"And what exactly do pineapple trees look like?" Juliette, about to burst, prompted.

"You know. Kind of like palm trees or something I guess. What? Wait. Are you telling me that there is no such thing as a pineapple tree?"

"Bro," Joel laughed, quickly accompanied by the two girls, "I'm so disappointed in you right now."

"Seriously? No pineapple trees? Huh! Who knew?"

"Pretty much everyone, babe," Emma smiled.

"But bananas grow on trees, right," Matthew questioned, sounding surprisingly uncertain.

"Yes, Matt, bananas grown on trees," Juliette confirmed.

"Whew! That's a relief," Matthew chuckled.

"Technically, they're not actually trees, just really large plants," Joel corrected.

"Don't mess with me, man!" Matthew protested.

The friends walked along for over half an hour. They had begun to question whether they should consider turning back when Joel spotted another orchard to their right.

"Do you think that's the one we're looking for?" he asked.

"Only one way to find out," Emma answered. "Let's go take a look."

A few minutes later they stood at the edge of the grove. "It's definitely olives," Juliette observed, feeling grateful that the fruit was in season. Identifying these plants purely by their leaves was not something they were likely to be successful at.

"Silas said the box was in the middle somewhere," Matthew recalled.

"Let's check it out," Joel said, eagerly striding into the olive grove. "Let's split up a bit and cover more ground."

"Okay, but don't wander too far away. Joel, you head over there. I'll go off this way a bit. Juliette and Emma, you two go more or less up the middle."

"Got it."

"Sounds good."

"Okay."

As she walked along, Emma examined the trees in the orchard more closely. She had never seen olives quite so large before. Most of the trees bore black olives, although some were green and every so often she'd come across a plant where the fruit had a bluish tinge to it.

"Hey guys, over here!" Matthew called out a few minutes later. "I found it."

The others joined their friend next to what looked like a birdhouse mounted on a fence post. Matthew opened up the front of the house exposing the hunter green box inside. He pulled out the scanning device and rested it on the brass plate inside the box.

"Finally, some good news," he stated with a slight sigh.

"What is it?" his girlfriend asked.

"According to this the last destination of this portal was the workshop."

"Which means it must have been Tara or Silas who used it," Juliette concluded.

"Exactly."

"It also means," Joel theorized, "That Morgan has yet to test out the key to this realm. And now when she does she'll be stuck."

"Feels nice to actually be ahead of her for once," Matthew chuckled.

"It sure does," Juliette agreed.

"Is it wrong that I would feel disappointed if she got trapped in such a beautiful world as this?" Emma asked. No one answered, mostly because they all felt the same.

"Well, let's not blow our lead now," Joel reminded. "What's our next destination?"

"I think we should make a quick stop back at home and see if there's any word from Silas. We haven't crossed paths with him in quite a while. Then," Matthew pulled out the Mr. Spiffy's keychain and located the nullification key. He counted clockwise, five keys over, and slid that key into the bottom of the scanner. "Looks like we're headed to Demesne."

"Hmm," Emma sighed. "Why is it that the most calm and peaceful world we have visited is also the world that we get to spend the least time in?"

"We can come back for a longer visit when this is all over," Matthew suggested, "but for now let's get out of here before we encounter any unwanted guests."

"Good point, sweetie."

Matthew placed the black key in the brass plate and turned it. After removing the nullification key he inserted the key for Earth and held tight to Emma's hand. Joel and Juliette grasped Emma's other hand and all three gave a slight nod indicating they were ready to move on. Matthew turned the key and light filled the center of the orchard momentarily before it gently faded away leaving only the birdhouse and olive trees behind.

The Heritage Key

- 14 -

From Bad to Worse

Silas and Nicolas took a good chunk of the afternoon to make their way down to Theta Quadrant. Thankfully by mid-afternoon the predominant flow of traffic shifted and made their progress slightly faster. The afternoon was nearly over by the time they reached the southernmost part of the quadrant. Nicolas led the way through the twisting streets on their way to Morgan's hiding place. Silas was thankful for his reluctant guide as the roads of Rend were extremely difficult to navigate, not only because they were narrow and closed in, but even more so because there was virtually no signage to indicate which street was which.

"It feels like we're walking in circles," Silas stated in frustration.

"I assure you we're not. You know how the streets are here. It is true that we are taking some shortcuts that are technically longer in distance, but the streets are less crowded, which means we can move faster and come out ahead. Trust me."

"There is some logic to that I suppose. How much further?"

"Not far," Nicolas answered. "In fact, it's right there."

"Finally!" Silas cheered, examining the factory's exterior. "Doesn't seem to be much action over there. No guards or patrols that I can see."

"Okay, so, I'll just take my payment and be on my way."

"Not so fast," Silas cautioned. "We agreed on money for results, remember."

"Yes," Nicolas replied defensively. "You wanted to know where she was and I brought you to her doorstep. What better results could you want?"

"The only thing you've done so far is take all day leading me to an unidentified building. When I see Morgan, you'll get your credits."

"What? You don't trust me?"

Silas gave the shop owner a sardonic look and said, "Come on."

The two men crossed the narrow street and moved toward the factory door. The handle turned easily, and the door swung open. Silas moved inside with Nicolas in tow. The door slammed closed behind them, leaving them in a pitch-black space. With a soft click a light appeared, emanating from Nicolas' headgear.

"Find the light switch," Silas instructed, still hanging on to the shopkeeper's sleeve.

Nicolas let out a deep sigh as his switched on the building's interior lights. Silas looked around in total disbelief. The factory was completely empty except for a couple empty crates on the far side of the room. Furthermore, by the accumulation of dust on the floor, it was clear that the two of them were the first people to set foot inside in quite some time.

"What is going on here," Silas demanded, tightening his grip on Nicolas' arm.

"I...I...I don't know. Perhaps, my source was wrong."

"I don't buy it. You've been stalling me from the moment I walked into your shop. I thought we were taking the long way around to get here. Now I know why. No wonder you were so anxious to get paid before we came in here!"

"You don't understand."

"You're absolutely right. I *don't* understand," Silas fumed.

"Morgan came to my shop, day before yesterday," Nicolas explained. "She told me you would be coming to Rend to look for her. She said she would buy out my entire inventory if I would keep you here as long as possible."

"So, you double-crossed me for the sake of a big sale?" Silas asked incredulously.

"No. When I told her I wouldn't do it, she said she would kill me if I didn't delay you long enough. I'm so very sorry. I know it was wrong. You have always been kind to me, but she terrified me."

"I understand," Silas said, softening his tone and releasing his grip. "You should have just told me when I first arrived. I've always treated you fairly Nicolas."

"I know, I know. I was just scared. I'm so sorry."

"There's not much to be done about it now. If you want to make it up to me, get me to Iron Street in the Aeta Quadrant as quickly as possible so I can return to my world and hopefully pick up Morgan's trail again."

"Silas," the merchant said timidly. "There's something else you should know."

"What is it, Nicolas?" the carpenter asked anxiously – partly because he wanted to know what other information his friend had been concealing and partly because he did not want to waste another second standing around talking.

"She ... she wasn't alone."

"Yes, I know. She has recruited a number of thugs to travel to the realms with her. She leaves them behind to do her dirty work for her."

"No, it's not like that," Nicolas insisted. "The man she was with is from Rend. I don't know who he is, but he was definitely a local."

"How could you tell? What kind of mech did he have?"

"That's just it, he didn't have any. Not one single piece of machinery implanted anywhere, at least not that I could see anyways. That's what made him stand out. That and the fact that he was six foot four and full of muscles. But for a guy who didn't look at all like he should fit in, he completely fit in, if you know what I mean. Like he had been here a long time."

"Yes, that is strange indeed. Nicolas, I need you to use those contacts of yours again," Silas stated firmly, "for real this time. Find out everything you can about the man she was with. Track him down if you can, but don't approach him on your own do you understand?"

"Sure, but I don't think that will be a problem."

"Why do you say that?"

"Because I heard them talking and, well, it sounded like he was leaving Rend with her."

"All the more important that I catch up with her then. I must get to Iron Street immediately!"

"Follow me."

"Wait," Silas halted in mid-step as a distraught look swept over his face like an avalanche. "Did this man have a name?"

"Yeah, I think she called him Zander."

Silas's pale face stared blankly into the air. After a moment, both his skin tone and resolve returned, although he was still visibly distressed by the recent revelation. "We have not a second to lose."

* * *

"I told you I would get you here," Morgan beamed with delight.

"I didn't think it was actually possible, you clever girl," her companion said with a sly grin.

"We need to get out of here before…"

A bright light filled Tara's apartment as the four friends entered through the gateway. Juliette squeezed her eyes shut, shielding them from the intensity of the gateway's glow. She felt the ground solidify under her feet indicating they had arrived, and she could sense the light had faded away. She was about to open her eyes when she was jerked forward violently and spun around. She could feel the tight grasp of a beefy arm around her chest and the cold razor sharp edge of a metal blade pressed against her throat. She started to struggle against her captor's grip, but suddenly a sharp pain erupted in the back of her head and she faded into darkness.

"Let her go you ugly brute!" Joel shouted venomously.

"Calm yourself, boy" the titan of a man holding Juliette's unconscious body sneered.

"The four of you have become a rather annoying fly in my ointment," Morgan crowed. "That ends now. Stop making a nuisance of yourself and your friend will be fine. Better yet, give me the workshop key and I'll release her right now."

"We don't have it," Matthew stated firmly.

"Then get it, and bring it to me, before it's too late … for her," Morgan smiled devilishly. "Don't follow us, or she'll regret it."

Morgan backed out of Tara's apartment as the man tossed Juliette's limp body over his shoulder like it was an oversized pillow.

"We have to go after them!" Joel insisted.

"We can't," Matthew countered, holding his friend back.

"You heard what she said, Joel," Emma spoke soothingly. "If we follow her we're only putting Juliette at greater risk."

The three friends were still debating what to do when the portal activated once again. As the light faded away, Silas looked around the room and saw the visibly distraught companions.

"Matthew?" Silas asked gently. "What has happened? Where is Juliette?"

"Morgan got the jump on us. She was here waiting for us when we arrived. She and the brute she was with took Jules."

"Oh no," the carpenter gasped.

"No," Emma said thoughtfully. "I don't think she was waiting here for us. She seemed caught off guard by our arrival. Perhaps taking Jules was more of a makeshift escape plan rather than a premeditated ambush."

"That would make sense," her boyfriend agreed. "You would have thought that if it was a planned attack she would have brought more men and taken us all out."

"What does it matter?" Joel decried. "Jules is gone either way. That's all that matters!"

"I'm so sorry, Joel," Silas offered sympathetically. "This is all my fault, I should never have gotten you kids involved."

* * *

An oversized duffle bag unzipped and Juliette caught her first glimpse of the outside world in over an hour. Even as her eyes adjusted to the light she could tell something was not quite right. At first she thought perhaps it was just late in the evening, but she soon realized it was more than that. A beefy hand wielding a six-inch blade reached into the duffle bag and deftly cut the ropes around her hands and ankles. Before she could attempt to wriggle her way out of the bag she was engulfed in a bright light.

When the light faded Juliette worked her way free of the severed ropes and scrambled out of the duffle bag. The air was dank and humid, and the light was much dimmer than it had been moments earlier – or perhaps that was just her eyes readjusting after the portal light. Juliette thought she had somehow been transferred to a different realm. She stood up and examined her surroundings. She found herself in a room with walls carved from black stone. There was an opening at one end of the room. She ran towards what she hoped would be freedom, but as she drew closer the iron bars blocking her escape came into view.

She reached the cave's entrance and looked out through the bars. The man who had grabbed her in the apartment stood several yards away next to a small wooden platform, still holding the knife. Morgan stood nearby, behind a stone column with some sort of device mounted on top. She smiled with insidious delight.

"Welcome to your new home," Morgan sneered, "*Jules.*"

Juliette searched for a sharp and sarcastic comeback, but none came to mind. She was so disoriented by her surroundings and distraught about her situation, the best she could muster was a spiteful, "I HATE YOU!"

"I'm crushed," Morgan laughed gleefully, removing a key from the device and strutting around the control panel to stand next to her companion. Juliette let out a vicious scream the only expression of her rage and frustration that felt appropriately intense.

"She's a feisty one!" Zander noted. "I could fix that."

"They're all just kids," Morgan explained. "They're pests more than anything.

"Kids or not, they're not going to stand in our way. Nothing is going to stand in my way. I've waited too long," he said bitterly.

"But now that I've found you, nothing can stop us. I searched for you for so long, I almost gave up hope."

"I don't even know how long it was," Zander said, taking on a more reflective, less angry tone. "Maybe decades?"

"Too long, my love," Morgan smiled. "Much has changed since you were exiled but the history lesson will have to wait. Silas has been more pig-headed than I expected. I was sure he would give up anything for Tara."

"He will, eventually," Zander mused, "as soon as he realizes he can't win."

"That time will come much sooner now that you are free."

"I have escaped Rend, but I won't truly be free until I hold the workshop key in my hand and that snake, Silas, is behind bars with his wife," the imposing man stated, his voice dripping with vitriol. "No, wait. Behind bars *like* his wife."

"We're almost there," Morgan smiled, opening the lid of the black box that sat on a small shelf at the side of the control panel. "That old man has already lost, he just doesn't know it yet."

Juliette watched her two adversaries disappear into the gateway, then turned around reluctantly to examine her new surroundings. The walls, floor and ceiling were smoothly carved out of the same black stone that she had seen erupting from the ground outside. At the midpoint of the room there was a small wooden table and chair against one wall and a narrow bed against the opposite wall. At the far end of the room was a metal toilet, metal sink, and a showerhead protruding from the wall.

Suddenly a sound caused her to spin around and look behind her, but she saw nothing. The room was empty and no one could be seen outside. Juliette cautiously moved back toward the iron bars of her cell. A small rock flew through the air, bounced off a bar and crashed onto the stone floor. Juliette took a few more steps closer to the cave entrance.

"Hello?" a voice gently called. "Are you there?"

* * *

"What are we going to do?" Joel shouted as he closed the door to his apartment. It was the same question he had asked dozens of times as they walked from Tara's place to his. "What are we going to do?"

"We'll get her back, buddy. I promise," Matthew consoled.

"How?"

"I haven't figured that part out yet, but we will."

"I apologize, Joel," Silas said contritely. "This is all my fault. I should not have involved you folks in my problems."

"You don't have to apologize," Emma said. "We volunteered, remember."

"Nevertheless, I should have realized the danger of returning to Tara's apartment. I should have known that eventually Morgan would try to ambush us there. I was so preoccupied with getting Tara back I wasn't thinking clearly, and now things have gone from bad to worse."

"How could you think of anything else?" Emma sympathized.

"Why don't we do the same thing to her?" Joel suggested. "She's got to come back eventually right? Why don't we just sit in Tara's living room with a shotgun and wait for her to show up?"

"I'm not so sure," his friend replied. "My guess is, now that she's got the jump on us once, she'll be expecting us to try something similar. In which case she'll avoid returning to earth at all costs, I suspect."

"That's very possible," the carpenter agreed. "She has been a step ahead of us from the beginning. I can't see her making that kind of foolish mistake now."

"But doesn't she have to come back, in between each realm she visits, to pick up a couple new bad guys to take with her to the next world?" Joel inquired.

"That's a good point," Matthew concurred.

"Yes, I've been pondering that myself," Silas answered. "I have a feeling that her most recent visit to Tara's apartment is the first time she's been there since she kidnapped you, my dear," he said, putting his hand gently on Emma's shoulder.

"And when she returned this time she had a pretty good hunch that we were all off in other realms," Matthew added.

"Exactly," the carpenter agreed. "Which means she must be keeping all the prisoners she freed from Garda in one of the other realms she has a key for."

"Well, that's a relief," Joel responded.

"Not really," Emma disagreed. "Because that means one of these times we could arrive in a world full of who knows how many of her henchmen."

"Very true, Emma. That is why the three of you need to be extra cautious when arriving in new worlds from here on out."

"Yeah, but the upside is," Matthew theorized, "if we do end up in that world, once we use the nullification key all of Morgan's hired muscle will be trapped and of no use to her."

"If they don't kill us first, you mean," Joel dryly remarked.

"If that is true, then I would say she won't come back to earth unless she's really desperate," Silas reiterated. "At least not until she has secured the workshop key."

"Does that mean it's safe for us to continue to use that gateway then?" Emma asked.

"I wouldn't count on it," Joel warned.

"Agreed," Matthew said. "We should avoid arriving in Tara's apartment as much as possible. Just in case."

"Can't you just make some new keys that open the gateway somewhere safer? Somewhere that we know Morgan won't be waiting for us?" Emma suggested.

"I wish I could," Silas sighed. "To do that I would have to carve a new door and that takes more time than we have. It is a moot point anyway, because I don't have access to my workshop."

"What do you mean?"

"What?"

"What are you talking about?"

"I don't have my key to the workshop anymore," the carpenter explained. "I did not want to be captured with it on me, or be tempted to give it to Morgan for the promise of Tara's release, so I hid it away."

"We could just go get it," Joel suggested.

"But, what if Morgan has people watching us?" Matthew asked. "We could lead them right to the workshop key!"

"So, what *do* we do?"

"We keep traveling through the realms," Matthew stated resolutely. "We get them all locked down with the nullification keys and Morgan will run out of places to hide."

"Then what?" Emma asked.

"Then we go back, one world at a time, until we find her," Silas confidently answered.

"And what about Jules?" Joel asked.

"I know this doesn't make it any easier," his friend began, "But, Morgan took her for leverage. If she harms Jules, she loses that leverage."

"Or maybe it's already too late and we just don't know it yet!"

"Silas' plan is still our best chance of getting Juliette back," Emma agreed.

"I suppose you're right," Joel reluctantly conceded.

"Hey, wait a minute," Matthew interjected. "Where do you suppose Morgan is holding Jules?"

"Could be anywhere."

"Could be," Silas said thoughtfully, "but I suspect she took Juliette to Garda and put her in a cell, just like Tara."

"That's what I was thinking too," Matthew said. "Which means either Morgan is trapped in Garda now or you didn't use a nullification key in the box the last time you visited."

"No. No, I didn't," Silas confessed. "Unfortunately, the unique properties of the realm prevent the box from being deactivated. The ancients created it that way."

"Well, I guess we'll have to trap her somewhere else," Matthew stated determinedly.

"Where to next?" his girlfriend asked.

"Our next key is for some place called Demesne."

"I, on the other hand, will head to Nyumbani," Silas explained.

"Sounds good," Matthew replied. "Remember, our goal is to lock down as many realms as we can, as fast as we can, not only to trap Morgan but also to make sure she brings her goons to terrorize as few worlds as possible."

"Right," Emma agreed. "And, just to be safe, we should only return to Tara's apartment when absolutely necessary."

"Indeed," the carpenter concurred. "Good luck, my friends." With that he walked over to the coffee table, opened the box, inserted a key and passed through the gateway. As soon as Silas was gone, the others moved to the living room. Matthew selected the next key on his ring.

"Everyone holding on? Okay, here we go!"

– 15 –
Sand Trap

"Yes, I'm here," Juliette answered tentatively.

"Are you okay? Did they hurt you?" the voice asked, sounding genuinely concerned.

"I'm fine. A little confused, but fine."

"What is your name, dear?"

"My name is Juliette. And you?"

"I am Tara."

"Tara? As in Silas' wife, Tara?" Juliette asked excitedly.

"Yes," Tara answered sounding equally enthusiastic. "How do you know my husband?"

"Oh, crud."

"What is it? Did you hurt yourself?"

"No. I just realized where I was," Juliette explained. "If you're Tara, then this is Garda and that really sucks, because according to Silas we are hopelessly stuck here."

"Stuck, yes. But not hopelessly so. My Silas will find a way to get us out."

"I hope you're right."

"So, how *do* you know Silas?"

"Oh, well, my friends and I were trying to help your husband capture Morgan. Obviously, we haven't been as successful as we would have liked to have been."

"Nevertheless, I appreciate the effort."

"Don't mention it," Juliette smiled weakly. "Hey, can I ask you a question?"

"By all means. What is it?"

"These are the cells designed by the ancients to hold all the criminals from all the realms, right?"

"Yes, I suppose you could say that."

"So, is there like a caretaker or something around we might be able to convince to help us?"

"No, I'm afraid not. There is no one in Garda but the prisoners."

"You mean you just leave people here to starve to death?"

"No, no. Food is provided automatically. Three times a day, a small gateway will deliver food to the tables of every occupied cell. It is all automated and can run unchecked for years."

"Well, I guess that's good to know."

"Be thankful for small blessings, right?"

"That's one way of putting it." Juliette examined the bars and thought for a moment. "Is there any way to open these bars?"

"No, my dear. Not at all," Tara explained. "The bars don't open, ever. They were driven deep into the rocks and welded in place. The only way in or out of these cells is by use of that control panel over there, and unfortunately Morgan has the only key."

"How did she figure out how to run that thing? And how did she even know to bring you here in the first place."

"Some of the prisoners here have been around a very long time. They have seen the control panel operated on many occasions and were more than happy to explain it to her in exchange for the promise of their freedom. Besides, it's really not that complicated."

"I suppose."

"As far as how she knew to bring me here, well, that is my fault, I'm afraid. Before Silas started having suspicions about Morgan's intentions, I told her all about this place. I even brought her here once."

"Why would you do that? It's not really an ideal vacation location."

"No, not at all," Tara chuckled at her new friend's observation. "I came here regularly to bring fresh food and flowers to the inmates."

"I thought you said the food was automatically provided."

"It is. Food that will keep you nourished and healthy, but it's not the same as fresh fruit or a really good burger. I felt bad for the prisoners here and thought I could do a little something to make their existence just a little less miserable. I mentioned it to Morgan once and she asked if she could tag along some time. At that point I had no reason to doubt her and I thought, "What's the worst that can happen?""

"I guess now we know," Juliette remarked, then quickly added, "I'm sorry, I didn't mean that like it sounded."

"Don't worry, dear. I have no misconceptions of who holds the blame for all this. And I know it's Morgan, not me."

"That's good. It does no good to beat yourself up over things you can't change, right?"

"That is very true," Tara agreed. "But not always so easy."

"Ain't that the truth?" Juliette snickered, then tentatively asked, "So, you didn't have any idea Morgan was going to do this?"

"No, none. Well, at least not at first," Tara answered with heavy sadness in her voice. "The Morgan I knew was nothing like that woman who was just here. We were the best of friends. If I had even remotely thought something like this could have happened, we would never have revealed Silas' craft to her."

"What happened?"

"I don't know. She changed. Inexplicably," she answered and then gave it some more thought. "I honestly don't know if her lust for power caused her radical transformation, or perhaps that's who she was all along, and she was just playing me for a fool from the start. I suppose it doesn't really matter at this point."

"Maybe we will get some answers once Silas and the others have tracked her down," Juliette offered optimistically.

"Maybe."

* * *

From the moment Silas arrived in Nyumbani his skin was pelted with grains of sand that had been sucked up into a whirlwind of a storm. The sandstorm was enough to leave any new arrival completely disoriented. Silas held his breath, hoping to protect himself from his harsh surroundings as he shoved his hand into the satchel and searched for something. A few moments later his hand emerged from the bag firmly grasping a pair of motorcycle goggles. He quickly put on the goggles, protecting his eyes from the barrage of sand around him, but doing very little to improve his range of vision.

He leaned heavily into the gale force wind to keep himself from being toppled over. He fished through the satchel again and pulled out a long piece of cloth, which he raced to wrap around his head as a make-shift kufiyah.

The process was painfully prolonged as the wind relentlessly blew the material around like a kite in a hurricane. Protected by the fabric draped across his face, Silas finally exhaled and then drew in a deep breath. He coughed a couple times attempting to expel the sand that had entered his nose and mouth upon arrival.

He chuckled at his own absent-mindedness. He had been so anxious to track down Morgan, especially in light of Juliette's abduction, that he entered the gateway before adequately preparing himself for the harsh environment on the other side. It was fortunate that he had the foresight during his last visit to the workshop to stock his satchel with the supplies for each world he planned to visit.

Not wanting to lose his way in the storm, Silas stretched out his arms and blindly felt the air around him. Even though he knew exactly where he needed to be headed, he realized it would not take much for him to get hopelessly lost in this squall of sand and wind. He cautiously inched his way around in a circular pattern until his fingertips finally touched something solid. Silas took a step forward and a wooden sign emerged from the barrage of sand. The sign, black with bright yellow letters, read:

You are trapped in a room. The room has only two possible exits: two doors. Through the first door, there is a room constructed from magnifying glass. The blazing hot sun instantly fries anything or anyone that enters. Through the second door, there is a fire-breathing dragon that incinerates all who enter. How do you escape?

Silas smirked under the kufiyah as he read the riddle he had written on the sign. The puzzle did have a solution, one he found particularly clever, even if he said so himself. The answer, however, was completely irrelevant. The carpenter had posted the puzzle merely as a distraction and a decoy to any who might stumble into this realm. The true secret of escaping the sandstorm was not found in the words at all. It was the orientation of the sign itself that pointed the way out.

He positioned himself with his left shoulder pressed tight against the sign. Leaning into the swirling wind he resolutely marched forward through the storm. The sand continued to pelt every inch of exposed skin like thousands of jabbing needles. He tilted his head down as he walked, hoping for slightly more protection from the granular bombardment.

After several minutes, which felt much longer than they actually were, Silas reached a rough sandstone wall. His hands felt around in all directions. The wall was taller than he could reach, but he had no interest in scaling it, as others might be inclined to futilely attempt. Instead, he shuffled along the edge, his body pressed tight to the stone, until he slid into a narrow opening.

Silas stepped into the alcove and fumbled for the handle of the wooden door that stood inside. As soon as the door was unlatched it slammed open from the power of the wind blasting behind him. The sand covered man slipped through the doorway and heaved with all his might to push the door shut.

With the door finally closed and latched behind him, Silas ripped the cloth down off his face and gulped in the clean air.

The sandstorm would have been entirely debilitating to anyone less prepared, which was its purpose. It took him a few moments to regain his breath. As he recovered, he glanced around the dimly lit stairwell. The storm continued to beat against the door, pushing sand through every tiny gap and crack. Small piles of sand and dust were building around the base and frame of the door

After fully regaining his breath Silas began to ascend stairs hewn out of the sandstone rock that had formed the exterior wall of the "storm pit." He reached the top and emerged into the bright sunlit surface. The carpenter still wearing his typical sweater vest, was starting to perspire from the intense heat of this realm. Even the slightest of breezes would have been a welcomed comfort as the temperature was enough to make a camel wilt, but there was not even a whisper of wind.

Silas removed the sweater, rolled up his sleeves and popped open a couple of buttons on his shirt. He walked toward a wooden split rail fence. The barrier was clearly weathered from the intense sunlight, but still sturdy. He gazed across the large crater it encircled. The pit was close to 100 yards in diameter, but its depth was indiscernible due to the swirling dust and sand.

Silas had installed the pit around the portal of this realm after he had become suspicious of Morgan. He had intended to create secure entry points on each of his worlds just in case someone unauthorized managed to sneak in. Unfortunately, that plan was hatched a little too late, as the sandstorm crater in Nyumbani was the only security measure he had put in place thus far.

The good news was that it seemed likely he had arrived in this realm before Morgan since there was no sign of her presence down below or in the stairwell. It was possible she was still down there somewhere, fumbling around in the dust. Even if that were true, he was still one step ahead of her and that felt very good for a change.

Silas walked closer to the rail fence and approached a nearby post. On the top of the post rested a black housing holding a large red button. He pressed the button firmly and watched the crater below. Gradually the whirlwind subsided and the dust and sand began to slowly settle back to the ground. After a few minutes the air was mostly clear and Silas could see all the way down to the bottom of the pit 50 feet below. He scanned the area closely but found no signs of any other visitors. He breathed a small sigh of relief but knew that this was only a very small victory in a much bigger battle.

Someone approached from behind and came to stand next to Silas. The casual gait of the man's approach indicated he was not afraid of the carpenter, nor should Silas be afraid of him. He was wearing a beige robe, similar in hue to the sandstone all around and spoke in a series of clicks, ticks, and guttural sounds.

"Oh, you were just coming to do that, were you?" Silas chuckled.

The man lowered the hood of his robe revealing his dark-skinned face and shaved head, then spoke again in the same foreign tongue as before.

"Every 30 minutes, just like I told you, eh? Excellent work. And there's been no sign of anyone caught down there?"

The man gave a short response in this native language which loosely translated meant, "No."

"Do you think someone could have made it out without you noticing?"

"I suppose it is possible," the man replied in his Khoisan-like dialect, "but it would be unlikely. The chances of finding the door during the storm are remote. And their arrival would have to be timed perfectly between my visits."

"Yes, that does seem very unlikely, indeed," Silas concurred. "But not impossible." He pressed the red button and watched as the wind began to swirl around and pick up velocity once again. "Keep an eye on it, Krotoa. Every 20 minutes now."

"Of course. In the meantime, let me escort you to my village."

"That would be wonderful," Silas grinned. He was certain he could find his way to the village on his own, but he would most likely take a more winding route and time was of the essence. If he was actually ahead of Morgan for once he wanted to stay that way. Besides, a little company on the journey was always comforting.

Krotoa talked of his family and recent events in Nyumbani as they walked over and around the large sand dunes which covered the terrain. Nothing terribly dramatic ever happened here. The Nyumbani were, for the most part, a very low key and relaxed people. Krotoa was one of the more ambitious members of the tribe, which is why Silas had selected him to oversee the checking of the pit. There were many others who might have agreed to do it but would not have completed the task with any sort of regularity or punctuality and Silas was unwilling to accept that. The sandstorm pit was a precaution against unauthorized visitors. It was designed to disorient and disable anyone who came through the gateway, however, the last thing he wanted was for someone to be seriously harmed by the safeguard.

As they neared Krotoa's village, Silas told him of Morgan's treachery and warned she might arrive with several others who could pose a great threat to the Nyumbani people. He considered telling Krotoa about the man Morgan had liberated from Rend but decided he needed to make sure his suspicions were correct first. Deep down he was certain he knew who the man was, he just couldn't bring himself to say it aloud. As long as it was unspoken he could pretend it wasn't true.

"We are almost there, my friend," Krotoa chimed in his native dialect.

"Excellent," Silas replied, chuckling to himself as he imagined what the others would have done if he had given Matthew the key to this realm. At the time he had thought of the sand pit and decided it was best to visit this world himself. The thought had not even crossed his mind how his friends from Earth would have responded to the Nyumbani's dialect. He chortled again as he thought, *Joel would probably manage just fine, somehow.*

"Welcome back to Engoshee!" Krotoa smiled broadly as the two men reached the top of a particularly large sand dune.

In the valley below stood what appeared to be several long sandstone monoliths, which seemed to run in impressively straight lines. The rock formations stretched out for hundreds of yards and from his perch atop the sand dune, Silas could count at least a dozen rows, one behind the other. The monoliths stood roughly forty feet tall and nearly double that in depth. The pair descended the far side of the dune and walked closer to the unique geological contours. As they approached, the scale of the monoliths grew increasingly impressive. Some portions of the rock wall remained in their natural state with rough and uneven surfaces. Most of the sandstone, however, had been elegantly carved away to give texture and design. Columns, beams, doors, and windows could all be easily identified. It was as if a long row of oversized townhouses had been petrified.

"Where is everyone?" Silas asked.

"Oh, it's school time," Krotoa explained. "My house is this way. Come on in!" he invited, opening a wooden door built into the monoliths surface. "Sweetheart, we have a guest!"

Silas stood at the entryway of the home. It was not at all what one would have expected from the exterior. The inside of the house was cozy and inviting. The walls had been chiseled perfectly smooth and then painted in warm colors. The stone floors had been covered with carpets and rugs, and there were meticulously crafted wood railings and furniture throughout the house.

"Oh, hello Silas!" a woman beamed as she scurried across the room and welcomed her guest with an enormous hug. "We haven't seen you in forever!" she added in her native tongue.

"It's wonderful to see you too, Laara."

"What brings you here? Just a quick visit? How long will you be staying? Will you be here overnight? I can have the kids make up the guest room when they get home from school. It's really no trouble at all," the woman offered, speaking so rapidly Silas could barely decipher what she was saying.

"That's very kind of you, but I cannot stay very long this time I'm afraid."

"Oh, sounds serious. On a mission, are you? Well, you must eat first. Come, join us for lunch. I insist. It should be ready in just a few minutes."

"I..."

"I won't take no for an answer," the woman declared. "Krotoa, go set another place at the table, please dear."

"Thank you, Laara," Silas conceded the argument he knew he had absolutely no chance of winning. "I would love to stay for lunch, but then I really must be on my way."

After his wife had retreated to the kitchen Krotoa led his guest into the living room. The area was very comfortable and homey with several large, soft chairs spread throughout. In the center of one wall stood a grand fireplace. Inside the hearth, a fire with blue flames roared. As he walked past, Silas could feel the cool air radiating out from the blaze.

"Wait here, my friend," the host instructed.

"I will go next door and ask Kitrich to return to the sandpit while we are occupied here."

"That's a good idea," Silas concurred. "Is there someone you can send to the exit portal as well? If Morgan slips in somehow, we need to know about it."

"I agree. I will go find someone reliable to keep an eye on it."

"Thank you, my friend. But be very clear to whomever you send. They are only to watch the portal and report back. They should not, by any means or under any circumstances attempt to engage with her."

"I understand," Krotoa said, lifting the hood of his robe and slipping back out the door.

* * *

By the time Krotoa had returned from his errands, the children had come home from school and Laara had finished preparing lunch. They all sat around a large oval table in the dining area and enjoyed a delightful meal of roasted sari-bird, which tasted very much like chicken, and an assortment of fresh vegetables.

"I see the hydroponic farms are still working well," Silas observed.

"Better than ever," Laara reported. "Last year's crop was one of our best ever and this year is looking very good as well."

For a moment, as they sat around the table making small talk, Silas began to feel like things were back to normal. This was just one of the hundreds of visits he had made to his realms enjoying friendship and conversation with their inhabitants.

"Mr. Silas, where is Ms. Tara?" the eldest child asked between bites of something resembling a carrot.

"Milva," Krotoa spoke quickly, with a look that every father has given their child when they have said something they shouldn't.

"It's alright," Silas replied gently, the illusion of normalcy shattered. "My wife was not able to come with me this time, Milva. But I really hope she will join me on my next visit."

"Ok," the young girl said nonchalantly, returning her attention to her meal. "I hope she does. I like her."

"I hope so too," Silas smiled gently at the child. "I hope so too."

"KROTOA!" a voice shouted as the front door burst open.

"What is it?" Krotoa urgently inquired, standing from his chair and rushing to the door, with Silas right on his heels.

"She's here! I saw her! She's here!" the young man reported with unbridled enthusiasm.

"You saw Morgan at the gateway?" Krotoa clarified.

"Yes," the out of breath young man huffed.

"*Which* gateway," Silas soberly asked.

"He was stationed at the exit portal," Krotoa explained.

"We must go. Now!" The three men ran out the door and sped toward the portal box's location.

"Eat your veggies, kids," Laara said as calmly as she could manage.

– 16 –
An Unexpected Welcome

"Halt!" a voice demanded as the trio of friends arrived through the portal. "Do not move."

"That's not a good sign," Joel quipped as the effects of passing through the gateway wore off.

"Not good at all," Matthew agreed.

The new arrivals were surrounded by makeshift stone walls that stood nearly eight feet tall. There was only one way in or out of the improvised room, through a narrow opening directly in front of them. Standing square in the middle of the doorway was a man holding a long spear with a very sharp point. Once the light of the gateway had dissipated the room was quite dim, which, combined with the bright sunlight beaming in from behind the man, made the features of the sentry's face quite difficult to make out.

"We come in peace," Emma offered gently, realizing she sounded like every alien B-film she'd ever seen.

"Don't move," the guard sternly warned again. "On your knees, all of you."

Faced with stone walls surrounding them and the spearhead in front of them, the three companions had no choice but to comply. As they slowly sank down to their knees the silhouettes of two others could be seen skirting around the guard with the spear. They moved quickly and with the noticeable clanking of metal. Almost immediately the men were behind the bewildered friends and began tightly securing the off-worlders' hands with iron shackles. Once the visitors were secured, they were lifted to their feet and pushed out of the stone chamber.

"We were warned of your arrival," the guard with the spear explained, his voice laced with suspicion.

"Warned of our arrival?" Matthew asked. "By who?"

"Who do you think?" Joel responded dryly.

"Fortunately, we had just completed the containment walls when you entered our world. You will come with me."

The man began to lead the way through the tall trees that surrounded the entry portal. Emma noticed a few men staying behind to finish fortifying the stone walls. It was the three men directly behind them, however, each with swords drawn, that held most of her attention. In addition to their weaponry, each man was wearing heavy chainmail armor from head to toe.

"Did we just land in Camelot?" she whispered.

"I was just wondering the same thing," her boyfriend replied.

"Well, the knights of the round table don't seem too friendly at the moment, that's for sure," Joel noted.

"No talking," the lead knight demanded.

The entourage walked through the woods for 15 or 20 minutes before stepping out into a large clearing. The guards did not speak a single word to their prisoners or to each other the entire time. The man out front never even turned around to look at his captives. The men behind kept the tips of their swords firmly pressed against the small of the traveler's backs.

"Well, dip me in cheese and call me fondue," Joel gasped. "Would you look at that?"

"It's amazing!" Emma gawked in wonder at the massive stone fortress looming ahead.

"Is that ... a castle?" Matthew asked in disbelief. It was not so much the existence of a world with castles in it that struck him. By now he had come to expect just about anything from the realms they visited. And yet the size and grandeur of the edifice had still taken him aback.

The guard in the lead gave another stern prohibition of all chatter as he continued to march them onward. It took several more minutes for the group to near the castle itself. As they drew close it was evident this stronghold was well fortified, and a great number of men were at the ready to defend it. Finally, the party stood at the edge of a wide moat waiting for acknowledgment from someone within the fortress walls. Eventually, the guard caught sight of someone, although Matthew could not spot the gatekeeper himself.

"Commander Cyfus, returning with captives caught entering through the gateway," he called out in a loud and brusque voice. "Prisoners are secured and prepared to meet their fate."

"Hey, just wait a ..." Joel objected, but was cut short by a firm shoulder check and icy stare from Matthew. As a result, both had the swords behind them pressed a little harder into their backs momentarily to reinforce the limits of their permissible behavior.

There was no audible response from inside the castle walls, but a few moments later an enormous drawbridge made of oak planks several feet thick, reinforced with iron, began to slowly lower toward them. The bridge took a few minutes to completely descend. Once down, the three friends could see a large number of men, dressed in armor and brandishing weapons like those they had been originally greeted by, standing in the entryway to the castle. The knights stood side-by-side, twelve men across and three rows deep, spanning the entire opening. The chevaliers marched forward about fifteen paces and then stopped abruptly in unison. The battalion held their position, weapons drawn, as a massive iron gate slowly descended behind them sealing off the entrance.

An Unexpected Welcome

Although none of them dared to say it out loud, it was painfully obvious to all three that, for whatever reason, their arrival was not in any way welcomed. Deep down they hoped that this was simply a misunderstanding like they had experienced in Bhal and that once they had a chance to explain who they were and why they had come to Demesne, Cyfus and the others would understand and assist them in their mission. If they were being honest, however, they all felt like this was something different and a positive resolution was not apt to be easy to come by.

"Come," Cyfus instructed in his usual curt manner.

Assisted by a nudge of the swords held by the knights behind them, the three friends dutifully moved forward onto the bridge. At the same time, the three dozen soldiers in front of the gate began marching forward again. The two groups met in the middle of the bridge. Cyfus halted his party and walked ahead to confer with the commander of the drawbridge garrison.

This was the first good look the travelers had of the local inhabitants, other than Cyfus' back. Rather disappointingly, all the knights wore helmets with visors that obstructed any view of their face. Unlike the men from the portal who wore only basic chainmail, the drawbridge garrison wore armor reinforced with plate metal across the chest and torso. After a brief discussion, which the visitors could hear none of, Cyfus turned back and waved to his men.

Matthew, Emma, and Joel felt the all too familiar nudge of the sword's tip pressed sharply into their backs. They moved along trying hard to fight off the growing sense of foreboding that steadily grew within them with each passing second. As they neared the garrison, a half dozen knights marched out to meet them. The portal guards stepped back as the drawbridge knights surrounded the nervous off-worlders and continued to march them forward. As they approached, the rest of the battalion gave way, allowing the knights to march the three friends into the center of the formation. With startling precision, all the cavaliers turned about and began marching back toward the iron gate of the castle. The gate slowly lifted, just high enough for the company to march under and then began lowering again as soon as they moved through. Matthew could hear the drawbridge being raised as well, although he could not see anything other than the armor of the men surrounding him.

Ten or fifteen minutes later the three friends found themselves alone again. They had been deposited in a dank and musty cell with a particularly pungent aroma. Although all their guards had gone, the off-worlder's hands were still bound and, once in the cell, their escorts had shackled their legs in irons as well.

"Well, isn't this just ducky?" Joel exclaimed.

An Unexpected Welcome

"Not the reception I was hoping for, that's for sure," his friend agreed.

"I'm sure, eventually, they will take us to whoever is in charge of this place and we will have an opportunity to explain ourselves," Emma responded, trying desperately to sound more optimistic than she felt.

"I hope you're right, Em, but so far things haven't really been going our way."

"We can't just sit here and wait for something to happen," Joel insisted. "The longer we're here, the further ahead of us Morgan gets. And the less chance we have of ..." His voice cracked and vanished as he couldn't bear to verbalize the thought that weighed so heavily on his mind.

"I know, buddy," Matthew comforted. "We *will* get her back. I promise."

"I appreciate the thought, Matt," Joel said, sniffling back the tears, "but it would be a lot more reassuring if we weren't shackled in some pee-soaked medieval dungeon."

Matthew tried to think of some more comforting response, but he knew he had none. His friend was right. As much as he'd love to promise that it was all going to work out okay, at the moment he wasn't completely convinced that was true and he certainly had no idea how to make it happen.

"We can't do anything about where we are now," Emma stated calmly. "We just have to be ready when our opportunity comes and make the most of it."

"How do we do that?" Joel probed.

"This place seems pretty 14th century, which likely means I'm not going to get much respect," Emma postulated. "So, it's likely best that one of you guys does the talking, and no offense, but Matthew is less likely to lose his cool and say something that gets us in even more trouble than we are already in."

Both the guys glanced at each other and exchanged looks of knowing agreement. "Okay, what else?"

"The best thing we can do is not give them any more reason to think we pose any kind of threat or danger to them. Or even a hassle or a headache for that matter."

"She's right," Matthew agreed. "The best thing we can do now is not cause a ruckus. The last thing we want to do is get any more on the bad side of these guys than we already are."

"You're probably right, but just waiting and doing nothing is killing me!"

"I know. Let's rest up, maybe even get some sleep so we're sharp and ready to go when we finally get a chance to plead our case," Matthew suggested.

"Fine," his friend conceded. "Would you like to lean against the icy cold stone wall or lay on the urine-soaked hay?"

"Gross," Emma scoffed.

An Unexpected Welcome

"Don't get mad at me," Joel protested. "I didn't do it. I am, however, regretting that grande mocha I drank just before we left."

"What are you doing, Em?" Matthew asked.

"Trying to figure out which way the floor slopes," his girlfriend replied. "There's no way I'm sleeping downhill from him!"

They all enjoyed a much needed but short-lived chuckle and then proceeded with their plan of trying to rest and sleep while they had the chance. Matthew sat down and leaned back against the cell bars and Emma laid down with her head on his lap. Joel stood for a long while peering out the small barred window at the night sky, but eventually slumped down against the wall and drifted off.

* * *

In the morning, Matthew caught the attention of a guard passing by their cell. He begged the man for some food, as none of them had eaten since noon the previous day and all their supplies had been confiscated upon arrival. The guard seemed to pay no attention to the prisoner's plea and continued to walk by. He returned a few moments later holding a round loaf in one hand. The knight haphazardly tossed the bread towards the cell. Being caught unprepared, Matthew was not able to reach his hands through the bars quick enough to catch the bread. The hurdling loaf bounced indiscriminately off the iron rods and landed on the stone floor a few feet away.

Joel, being both the tallest and lankiest of the three, immediately raced over to the front of the cell and reached his arm through the narrow opening as far as he could. His face was mashed against the bars as he strained for every inch of reach he could manage. Despite his best efforts the bread sat in a puddle on the floor just beyond his grasp.

"Come on!" Joel shouted in frustration.

The guard, with a look of complete indifference, snarled at the prisoner's outburst for a moment and then, reluctantly, sauntered back toward the cell. He tapped the loaf with his muddy boot just enough to move it a couple inches and walked away again. Joel stretched out his arm again and managed to, with the tips of his fingers, nudge the bread close enough to grab hold of and retract it into the cell. He did his best to brush off the dirt and mud. He tore off a big chunk and then tossed the rest to Matthew and Emma.

"The Food Safety Inspector would shut down my trucks if he saw this," Joel smirked, "but I'm starving."

"I'm just trying not to think about it," Emma cringed.

"At this point, I think we better take what we can get and be grateful for it!" Matthew said taking a large bite out of his chunk of the loaf.

An Unexpected Welcome

It was a frustratingly long time before anyone else visited the dungeon. Matthew guessed that it must be close to noon based on how long the sun had been up. This time it was the commander of the garrison who had talked with Cyfus before leading them into the castle. He had brought with him several of his men as well.

"I am Etwin," he announced in a firm, but not entirely unfriendly tone, "I have come to escort you to your assessment."

"Assessment?" Matthew questioned. "What do you mean, assessment?"

"Your punishment will be determined and carried out," the knight flatly explained.

"Wait just a cotton pickin' minute!" Joel protested. "Punishment for what? We didn't do anything except show up!"

"Chill out, Joel," Emma said calmly, gently grabbing his shoulder and pulling him back from the bars.

"Will we have an opportunity to speak at this assessment?" Matthew inquired. "To plead our case and ask for leniency?"

"I believe you will," Etwin replied, seeming to soften ever so slightly in response to Matthew's apparent compliance. "Now, move to the back of the cell and stand with your face to the wall as my men come in and prepare you for transport."

"As you wish," Matthew bowed his head slightly. He wasn't sure why he did so, but it seemed like the right thing to do. Etwin again seemed pleased by Matthew's cooperation, which felt like a good thing for the off-worlders. "Joel," Matthew whispered as they took the requested position. "This could be our opportunity, but only if you keep your cool."

"I know," his friend conceded. "This could also be the end."

"I know," Matthew admitted.

"No more chatter," Etwin called out, sounding almost like a request rather than a demand. "Let's go. The council will be waiting for us."

The knights covered each of the prisoner's heads with a heavy burlap sack and then led them out of the cell. The journey to the council room took quite some time as Etwin led them down a long and looping path, likely to ensure the prisoners gained no knowledge of the layout of the castle. Should they ever manage to escape, he undoubtedly wanted to make sure they would not know where to go and certainly not the best route to get there. Fortunately, this time the guards were simply leading their captives with a firm hand on their shoulders, rather than a sword point in the back. After what Matthew guesstimated to be about twenty minutes of wandering along, blinded by the thick hood, they came to a stop.

"The prisoners, as requested," Etwin announced. "They arrived at the portal yesterday afternoon, unannounced and without proper authorization. I present them to you for your judgment and sentencing."

"Matt?" Joel anxiously whispered through the burlap.

"Hold on," Matthew instructed, hoping desperately that was the right thing to do.

"Remove their masks," a woman's voice commanded.

The hoods were removed and the off-worlders squinted as their eyes adjusted to the bright light of the council room. The room itself was magnificent. High vaulted ceilings supported by tall columns of stone. Frescos, mosaics and large stained-glass windows covered the walls. Grand statues and podiums with ornate pottery atop them lined the room. But without a doubt, the focal point of the chamber was a large oak table covered in a rich purple cloth that stood at the front of the room. The table sat on a platform elevating it off the ground several feet, and behind it stood seven high-backed ornate chairs. Upon the chairs sat the council members, wearing flowing robes over leather body armor, all of whom were unmistakably female.

As the three friends examined the room they saw in the council members their first glimpse of a Demesnian without helmet or mask. The facial features of the council members were all relatively similar to one another and not extremely different from people on earth. There were a few noticeable variances. The Demesnians' heads were slightly more elongated, as were their noses and ears. The most striking difference, however, was found in their skin tone. Not only did the people of Demesne have skin of a different color than humans, but they also had a wide variety of skin colors amongst themselves. Each of the council members represented one of the seven clans of the realm. Clans could be easily identified by the different pastel hue of their complexion. Their skin also appeared to be slightly translucent, allowing shimmers of light to flood across their faces periodically in response to elevated emotion.

"Have the prisoners step forward," the woman in the center and slightly larger chair instructed. The three off-worlders were pushed forward to stand in a black square inlaid in the tiles of the floor. "You have been found guilty of entering our lands without our consent and with devious purpose and intent. We will now deliberate your sentence."

"Matthew!" Joel said, teeth clenched.

"Excuse me," Matthew spoke up, taking a step forward, but making a point of remaining within the black square.

The woman with the rose-colored skin in the center chair shot an icy look at the prisoner. "You were not called upon to speak."

"I understand," Matthew continued cautiously. "And I apologize if I am breaking protocol, but we are not familiar with your customs and no one has instructed us on the proper way to represent ourselves."

The woman's look softened. "You may proceed. Briefly."

"Thank you," Matthew replied as courteously as he possibly could. "My name is Matthew, Matthew Sinclair. These are my friends Emma and Joel." His introductions seemed acceptable, so he continued on. "Would it be inappropriate for me to ask your name?"

There was an uncomfortably long pause. "No."

Matthew looked at his friends in bewilderment. "Pardon me, but, do you mean *'No I cannot ask'* or *'No it would not be inappropriate?'*"

The woman seemed momentarily amused by Matthew's confusion, but quickly regained her solemn composure. "My name is Agitha."

"It's a pleasure to meet you, Agitha."

"Seriously? *This* is a pleasure?" Joel said under his breath.

"I fear there has been some misunderstanding about our intentions. We mean you absolutely no harm or ill will. We are friends of Silas, and he is the one who allowed us to travel through the portal to arrive in your wonderful land."

"You speak persuasively, Matthew Sinclair," Agitha replied pensively. "I could very well be won over by your words."

"That sounds promising," Emma whispered.

"If I were not certain that you speak nothing but lies!"

– 17 –
A Tale of Two Tales

"Okay," Matthew said, as he turned and whispered to his friends. "Clearly this is not going well. Time to call an audible." He turned to face the council once again and respectfully bowed his head. "If the council would graciously permit it, Lady Emma will speak on our behalf." Matthew took a step back and gently nudged his girlfriend forward. "You've got this Em."

"Oh, crud," she murmured.

"Lady Emma," Agitha addressed her with noticeably greater deference than she had given Matthew, "there is nothing more you can say."

"If the council would permit me just a few minutes to explain. There seems to have been a grave and very unfortunate misunderstanding."

The council head pondered the situation for a minute and then reluctantly said, "You have a brief moment to say what you need to say, but I will caution you that this council will not be easily swayed."

"Thank you," Emma smiled politely. "You are very gracious."

"Proceed."

"As Matthew said, we are friends of Silas. He was the one who sent us to your beautiful land. We are here to warn you of a great danger."

"This is a clever ruse, Lady Emma," Agitha replied. "But we have already received this warning and have taken the necessary precautions, which is why you stand before us today."

"I do not understand."

"Sometime prior to your arrival, another traveler came through the gateway. This traveler also claimed to be a close friend of Silas, an assertion we are much more inclined to believe because she has visited our realm before as a companion of Silas and Tara."

"Oh." Emma looked at her two friends who both wore the same expression of defeat.

"As we say in the food business: I think our goose is cooked," Joel lamented.

"Perhaps it's time to change tactics," Emma whispered and then turned back to face the council again. "Time to go on the offensive," she encouraged herself under her breath. "And who in their right mind would take the word of four, um, I mean three strangers over the word of someone who has been personally endorsed to them by Silas himself."

"You have an odd way of arguing your point," Agitha interjected.

"And I assume that when Morgan came through the gateway she warned you that others might follow. Not just any others, but I'm guessing she described us in great detail and told you to not take any chances should we appear."

"Indeed, she did," the head of the council confirmed, but for the first time since they had arrived Emma sensed the tiniest hint of curiosity. And curiosity makes people want to hear more.

"That makes sense I suppose," Emma continued her argument. "After all, it could be that even with a few words we would be able to delude a wise council like yourselves." She glanced back briefly at her two friends. "Yeah, I don't think so."

"What is your point?" the blue-skinned council member to the left of Agitha demanded.

"It just seems to me that if I were trying to deceive someone I would make sure that the only people who could expose my lies were never allowed to speak. Now that sounds like a cunning plan to me."

"Your point is well taken," Agitha conceded. "However, all you have proven is that it is not prudent for us to trust either you or ..." She paused a moment and replayed the dialogue of the last several minutes in her mind. "I did not tell you that the person who preceded you through the portal was named Morgan."

"No," Emma concurred, finally feeling like she was gaining ground. "But you didn't have to. We know Morgan all too well. We have been helping Silas pursue her through all of his realms."

"Impossible. Only Silas has access to his realms," the council member with the pastel orange skin objected.

"Not just Silas. Tara had portal keys as well. That is, until Morgan kidnapped her, imprisoned her on Garda and stole her keys."

There was an audible gasp from the council members at Emma's bold assertion. After a few moments of contemplation Agitha quietly conferred with the other council members and then addressed the off-worlders.

"You have given us much to ponder, Lady Emma. We will adjourn to deliberate. You and your friends will be remanded until the council can reach a decision on how to proceed."

"Thank you," Emma said politely as the council members stood to leave.

"Um, excuse me," Joel spoke up. "Um, if it wouldn't be too much trouble, would it be possible for us to be remanded to somewhere with a, what would you call it, a latrine? Please?"

Agitha chuckled slightly. "I'm afraid we have no latrine to offer you, sir. Would a toilet and bath suffice?"

Joel's face flushed red, "Um, yeah, I think we could make do with that. Thanks."

* * *

"Feel better?" Matthew asked as Emma emerged from the bathing room.

"SO much better," his girlfriend smiled brightly. "Remind me to thank Silas for including the essential amenities in his medieval world."

"These digs certainly are a step up from last night," Joel observed.

The three friends were being held in a large bedroom with a private bath. There were, of course, guards posted at the door who would randomly enter the room without any notice to ensure their guests were not up to something. There were several windows on the outside wall, but most were too narrow for anyone to attempt to slip through. The room was also on one of the upper levels of the castle, which meant that even if someone were able to get outside there would be nowhere to go but down – a long, long way down.

"You did great out there today, Em," Matthew said, giving his girlfriend a hug. "I'm pretty sure we're being watched," he whispered in her ear, "be careful what you say."

"Thanks, Matthew," Emma smiled as the hug ended. "I just hope it was enough."

"Well, they're thinking about it instead of sentencing us, so that's a big step up I'd say."

"Yeah, but we're wasting time," Joel reminded. "They confirmed that Morgan arrived here before us. That means she already has a huge head start. For all we know she could have left this realm already and moved on to who knows where."

"Joel's right," Matthew stated. "The longer we stay locked up here the more damage she can do."

"And the worse our odds become of getting Juliette back."

"You guys are right," Emma said sympathetically, "but we don't want to waste whatever goodwill we've managed to accumulate by doing something stupid."

"Emma's got a point, Joel. We made progress today. We'll keep talking with them and we'll keep making progress."

"You always say, Emma's right," Joel scoffed in jest.

"That's because she usually is."

"Hey! What do you mean usually?" Matthew's girlfriend protested.

Just then the door opened.

"Come on, guys," Joel protested. "Another random inspection? Seriously, we're not up to … oh, Lady Agitha. So nice to see you again."

"That one is odd," Agitha stated, and then cracking a smile added, "But I kind of like him."

"Agitha, has the council reached a decision?" Emma asked.

"Are they going to let us go after Morgan?" Matthew followed.

"I'm afraid not," Agitha stated as she moved further into the room and signaled for the guard to close the door behind her. "We seem to have come to an impasse."

"What is the problem?"

"There are some who were persuaded by your side of the story. They feel like we should set you free, perhaps even offer you aid in your pursuit of Morgan."

"I like that idea," Joel burst out.

"But only some?" Emma perceptively inquired.

"Yes, only some," Agitha confirmed. "There are others who hold fast to the idea that Morgan's version of events is the truth and believe as long as you are alive and in our world you are of immense danger to us."

"Okay," Matthew said optimistically. "We can work with that."

"How so?" the head of the council inquired.

"If some of your people don't feel safe with us here, we will leave."

"We cannot simply release you," Agitha objected.

"That's fine," Emma jumped in. "You don't have to free us, just let us go."

"I don't understand."

"Commission however many of your knights you need to feel comfortable to escort us to the exit gateway. They can march us right up to the box at spear point if need be."

"That's right," Joel affirmed. "We'll play nice. We'll open the gateway and we're out of your hair forever. We cause any problems along the way and we're shish-kabobs."

"Demesne will be safe," Matthew argued, "and we'll be someone else's problem."

"Hmm," Agitha said thoughtfully. "That is a very wise and prudent compromise, which makes me more prone to believe your intentions are noble. It is also exactly what I recommended to the rest of the council."

"Yes!" Joel shouted, unable to control his enthusiasm. "When do we leave?"

"The exit gateway is some distance from here. You will set out with my men at first light. I will have some food brought up to you this evening, but you must remain confined to this room."

"I can live with that," Joel agreed happily.

"Thank you, Agitha," Emma said kindly.

"Your men took all of our supplies when we arrived," Matthew stated. "We will need those back before we leave."

"I will see that they are brought to you." Agitha started toward the door and then turned back toward the off-worlders. "Be cautious," she warned. "Not everyone was content with this concession. There are some who grew very fond of Morgan during her previous visit and therefore do not find your story credible in the least. They are very loyal to her. I do not expect that they will cause any trouble, but I cannot guarantee they won't."

"Thanks for the warning," Matthew replied. "We'll be careful."

"And when this is all over," Emma added. "We will come back here with Silas himself, so you and all your people will know beyond all doubt that you made the right choice."

"I look forward to that day, Lady Emma," Agitha smiled gracefully and then exited the room.

* * *

The next morning the three friends stood in the castle courtyard in front of the drawbridge gate surrounded by more than a hundred armored knights. Matthew searched through his backpack to ensure everything was still there. He was especially relieved to find that his Mr. Spiffy's Car Wash keychain still held all seven of the keys Silas had originally given him. He pulled out the device and quickly scanned each key to make sure they were all authentic and in the same order on the key ring. It would be most unfortunate, he thought to himself, to wind up trapped back in Bhal with no means of escape, just because someone here had inadvertently shuffled the keys.

"Wow!" Joel gawked. "This is quite the send-off. It's nice of you to send all these men with us to keep us safe."

"Oh, they are not here to keep you safe," Agitha corrected with a sly grin, "they're here to make sure you leave."

"Oh," Joel replied sheepishly.

"Thanks again, for everything."

"You're most welcome, Lady Emma. Do take care. Etwin and twenty of his men will escort you to the exit gateway. I hope your journey is highly uneventful and that, if you are indeed telling us the truth, you are most successful in your quest."

"Thank you," the three friends chimed in unison.

"By the way," Matthew said softly. "Nice outfit, Em."

"Thanks," Emma smiled precociously, glancing down at the leather body armor Agitha had gifted her. "Agitha figured if I was going to keep traveling with you two hoodlums I might need some protection." All three off-worlders had also received heavy wool cloaks to wear on their journey through the land which was often cool and drizzly.

"Commander," Agitha called out. "They are under your keep."

"Yes, ma'am," Etwin acknowledged. The commander called out to the men under his command, most of whom were from his green-skinned clan, "Company move out."

With that, the iron gate gently rose, and the knights began to march forward. Matthew, Emma, and Joel marched in step with them, grateful to be doing so without swords pressed against their spines. Their hands and feet were also free of restraints, but none of them had any doubt the knights had been given strict orders to take them down at the first sign something was awry.

"How long will it take us to reach the exit gateway?" Matthew inquired.

"If we keep a steady pace we should reach there by late afternoon. If all goes well," Etwin answered.

"Is there any reason to expect that all wouldn't go well?" Joel asked.

"There's always the possibility."

"Like what?"

"If we have to stop to defend ourselves from an animal attack, that might take extra time. If the river is running particularly fast we might have to travel downstream to cross. If one of you falls off a cliff and breaks a leg you'll have to be carried. That will slow us down."

"Do you really think that could happen?" Joel questioned nervously.

"Naw," Etwin replied. "The river's quite slow this time of year." He guffawed heartily and then moved to the front of the troop to lead the way.

"Well, he's in a much better mood than he was a couple days ago," Joel murmured.

"Agitha told me she chose Etwin to lead us to the portal because he believed our story," Emma explained. "She instructed him to select other men who would be willing to defend us if trouble should arise."

"What are the odds of that?" her boyfriend asked.

"I think Agitha believed it was possible."

"Let's hope she's wrong."

* * *

After hiking through the woods all morning the company stopped by a small stream. Rations of bread, smoked meat and cheese were passed around for both the knights and the off-worlders to enjoy.

"This is such a beautiful place," Emma observed as she sat at the edge of the forest.

"It's your kind of place, alright," Matthew chuckled.

"Hey, guys," Joel called out from the stream's shore. "Check these fish out. They're like all kinds of neon colors. It's wild."

Matthew was about to walk over and see what his friend was talking about when he heard a series of whistles and whirs. A barrage of arrows came streaming over from the far side of the water striking many of the knights who had let their guard down as they ate.

"Get down, Joel!" Matthew screamed. He then grabbed a shell-shocked Emma and pulled her back into the moderate safety of the treeline. The two crouched down behind the trunk of a large tree. Matthew glanced out and saw that Joel had managed to dive behind a sizable rock near the shoreline.

After several additional volleys the barrage of arrows ceased. Over half of Etwin's men had been

"Archers, bows at the ready," Etwin commanded. "Target the woman on the shore. Be prepared to release on my command."

Matthew stepped to the very edge of the treeline making himself fully visible to all those on the far side. "I think we should talk," he shouted.

"I assume you have your archers targeting me," Morgan called back. "At least the few archers who are still able to stand."

"Every last one of them," Matthew said with all the confidence he could muster. "Your guys mostly missed anyway. And I assume yours are doing the same to me."

"Indeed they are."

"Well," he said stepping nervously out into the open. "I guess that means we can talk."

- 18 -
Truce

Silas slowed his pace as he approached the exit gateway. He looked around cautiously. If Morgan had left any goons behind, he had no desire to be blindsided by them.

"Who are you looking for?" Krotoa asked.

"Morgan has a habit of leaving several thugs behind to cause havoc," the carpenter explained.

"I only saw one," the young man stated. "One really big guy."

"What will you do now?"

"We've been chasing Morgan through the realms," Silas explained, still looking around nervously. "Every time we leave a realm we lock the portal box, so it can't be used anymore."

"Which means if Morgan is in that world," the young man surmised.

"Or enters that realm at some later point in time," Krotoa added.

"Right," the young man agreed. "She would have no way to escape."

"Exactly," Silas confirmed. "Once she is trapped in one single realm, we will do what is necessary to apprehend her and bring her to justice. We will retrieve her keys and free Tara and Juliette."

"Who's Juliette," the young man asked.

"It doesn't matter at the moment," the carpenter stated determinedly. "What matters now is that I follow Morgan and lock this gateway behind me immediately."

"Good luck, old friend," Krotoa smiled.

"Not so fast," a voice boomed behind them. "Step away from the box you weaselly snake."

Silas instantly knew who the voice belonged to, even without turning around. He quickly weighed his options. He could make a run for it and hope that he got to the box, found the right key and opened the gateway before the large man caught up with him. Unfortunately, the odds of success for that plan were extremely low. There simply wasn't enough time. By the time he got to the box, listened to the keyhole to discern Morgan's new location, found that key – if it was one he possessed – and opened the gateway, the man almost certainly would be upon him. At best the man would travel through the gateway with him. And there was virtually no chance he could do all that and use the nullification key as well. More than likely the man would be upon him before he could do any of it and once he was overpowered, which he most certainly would be, the man would not only have Silas as a prisoner but all his keys as well.

"Run!" Silas called out. The three men scattered with great haste looking for cover wherever they might find it.

"You've got nowhere to go," the man shouted after them as he sauntered toward the box. "You can't leave without the box, Silas. And you ain't getting it away from me. You're done taking what's rightfully mine."

Silas had found cover behind a nearby stack of crates. He peered around the edge just enough to see the man take up a position directly in front of the box.

"I can wait," the man crowed defiantly. "Morgan will be back, and when she gets here I will tell her your whole pathetic plan. Then we'll go visit your honey on Garda and take care of her."

"Noooo!" Krotoa screamed and rushed toward the man from his hiding place.

With one, almost casual, sweep of his arm the man sent the Nyumbani flying across the courtyard and crashing into a couple of water barrels, which shattered upon impact. Silas glanced over to where Krotoa had landed and was relieved to see him moving slightly. The young man who had first alerted them scurried out to assist Krotoa to safety.

"You've got some loyal friends, Silas," the man mocked. "I wonder how loyal they'd be if they knew the real you? If they knew what you had done? If they knew you like I do?"

"No one else needs to get hurt," the carpenter shouted from behind the crates. "This is between you and me. Leave them out of it."

* * *

It was a rather strange thing, Matthew thought as he walked down the beach, to feel such passionately negative feelings about someone you've hardly ever met face to face. The truth was, most of his angst toward Morgan was second-hand. She had betrayed and kidnapped Silas' wife. She had ambushed them and taken Juliette, who was his friend and Joel's entire world. She had crossed paths with Emma a couple times, none of which went well. Her archers had just taken out half of Etwin's squad. Of course, it wasn't much more than twenty-four hours ago when Etwin and all his people were ready to sentence Matthew and his friends to possible death without even allowing them to speak in their own defense. That's not to say he wasn't thoroughly convinced that the woman he was about to speak with was a malicious sadist. It's just that most of his very strong and angry feelings about her came to him indirectly through other people.

Matthew reached the shore of the stream and looked across at his foe standing 15 or 20 yards away. He stared at her with all the intensity he could manage. She clearly had the advantage here and he felt it. He was just trying not to look like he felt it.

"That wasn't necessary," he shouted across the water. "Those men weren't sent to capture you, they were simply escorting us to the gateway."

"Dear boy," Morgan said in a kinder voice than he had ever heard escape her lips. "The water is far too loud, and I have no desire to shout an entire conversation. Why don't you wade across to my side and we can speak like civilized people?"

Matthew was certain Emma would grab Etwin's bow and shoot him herself if he attempted to cross to the other side. "I don't think so."

"Come now," she smiled in a way that was much less devious than he expected. "The water doesn't appear that deep. I'm sure you could navigate it just fine."

"Sorry," Matthew smirked and gestured toward his beat up, old Nikes. "New shoes. I simply couldn't bear to get them wet."

"Hmm. Very well. Please tell your archers not to shoot. I would hate to die before our conversation even begins."

Morgan stepped gingerly into the stream and began making her way across to the other side. Matthew turned back to the woods and motioned with his hands for Etwin's men to hold their fire. He quickly turned back to keep his eyes trained on Morgan as she navigated her way across the water. Shouting at one another across the stream would have, without a doubt, made communication more difficult, but standing face to face with her made him much more uncomfortable. Morgan reached the shore and strode calmly toward Matthew.

"See, now was that so hard?" she asked. "Come on, let's sit down over here." She walked over to a pair of large rocks just up from the water's edge. She sat down on one of the stones and then looked up at Matthew with a surprisingly gentle smile. "Is this okay, or would your men prefer I sat over here?" She moved to the other rock and sat down again. "Why must these things always be so terribly complicated? Talking shouldn't be complicated, don't you agree? But I suppose it usually is, isn't it?"

Matthew was still standing uncertainly by the water's edge. This meeting was not going as he had expected it to. Morgan was not acting at all as he had expected her to. His mind raced. What was her angle in all this? She obviously had one. There is no way she was this charming. He couldn't even believe that thought had entered his mind.

"Come on, Matthew," Morgan called gently. "Archer's fingers get tired and I, for one, would like to finish this before someone fires off a random shot and starts Armageddon on this beach."

"Agreed," Matthew said, cautiously sitting on the rock across from Morgan.

"I had always thought that mutually assured destruction during the Cold War was such a strange philosophy. But sitting here now, I understand how people end up there. Let's hope it keeps us both alive."

"Enough philosophizing, what do you want?"

"First," she answered in a measured tone, "I want to apologize. I am truly sorry for the injuries your men sustained. For what it's worth, I gave specific instructions to my archers to only aim for legs or arms and to inflict no mortal wounds."

"Well, aren't you just a real saint?" he scoffed sarcastically.

"I know that you must have a terrible opinion of me, and rightfully so after what I've put you and your friends through."

"Yes, I do. Yes, you have," Matthew replied, feeling slightly guilty for being so blunt when his counterpart appeared to be going to great lengths to be civil.

"But I want you to understand, I'm not a bad person." Matthew stared at her in disbelief. "I know it must be hard for you to see that, but it's true. I'm not a bad person, but I am a desperate one. And desperate people do desperate things. Just think about it. Your friend back there, Joel is it? I bet he's a pretty decent guy most of the time, right? I also suspect you must have had to virtually tie him to a tree to stop him from coming out here and ripping me to shreds with his bare hands."

"You did kidnap his girlfriend," Matthew pointed out.

"I did, and now he's desperate to get her back. And desperate people are capable of things that the normal version of themselves would never in a million years consider."

"Okay," he conceded, "I see your point, but the difference is, Joel hasn't ripped you to sheds, yet."

"No, he hasn't, because he's got a friend like you to keep him from going too far."

"As I understand it, you used to have a friend like that too. If you'd like to talk with her, you can find her in a cell on Garda – right where *you* left her."

"I thought Tara was that friend for me, but I was mistaken," Morgan stated sadly. "I was mistaken about a lot of things."

Matthew glanced back at the treeline where he knew his friends were watching and wondering what was being said. He was confident the conversation wasn't going anything thing like they would possibly be imagining. "So, you're telling me, in your mind, you're a good person who's been forced to do some bad things out of desperation?"

"That's precisely what I'm telling you, Matthew."

"And what unbearable atrocity has made you so desperate?"

"Not what, Matthew, who?"

"Who?"

"Exactly." Morgan paused a moment to collect her thoughts and then continued, "What has Silas told you about how he learned to create worlds like this one?"

"He told me he was chosen by the previous craftsman and taught how to carve the doors and boxes to make new realms," Matthew explained. "He also told me that you befriended his wife and, because they *thought* they could trust you, he showed you some of the worlds he had made.

That's when you decided you wanted it all for yourself and plotted against them."

"And how, exactly, did he say the craftsman selected him?"

Matthew hesitated momentarily. Morgan had put him at ease, but he did not want to reveal too much. This could all be a fishing expedition as she searched for some key piece of information she needed to gain access to the workshop or even create worlds of her own.

"Okay," Morgan smiled knowingly. "I can see you don't want to tell me too much. Let me see if I can guess. A special key led the craftsman to Silas and that's how he knew who to select as his apprentice?"

"For argument sake, let's say, yes."

"Well, that's true. That is how a new apprentice is selected. What Silas failed to mention, however, is that the key doesn't select only one person. The key always leads the craftsman to at least two candidates who possess the Heritage. The craftsman then puts all the potential apprentices through a series of tests to evaluate their abilities and to assess how they will use their gift if they should be the one chosen."

"Fine," Matthew replied, suddenly feeling slightly off balance in the discussion. "So what if

Silas wasn't the only potential candidate. He was the one who was chosen and that's what matters."

"Yes, you're absolutely right. It does matter who was chosen by the craftsman."

"Yeah, so that settles it then."

"Not quite. At the time Silas was selected, the other candidate was a man named Zander."

"Okay?"

"Zander and I had been friends since we were little. We grew up in the same neighborhood. We even lived next door to each other for a while," Morgan's voice took on a sadly nostalgic tone as she spoke. "Everyone always teased us that we would get married when we grew up."

"So, what happened?" Matthew was caught off guard by his response of genuine interest as opposed to a sharp-witted jab.

"We became High School sweethearts," Morgan recalled. "And then, College sweethearts. Zander was my whole world back then. I couldn't imagine ever being without him. We had talked about getting married at the end of our senior year. He just hadn't got up the nerve to pop the question yet."

"I see."

"Then everything changed. He got really busy with projects and appointments I knew nothing about. He gave me evasive answers when I asked him about it. He assured me that everything was fine. In fact, more than fine, he said. He promised that soon he would be able to tell me everything and our lives would be changed forever. I just assumed he was trying to plan out some super romantic way to propose or something, so I didn't press him on it."

"But that wasn't it, was it," Matthew guessed. "He was training with the craftsman."

"Yes, that's exactly what he was doing, but, of course, he had been sworn to secrecy about it. He couldn't tell anyone, not even me until the process was over and he had been accepted as the new apprentice."

"But he wasn't chosen, Silas was."

"Yes, that is Silas' version of things."

"What are you saying? That Silas is lying?"

"I'll let you decide that for yourself," Morgan said and then paused to regain control of her emotions. "All I know is that Zander went out one night to work on his mysterious 'project' and I never saw him again."

"That doesn't mean Silas is at fault. Maybe, when Zander found out Silas was chosen over him, he couldn't take it and ran off. Maybe he was too embarrassed to face you. Maybe he was too ashamed because he failed. Maybe he refused to take no for an answer and the craftsman had to take matters into his own hands. There are a million possible explanations. It could have nothing to do with the Heritage. Maybe he was never a candidate. Maybe he had another girlfriend on the side and ran off with her. Maybe he flunked out of school. Maybe he was on drugs. There's no way to know. There is no proof that Silas was involved at all!"

"I suppose it could have been any of those things," Morgan conceded seeming more fragile than Matthew had imagined her capable of. "But you are wrong about one thing, Matthew."

"What's that?"

"I do have proof," she said as she removed an aged and worn envelope out of her pocket."

"What's that?"

"When Zander disappeared, no one knew where he was. Not me, not his friends, not his family, no one. His parents called the police to investigate, but they found no leads at all. It was like he just vanished into thin air they said. Eventually, they stopped looking and we all gave up hope. His parents called me a month or two later and asked me to stop by their house. When I got there, they told me that the police had just dropped off all the things they had collected from Zander's dorm room during their investigation. Among his belongings was a birthday present for me, all wrapped up nice with a bow."

"That's sweet, but I don't see how that..."

"Zander disappeared in October. My birthday is in July."

"So, it was a really belated birthday gift," Matthew suggested incredulously. "What was it?"

"It was still wrapped. The police had not even bothered to open it. Inside the package was a book.

It was a lovely hardbound copy of Hamlet, written in the original old English."

"You're a Shakespeare fan?"

"Heaven's no. Can't stand it. Neither could Zander, which is what made it so bizarre."

"And? I presume there was more. Was that envelope in it?"

"I knew he must have chosen that particular book for a reason. The story is all about betrayal and being double-crossed so I thought maybe this was his way of telling me there was foul play involved in his disappearance. At first I thought I was just deluding myself to deal with my grief. But then I noticed seemingly random letters on random pages had been circled. I searched through the book and looked for all the circled letters. When I was all done the letters spelled *'undercover'*."

"Maybe that was his way of telling you he had taken a job as an undercover cop," Matthew suggested. "Maybe he was sent on a deep cover assignment and didn't have a chance to tell you. Later, he had his handler to slip the book into his belongings before they were returned to his parents."

"Yes, I considered that possibility too," Morgan admitted, "but then, almost on a whim, I examined the covers of the book itself. I could feel a lump under the paper glued to the inside of the back cover. When I removed the paper I found this," she declared holding up the envelope once again.

"What does it say?"

"Here," she said extending the envelope to him, "read it for yourself."

* * *

"What do you mean, she gave him a letter?" Joel exclaimed. "Are they pen pals now or what? What in tarnation is going on down there!"

"I don't know," Etwin replied, glancing once again through his spyglass. "The conversation seems quite cordial actually."

"Yes," Emma responded anxiously. "You've already said that, several times."

"I apologize, it's just that from the way you spoke of her before it seemed as though you were lifelong foes. However, the two of them seem to be getting along quite well."

"Yes, I know, very cordial," Emma groaned in frustration. Her angst was not with Etwin's reporting, but rather with being helplessly stranded on the sidelines while Matthew was out sitting face to face with *her*. On the other hand, perhaps she should be grateful that things were seemingly going so well, as opposed to how she thought this streamside summit was destined to end. If it was a choice between uncomfortably cordial and unmitigated disaster, this was certainly the better of the two options. Deep down she knew that, but she didn't have to like it.

"Perhaps she is not as evil as you believed her to be," Etwin hypothesized.

"Dude, did you forget the part where she just shot all your men without warning?"

"Yes, that is difficult to overlook."

"How much longer is this going to go on?" Emma questioned rhetorically.

"What's happening now?" an equally impatient Joel asked.

"He's reading the letter."

– 19 –
A Sign of Good Faith

"That is Zander's handwriting," Morgan verified. "I would know it anywhere. He used to leave me notes all the time. The letter is, without a doubt, from him."

"Let me see," Matthew said, taking the envelope and removing the paper inside. "*'My dearest Morgan,'*" he read. "*'If you are reading this, something has gone terribly wrong. I thought I was opening the door to a great life for us, but now I fear I have only put us in harm's way. I am not supposed to tell you any of this, but if you are reading this letter it means I am gone, and I need you to know why. Several months ago, I was approached by a man who told me I was a candidate for a very prestigious job. He began running me through a series of tests and training exercises. What I discovered is truly unbelievable. Morgan, there are many other worlds out there and this man is going to teach me how I can travel to all of them and maybe someday even create new ones myself.'*" Matthew looked up from the letter and said, "This is all very touching, but I don't see how it changes anything."

"Keep reading, Matthew."

"Alright, where was I? Blah, blah, blah create new ones myself. '*The training is almost complete.*

There is one other candidate and very soon we will find out which one of us gets to move on and become Phineas' apprentice. I am quite certain that I have the edge over the other fellow. But I'm starting to get nervous. Not that I won't be chosen. I'm worried about what Silas will do if I am. The other day he said he thought maybe he should strand me in one of the realms Phineas had created, with no way out so the apprenticeship would go to him. He played it off as if he were joking, but I'm not entirely sure he was. If I have disappeared I suspect this is exactly what has happened. Do not, under any circumstances, go looking for Silas. He is as cunning as he is cruel, and he has a silver tongue that can persuade you of almost anything. The last thing I want is for you to get stranded somewhere as well. Knowing Silas, he would never strand us both in the same world. I just needed you to know what happened to me. Do not go after Silas. Stay away from NYU. And if anyone comes around asking about me, don't say anything about this. As long as they think you don't know anything you are not at risk. I love you, my sweet' ... and then it gets all mushy."

"There is your proof," Morgan declared confidently. "The noble Silas exiled my Zander to some strange realm, just to win the craftsman's apprenticeship. Once he learned how to craft worlds of his own there was no chance Zander would ever be found."

"That's right. Tara told me that the workshop was the access point for all the realms Silas and the others had made. If Zander wasn't in one of the realms on Tara's keychain I would need access to the workshop."

"It's an intriguing story," Matthew admitted. "But..."

"I know I've given you no cause to believe me. I have done terrible things. I hardly recognize myself at times. But I just got so desperate when my chance to find Zander started slipping away, and then everything just spiraled completely out of control. The next thing I know I'm holding on to innocent hostages and ordering a bunch of knights to fire arrows on another bunch of knights across a river. That's when I realized it needed to stop. I needed to stop."

Matthew pondered it all for quite some time. He really wasn't sure what to make of Morgan's story. It was plausible, but he still struggled to trust her. On the other hand, if he was in her shoes and Emma had been exiled he would move heaven and earth to get her back. In his heart he knew that he might do everything Morgan had, and more, if that's what it took.

"So, what do you want?"

"I need time. Time without you and your friends chasing me and stirring up the locals against me. Time to stay one step ahead of Silas."

"Is that all?" Matthew asked skeptically.

"No, I need your help to convince Silas to give me the workshop key."

"That's not going to happen. He," Matthew caught himself before revealing that Silas no longer had the workshop key in his possession. "He won't give that up."

"I need you to try and convince him," Morgan pleaded.

Matthew again mulled things over in his head. He was starting to feel legitimately confused about what the truth was and who was actually telling it. "Let's just say, for argument sake, I were to believe you, which is still not a given at this point. I would need a show of good faith on your part."

"Well, my archers haven't shot you yet, that's a good sign, isn't it?" Morgan said with a quiet snicker. "What did you have in mind?"

"Jules," Matthew stated firmly. "You have to release Jules. Not later, but right now. When you leave Demesne you head straight to Garda and you return her to earth, do not pass go, do not collect two hundred dollars. If Jules isn't waiting for us, one hundred percent safe and sound, when we get back to earth, all bets are off."

"Done," Morgan confidently replied. "I never meant to take her in the first place. You guys came through the gateway right after us and I needed a safe escape. However, I need your word that when I do, I will not be walking into an ambush."

"You have my word, you won't be."

A Sign of Good Faith

"Then, you have my word, I will."

"If you return Jules we can continue the discussion, but I am still not making any promises. I need to dig deeper into Silas' side of the story and figure out which one of you I can really trust."

"I understand completely. I'm just grateful that you were willing to hear me out."

"I'm glad I don't look like a pin cushion after this conversation. Please express my thanks to your archers for that."

"I will."

"I have to warn you," Matthew cautioned as he stood up to leave. "It's not just me that has to be convinced. Joel and Emma have to be on board too."

"And I expect that will not be an easy sell with either of them, and with good reason, I admit."

"Yeah, tickets on the Hindenburg is a tough sell. This is going to be something else altogether."

"I'm sure you will do your best," Morgan encouraged.

"I'll do my best to do what's right," Matthew clarified. "I'm just not totally sure what that is at this point."

"Fair enough," Morgan smiled. "Let's begin by seeing if we can both get off this beach without getting shot."

"Sounds like a great plan to me," Matthew grinned as he began to back his way up the beach toward the treeline. "By the way," he called out to

Morgan as she reached the water's edge. "For what it's worth, I kind of feel bad about making you cross the stream now."

She chuckled warmly and replied, "It was worth it."

* * *

"How was the tea party, Matt?" Joel asked sarcastically as Matthew stepped into the forest.

"What are you talking about?"

Emma ran to him and gave him a long hug. Then she pushed him back gently and said, "It's just that the two of you seemed rather ... cordial." She was annoyed with herself for not coming up with a better word to describe the meeting.

"Well," Matthew replied thoughtfully. "I admit the conversation did not go at all like I had expected."

"Yeah," Joel agreed with a notable edge in his voice. "She walked away in one piece, so it didn't exactly go as I expected either."

"Desperate people do desperate things. Things they normally would never consider," Morgan's words rang in Matthew's mind. "Yes, she did get to walk away this time," he said compassionately. "But so did I, so perhaps we can call this one a draw?"

"You're absolutely right, Matthew," Emma agreed, giving him another quick hug and then pushing him back again. "What were the two of you talking about? According to Etwin's play by play it sounds like you guys are besties now!"

"Play by play?" Etwin puzzled quietly.

"I have a lot to tell you," Matthew explained. "Morgan was not at all as I had expected her to be. At first I thought it was all an act. You know, a scam of some kind."

"But?" his girlfriend prompted

"But the longer I spoke with her the more I wondered."

"Wondered what?" Joel asked with a stern look that indicated he did not like where all this was going.

Matthew tempered his thought slightly, "I wondered if maybe she wasn't quite as evil as we originally thought her to be."

"I have not wondered that," Joel replied flatly.

"On the upside, she guaranteed us safe passage to the gateway," Matthew explained.

"And you believe her?" his girlfriend asked apprehensively.

"I think if she had wanted to she could have wiped us all out an hour ago. But she didn't."

"That's true, but it could all have been a ploy to gain our trust," Emma suggested.

"Yes, but would she go to all that trouble to gain your trust just to attack you again later? Is she that malevolent?" Etwin asked.

"YES!" Emma and Joel replied in unison.

"I don't think that's the case this time," Matthew suggested. "Etwin, can you give us clear directions to the gateway from here?"

"Certainly," the knight replied. "All you have to do is follow the stream, upriver, until you come to the highland bridge. Cross the water there and follow the trail on the other side. It will take you to the summit and the gateway box is there."

"Great. Then I want you to take your men back to the castle and get the injured attended to. We'll be fine on our own from here."

"Are you certain?"

"He's right, Etwin," Emma agreed. "If Morgan wants to take us out she can do it whether you're with us or not. And your wounded need to be cared for."

"Very well," the commander agreed reluctantly. "Good luck to all of you. I hope we meet again someday."

"We hope so too," Joel replied sincerely.

* * *

The three friends gathered up their belongings and started up the shoreline. Despite how well their meeting had gone Matthew couldn't help but stare across the stream and wonder if somewhere, just inside the treeline, there was a squad of archers poised and ready to fire. He could only imagine how his friends must be feeling. He knew they were anxious to hear more of what Morgan had said. He wasn't avoiding the discussion, he just wasn't really sure what to say or how to say it in a way that would be well received. They weren't there. They didn't see her, hear her. She was different, but how could he convey that to people who, for very good reasons, felt like she was evil incarnate?

"So," Joel finally prodded. "Are you gonna spill or what?"

"Sorry, guys," Matthew apologized. "We covered a lot of ground and I'm just trying to process it all."

"Well," Emma said, gently clasping his hand. "Why don't you tell us and then we can all process together."

"Alright, I'll do my best." Matthew pondered for one more moment how to begin and then said, "Okay, I have good news and bad news."

"I feel like we've played this game before," Joel quipped. "And I'm pretty sure last time we lost but go ahead."

"Okay, the very good news is that, as a sign of good faith, Morgan has agreed to release Juliette."

"Are you serious?" Joel asked in disbelief. "For real?"

"Yes," his friend confirmed. "On the condition that we will not lay a trap for her when she returns to Tara's apartment, she said she will bring Jules back."

"But we could end this whole thing right now," Emma suggested. "She won't know it's a trap until it's too late, and by then it would all be over!"

"Yes, I know that, Em. She does too. Which is why she would never release Jules unless I gave her my word she would walk away from the exchange."

"And she trusts you?"

"About as much as I trust her, but that's all we have to go on right now."

"That and the fact that if she had wanted to she could have easily taken us out back there on the beach," Emma conceded.

"It would have been a lot less hassle than setting up a double cross back on earth, that's for sure," Joel agreed. "So, when is she coming back?"

"Morgan said she would leave Demesne and go straight to Garda to release Jules. We're just supposed to go back to Tara's place and wait."

"I really want to believe it," Joel said, almost forcing the words out of his mouth. "But, I'm not sure I buy it. It makes no sense. It's completely out of character for her."

"Huh, yeah," Matthew replied reluctantly. "That's the thing about character, you're never really sure you've got it quite figured out."

"What is up with you, Matthew?" Emma probed. "Ever since your little streamside rendezvous you've been talking like you're not sure Morgan is the bad guy in all this."

"More like talking crazy, that Morgan's *not* the bad guy," Joel affirmed.

"I know," Matthew conceded. "And I know this is going to be impossible for you to understand, but ... she was different."

"Different how?" his girlfriend asked skeptically.

"She was," Matthew wrestled with completing the sentence, both because he knew how his friends would react, but perhaps even more so because he thought he might actually believe it. "She was...nice."

"Nice!" Joel cried in exasperation. "The woman who had her henchman hold a knife to my girlfriend's throat was 'nice'?"

"The woman who tied me up and threw me in the back seat of her car, was 'nice', Matthew?"

"I get it, guys. I was skeptical too," Matthew stated and then corrected himself, "I *am* skeptical. I assumed it was all an act. A ploy of some kind. But if it was, it was an Oscar-worthy performance. The entire time we talked she was pleasant, thoughtful, gracious, even, if you can believe it, gentle-spirited."

"I cannot believe it," Joel responded.

"Neither did I at first. But she was quite convincing."

"And to what did she credit this miraculous change in personality?" Emma demanded.

"Desperation."

"Yeah, she's desperate to get rid of us," Joel fumed.

"No, she claimed all the nasty stuff she said and did before was out of desperation."

"I don't understand," Emma said, softening in the slightest way.

"Joel, what would you do to get Jules back?"

"Anything. Absolutely anything."

"Would you lie? Cheat? Steal?"

"If that's what it took."

"Would you hold Morgan's closest friend hostage in order to barter an exchange?"

"I ... Come on. That's not fair. That's different. I'm talking about the life of someone I love, not some lustful greed for power."

"According to her, and remember, don't shoot the messenger, but according to her, it's not different at all."

"What do you mean, Matthew?" Emma asked.

"She claims she's not after power over all the realms. She says she's looking for her true love who has been stranded in one of these worlds for decades."

"And you believe her?" Joel asked skeptically.

"To be honest, I'm not sure what to believe," Matthew admitted. "But like I said, she was a totally different person. If I had never met her before today, I would not have questioned her story in the slightest. It seemed so completely genuine."

"I'm still not buying," Joel stated resolutely. "If any of that were true, Silas would know about it, and he would have told us."

"Hey, look," Matthew called out. "I think that's the bridge Etwin told us to cross." As difficult as the first part of this conversation had been, Matthew knew that discussing Morgan's version of events regarding Phineas' apprentice would prove to be infinitely more complicated to work through with his friends. He still found it almost impossible to believe himself. If Morgan's story was a lie, it was an extremely cleverly crafted one. Of course, the same could be said for Silas' rendition. Either way, he was happy to put the conversation on hold until they had reached the trail on the far side of the stream. It would give his friends time to ponder what he had told them about Morgan. And as far as the quandary about Silas went, they would have to cross that bridge when they came to it.

– 20 –
Fraught with Uncertainty

"Alright," Joel called back to his friends, "Etwin said the gateway is at the top of this trail. If we hurry we might get there before Morgan does."

"And then what?" Emma asked sympathetically. "We have to assume she has the same entourage with her she had back at the stream. What are the three of us going to do against all of them?"

"Emma's right. Our best move is to wait until after she is gone. Hopefully, her men will leave the box unguarded and we can slip in and make our exit."

"You want to just let her go?" Joel asked incredulously.

"It's not that, it's just…"

"What are you not telling us, Matthew?" Emma prompted. "I know you. You're holding something back."

"You're right," her boyfriend admitted. "But you have to promise me you'll hear me out before you make up your mind."

"I don't like the sound of that," Joel frowned.

"And bear in mind, I'm just relaying the information. I'm not necessarily endorsing it."

"But you're not necessarily denouncing it either," Emma questioned.

"I honestly don't know what I think."

"Well," Joel said softening slightly. "Spit it out and we'll figure it out together."

"Okay, but you're not going to like it."

* * *

The trio had almost reached the trail's peak by the time Matthew had finished recounting Morgan's rendition of history and how Silas had become the craftsman. Although it was understandably difficult for them to hear, Matthew's friends listened attentively and gave the matter fair consideration.

"I don't know what to think about all that," Emma admitted. "What you're describing doesn't sound anything like the Silas we know, but then again, how well do we really know him?"

"If he's lying, he's doing a bang-up job of it," Joel insisted.

"So is she," Matthew countered.

"I'll be honest," Emma confessed. "I want to believe Silas. I want Morgan to be the evil witch I've always thought her to be." She paused a moment, wrestling with her own thoughts. "But, if Morgan is telling the truth and I was in her shoes, I would do everything she's done and more."

"I agree," Matthew said. "And Silas seems like a good guy because we've always thought him to be a good guy. But, if we were on the other side of all this would we be just as furious at him as we have been at her?"

"I still think she's the villain in all this," Joel declared. "But, I admit I'm slightly less sure than I used to be."

"The problem is," Emma pondered. "How can we possibly know for sure? Both stories seem plausible. There's no irrefutable proof either way. One of the two is a brilliant pathological liar. The other is a tragically wronged victim. How do we figure out which is which?"

"We go home," Matthew replied.

"How does that help?" his friend questioned.

"We go home. If Morgan shows up and releases Jules, then we give her story a little more credibility. If we walk into another ambush, we write her off for good."

"Not the world's greatest plan, but it makes some sense," Emma conceded.

"Plus, if we're lucky we'll meet up with Silas again while we're there and we can question him some more and see if his version of the story still holds up."

The three all agreed that Matthew's plan, as imperfect as it was, was likely their best move at this point. They hiked the rest of the way up the trail in silence as each one tried to process things in their own mind. They all held on to the hope that, one way or another, Juliette might soon be free from her cell in Garda.

"There it is," Emma said, seeing the gateway box ahead.

"There she is," Joel scowled spotting Morgan standing nearby.

"Stay cool, Joel," his friend cautioned.

"Hello there," Morgan greeted cheerfully. "There's no need to fear, all of my men have gone. It's just me here now."

"Our deal still stands?" Matthew verified.

"Yes, yes," Morgan smiled. "I release the girl and you consider my request." She studied the three companions as they cautiously approached. "I can see that your friends have not been entirely convinced by my appeal."

"You could say that," Joel replied sternly.

"I understand, Joel. You are concerned for your sweetheart. Believe it or not, I know exactly how you feel." Joel's austere expression was unrelenting. Morgan lifted the box lid and inserted a key. "I'll see you soon."

Joel stared at Morgan as the anxiety of the moment erupted within him. "I'm sorry, Matt."

"Joel, no!" Matthew cried out. He reached out for his friend's arm, but it was too late.

Joel sprinted toward the box and dove to tackle Morgan to the ground. Unfortunately, he was a split second too slow. He made contact with her just as she turned the key and opened the portal. A bright light enveloped them both. A moment later the light was gone, and so were they.

"Oh crud," Emma said dejectedly. "Now what do we do?"

Matthew walked over to the box and opened the lid once again. He scanned the brass plate which confirmed the gateway Morgan had opened did indeed lead to Garda.

"What do we do now?" Emma repeated her question.

"She took Joel to Garda," Matthew stated. "We don't have the key to follow them. The plan hasn't changed. The best thing we can do is go home and wait. Hopefully, she isn't put off by Joel's antics and brings both him and Jules back to the apartment as promised."

"And if not?"

Matthew had no answer to that question, so he simply extended his hand and gently said, "Come on, let's go."

* * *

Even though the people of Nyumbani had no significant weapons, aside from basic spears and bows used for hunting, they almost certainly could have overpowered Zander, by sheer numbers. Zander was a large and strong man, especially when compared to the Nyumbani who were typically a little more diminutive than the average human.

Nevertheless, there was only one of him and a whole village of them. Silas instructed Krotoa to recruit all the able-bodied men and women in town and prepare them to make a rush at Zander. Even at his best, he couldn't possibly fight them all off. To increase their odds of success and limit the chance of Nyumbani injuries, Silas suggested waiting a day or two.

Zander had been guarding the box nonstop since his first encounter with Silas. He had not let it out of his sight for a moment, which meant he had had nothing to eat or drink other than the contents of a small canteen which had run out long ago. The heat of the Nyumbani sun beat down upon him constantly, as there was no night in this world. Finally, Silas decided the time had come.

The carpenter approached head on to where Zander was standing behind the gateway box. "I have not seen you in a very long time, old friend."

"Yes," Zander spit back, "And I imagine you wish you were not seeing me now. And we were *never* friends."

"When I heard that Morgan had taken a man out of Rend I knew it must be you, but I admit I was quite surprised. I have visited that realm frequently over the years. And every I time went I looked for some sign, some hint that you were still there – still alive. But there never was even a whisper."

"You *wanted* me to disappear," Zander scoffed. "I guess you did a better job than you thought."

"That was Phineas's decision, not mine," Silas countered, inching his way forward.

"So you say."

"You must believe me, I took no pleasure in it. Nonetheless, it had to be done, and I will not apologize for doing what was necessary." Silas took a few more tentative steps towards his adversary. "Just as I will do what is necessary now, to get Tara back and deal with you and Morgan once and for all."

"You can try," Zander scoffed defiantly, "but this time will be different. This time you will be the one to suffer."

"Oh, I think not," Silas grinned and then made a short series of clicking sounds.

Dozens of Nyumbani flooded into the small courtyard scurrying toward the box. Zander took up a defensive pose and started swinging his heavy fists in every direction. Several of the Nyumbani were knocked to the ground, but eventually numbers won out and Zander was taken down to the ground and subdued. Krotoa, sporting a fresh black eye and with a trickle of blood on his lip, bound Zander's hands and feet tightly, then rolled the large man onto his back.

Silas slowly walked up to the incapacitated man and looked him over. "I think not."

* * *

Morgan stumbled through the doorway at the bottom of the sand pit. It took all her might to force the door closed again against the power of the swirling wind. When she reached the top of the stairs she was greeted by five Nyumbani men with spears whom Silas had sent to await her arrival.

"Apparently you've been expecting me," she said dryly. "Take me to Silas."

"No more word," one of the Nyumbani insisted in broken English as he bound her hands. "We take to..."

"Take me to Silas? Yeah, I got that part already, let's get on with it."

The Nyumbani men marched Morgan across the dunes, into the village and led her directly to the courtyard where the gateway box was stationed. As she entered she could see Zander, still bound hand and foot, and tied to a wall at the back end of the square. Undaunted she continued to walk toward the box, where Silas stood waiting for her.

"It seems I've finally caught up with you," he announced.

"I'm not sure who has caught up with who, but here we both are, so let's just go from there, shall we?"

"You are far more bold than I remember," the carpenter admitted. "Nothing like the soft-spoken lamb who first befriended my wife."

"You're pretty much the same – old and tired."

Fraught with Uncertainty

"Enough dancing around," Silas said showing signs of frustration. "You have my wife. I have this man, who obviously means something to you, Lord knows why. I propose an exchange. Return to Garda. Come back here, with my wife and all the keys you have stolen, and I'll let the both of you go."

"Somehow I doubt that," Morgan replied incredulously. "You didn't let him go before, why would you do it now?"

"Very well, I promise to send you both back to Rend together, how about that?"

"Yeah, I don't think so. I have a counter-offer," Morgan smiled and held up her still bound hands. "Let's start with these."

"You may release her," Silas instructed.

"Much better," she said, rubbing her newly freed wrists. "Now, here's what *I* propose." She stepped forward confidently and looked Silas square in the eyes. "You release Zander, we leave, and you don't follow."

"Oh, dear girl, you have no idea ..."

"I wasn't done," Morgan interrupted.

"Why on earth would I allow that?" Silas scoffed.

"As I said, I wasn't done." Morgan's eyes revealed a slight glint as she explained further. "I have just come here from Garda. I left two of my friends there to keep an eye on things. Their names are Derge and Cazgon. You might be familiar with their work."

"Vile creatures, both of them."

"I left them with very specific instructions," Morgan explained calmly. "They are to guard the entry portal. If anyone other than me should come through, they are to deal with them as they see fit."

"I don't see your point."

"I also told them that if I do not return in 48 hours, they get to choose which one of them gets to pay your wife a visit and express my dissatisfaction."

"You wouldn't."

"I already did, but, if you let Zander and I go, I promise to call off the dogs, so to speak."

Silas pondered the situation for a moment, trying desperately to find an alternative that didn't require giving up the only leverage he had, but he came up empty-handed. "Very well," he said in defeat. "Release him."

Morgan smiled with delight as Zander was freed. They stood side by side as she opened the box. Silas and all of the Nyumbani watched helplessly as she inserted a key.

Zander leaned down and whispered in her ear, "You were bluffing about that whole Garda thing, weren't you. After all these years I can still read you like a book."

Morgan grinned. "Oh, and by the way, Silas, your friends will all be waiting for you back in your wife's apartment. I had a nice little heart to heart with them and filled them in on some of the details you seemed to leave out. I'm sure they'll have a number of questions for you."

Light filled the courtyard as the gateway opened. Silas rushed to the box as soon as the light faded. He opened the lid and laid his hand on the brass plate.

"Not again," Silas sighed. Allowing Morgan to slip through his fingers was a dagger to the heart. He had just started to believe that he had a legitimate chance to rescue Tara. Once again Morgan had outsmarted him, which was becoming an all too familiar feeling. Adding Zander into the equation made things that much worse. If Morgan got the key, she could wreak havoc on all the realms. But if Zander gained access to the workshop he would destroy worlds, create new ones, and worst of all, prevent Silas from ever entering the workshop, the vault or the other realms ever again. Silas' heart sunk at the thought. His shoulders drooped, his brow furrowed, and his mind raced to find some way to regain the upper hand. Deep down, however, he knew his best chance of saving his wife had just disappeared into the portal.

"What will you do now?" Krotoa asked.

"I don't know," Silas admitted, genuinely uncertain of his next move. "If she was telling the truth, then Garda is unsafe. I don't dare follow them to the realm of Skalla, at least not right away. Perhaps returning to earth is the best choice for now."

"What if she was trying to trick you into going back to Tara's apartment?" Krotoa postulated.

"I thought of that," Silas said. "It very well may be, but I don't know that I have any other choice at the moment."

"Good luck."

"Thank you. I feel like I need it now more than ever." Silas inserted the nullification key into the box and turned it. Then, with a deep sigh, he inserted the key for Earth and opened the portal.

* * *

"How long have we been waiting?" Emma asked.

"I don't know, maybe an hour," Matthew answered. "Maybe a little more."

"I feel so helpless just sitting here. Isn't there something we can do?"

"I can't think of anything and believe me I've tried." Matthew felt thoroughly defeated. Even though it was possible things would still work out, all he could think about was Joel disappearing into the gateway on Demesne. He should have grabbed him. He should have stopped him. Or perhaps, he shouldn't have said anything to him in the first place. Maybe he shouldn't have sat down to talk with Morgan and allow her to fill his head with all these conflicting ideas. The only thing he knew for certain was that he felt like a crushing weight had been placed on his shoulders and he was the one responsible for putting it there.

"How long do we wait before we decide that Morgan has stabbed us in the back and we move on?"

"I don't know," Matthew admitted. "To be honest, I can't even think about that. I don't know how we would move on. I don't know what we would move on to. I don't know anything anymore!" He collapsed onto the couch in frustration. "All I can think about is that if we lose Joel, it's all my fault."

"That's not true, babe," Emma comforted. "You warned Joel not to go. You told him to wait with us."

"Yeah, but I'm the one who screwed with everyone's head and got us thinking that maybe Morgan was actually one of the good guys."

"She still could be. We just have to wait a little longer." Emma could hardly believe those words had just come out of her mouth. She paused to have an internal debate over whether she had just said it to try and make Matthew feel better, or could it be she might actually believe it was possible.

"You're probably right. Maybe it's just taking more time than we expected to release Jules from her cell," he said, trying desperately to sound optimistic. "Let's give it a little more time and see what happens. If she doesn't show up in the next hour we'll ... Em, do you?"

"Yes, I see it too," Emma cheered excitedly.

A small light appeared in the center of Tara's living room and steadily grew. Matthew and Emma shielded their eyes from the intensity of the light. When the glow had faded, they opened their eyes to see who had arrived through the gateway.

"Matthew! Emma! Are you two okay?"

- 21 -
Welcome Home

Matthew and Emma stared at each other, not sure what they should say, or for that matter feel. Joy? Anger? Relief? Disappointment? Perhaps all of the above.

"Silas," Emma finally broke the silence, "welcome back."

"Thank you, Emma," the carpenter replied. "How did your journey to Demesne go?"

"It was not uneventful," Mathew answered in the most truthful way he knew how.

"Yes, a lot has happened," Emma affirmed. "How was your time in Nyumbani?"

"Most distressing," Silas confessed. "Perhaps we should move on from here and discuss things further at Joel's apartment."

"No!" Matthew responded much more adamantly than he had intended. "Umm, I mean we can't leave. Not yet."

"Why not?"

"Because we're waiting for Joel to get back," Emma explained.

"Why would Joel return here and not his own apartment?"

"Because," Matthew began, "we saw Morgan at the exit gateway in Demesne. Joel tried to grab her before she left, but he didn't quite make it and he was sucked into the portal with her."

"Then we should return to Nyumbani at once. I saw Morgan there only moments ago. If she took Joel with her he should still be there. But no – I used the nullification key there before I left. Do not worry though. My friends in Nyumbani will take good care of Joel. We will return to bring him home as soon as this is all over."

"Yeah, it's not that simple," Emma stated.

"Why not?"

"Because," Matthew said dejectedly. "Morgan didn't take him to Nyumbani."

"She didn't? Then where?"

"She took him to Garda."

"Garda! Heaven's no," Silas exclaimed. "But then, why – how are you expecting him back?"

"The truth is, we made a deal with her," Matthew explained.

"What kind of deal?"

"A deal that should have resulted in Juliette being returned to us," Emma replied.

"In exchange for what?" Silas asked dubiously.

"In exchange for hearing her out," Matthew said. "Nothing more."

"And you expected her to hold up her end of that deal?"

"We had hoped. We also hoped that Joel's last-minute quarterback blitz wouldn't mess things up."

"We're still hoping," Emma added.

"I'm truly sorry, but I fear your hope is gravely misplaced. The only deal Morgan lives up to is the one that benefits her most at that moment. It is folly to stay here any longer. She could return at any moment with who knows how many of her lackeys in tow."

"He's right, Matthew," Emma said gently. "If she does show up with Joel and Jules, they can find their way home on their own. If she shows up with a crew full of baddies, we're in no position to take them on."

"Fine, we'll go," Matthew conceded. "But first, I have to ask you a question. Who is Zander?" He had intended to be more subtle when questioning Silas, but the anxiety of the moment had gotten the best of him. "Who is he, Silas?"

"You *have* been listening to Morgan," Silas observed with sadness in his voice. "I will tell you everything, but please, not here."

* * *

"Okay," Emma said as they walked into Joel's apartment, "spill it." Seeing Silas' confused look, she clarified, "Tell us everything."

"I would ask you what Morgan has told you, but I suspect at this point you want to hear my side of the story, so you can decide who you are going to believe. I don't know what she told you, but based on what I just witnessed on Nyumbani, I suspect it was an incredibly devious tale."

"It was very convincing," Matthew admitted. "Which is saying a lot considering she was telling it to people who at the time completely despised her."

"I have underestimated her from the beginning. I see that now, and I am paying the price for it."

"Tell us about Zander," Emma prompted.

"What I told you about how I was chosen to learn this craft was all true. The previous craftsman – his name was Phineas – created a seeking door and encoded a key for it. As I said before, finding a new craftsman is a long process that is as much art as it is science. It takes months, sometimes years to properly vet a candidate. Most craftsmen go through multiple individuals with the Heritage before finding one worthy of becoming their apprentice."

"I understand," Matthew said, urging the carpenter to move on to the part of the story that involved Zander.

"Therefore, it should not surprise you that I was not Phineas' only potential candidate. He had three others before me. Zander was one of them."

"So, how did you defeat Zander to win the apprenticeship?" Emma asked.

"I'm not sure I understand the question," Silas replied sounding authentically confused. "A craftsman only pursues one candidate at a time. I did not meet Phineas until Zander had already been disqualified as a potential apprentice."

"I see," Matthew said thoughtfully.

"Zander had progressed very far in the vetting process. He had been told of the craft and notified that he was a potential candidate. He had even started some of the preliminary trials and visited a few realms."

"So, what happened?" Emma probed.

"Phineas told me he began to sense a lust for power and what he called a malevolence growing in Zander's heart. I think he saw some of the same things I began to notice in Morgan. Phineas told Zander that he would not continue to train him."

"Is it normal to get cut so late in the game?" Matthew asked.

"No, not normal," Silas admitted. "But not unheard of, so I'm told. You have to understand, the power we wield with this craft is immense. I am personally responsible for the lives and well-being of each and every person in all of the realms you have visited over these last few days. Those and countless more in realms you've never been to. Choosing the right apprentice is of critical importance."

"We get it," Emma said empathetically. She knew how they felt about the people they had met: those they had helped deal with Morgan's henchmen, and those they had abandoned to deal with things on their own. She could imagine that sense of responsibility growing exponentially for someone who had created the realm and visited it often.

"After Phineas refused to continue training Zander, the seeker portal led him to me. Eventually, he began to talk to me about the craft, to take me to visit realms and to learn how to craft doors myself."

"And what became of Zander?" Matthew inquired.

"Phineas' suspicions had been correct, but unfortunately he underestimated how devious Zander truly was. When he became suspicious that Phineas might end his training, Zander stole a key for the woodworks – that is what Phineas called his workshop. Phineas started to notice small changes in some of the worlds we visited, but he could not figure out why. One day as he was teaching me how to hear what key had last been used in a particular box he realized someone else had used that box to open a gateway."

"It was Zander?" Emma guessed.

"He was the only one who would possibly know how. We laid a trap for him and a few nights later he ensnared himself in it. Oh, he was so angry. I had never seen that kind of rage before. Phineas wanted to send Zander to Garda. He said it was the only way to protect the Heritage."

"So, he was one of the criminals Morgan freed from the cells?" Matthew surmised.

"No. Phineas told me that as the future craftsman it was my responsibility to decide Zander's fate. Perhaps I was too soft-hearted, but Garda seemed too harsh of a punishment to me. So, I exiled him to a realm instead. It was a realm he had started to create himself during his trials. I completed the door and sent him through the gateway making sure he did not have a key so there would be no way for him to leave."

"Until Morgan came along," Emma said.

"I don't know what Morgan told you, Matthew, but that is as much truth as I can possibly give you," Silas stated with a gentle smile that made it almost impossible to not believe him. "As for Morgan, I don't know what her connection to all this or to Zander is."

"I think I do," Matthew replied. "They say the best lies are the ones that are mostly true. In which case, I believe that Morgan was Zander's childhood sweetheart and girlfriend at the time Phineas found him. He was obviously jealous of you taking his place and, I suspect, was looking for a way to get rid of you."

"He also likely had a sense that you and Phineas had suspicions about him sneaking into the woodworks," Emma postulated.

"Exactly, which is why he left behind a note for Morgan to find, should he happen to mysteriously go missing. He told her just enough that she was able to eventually track you down and befriend your wife."

"Thus gaining access to the realms," Silas stated.

"It's possible at first, she was just looking for Zander," Matthew suggested.

"Or it could have been a vendetta against you from the beginning," Emma countered.

"Either way, once you started limiting her access to the realms she got desperate and took more drastic measures."

There was a long pause in the conversation as all three pondered the situation. Eventually, Silas spoke in his typical, amiable tone. "Did you find out what you were looking for, Matthew?"

"I think I did," Matthew smiled. "Actually, I really don't know. To be honest, you both tell really convincing stories. But in the end, you've earned our trust, she has not."

"I appreciate that. I can't imagine what it has been like for the two of you being thrown into all this. Being asked to help a crazy old man go on an absurd quest. No matter what happens, I owe all of you a great debt that I'll never be able to repay."

"Right then," Emma declared, feeling reassured, for the most part, that they were on the right side of things, "let's get to it. What's next?"

"When Morgan and Zander left Nyumbani they headed to Skalla. I did not dare follow right after them, but it should be safe by now," Silas suggested. "I will go there first, and then on to Duniya."

"We have two keys left as well," Matthew reported. "I scanned them earlier while we were waiting. They are gateways to Arispe and Sliabh."

"She's running out of places to hide!" Emma announced determinedly.

"Alright then," Matthew declared. "Let's get going."

* * *

"Whaaaat?" a woozy Joel questioned aloud. "Oh man, my coconut hurts." He attempted to clear the cobwebs and figure out what was going on. His head was throbbing, a lot. He had clearly been hit hard. Perhaps that's why his memory was still a little hazy. He looked around the dimly lit room that was still slightly spinning around him. He staggered toward what appeared to be an exit. When he reached the iron bars of his cell, it all came rushing back to him. He looked around outside but saw no sign of anyone. "Hello? Is anyone out there?" he called softly.

There was no response. He waited for a few moments and then called out again, slightly louder. There was no immediate reply, but he heard sounds of motion nearby. A few moments later a soft voice called back to him.

"Hello there. You're finally awake. That's good. I was starting to worry about you."

"Thanks. What's your name?"

"My name is Tara, and I suspect I'm the one who got you into this mess. Do you remember how you got here?"

"Yeah, I think so," Joel replied, still trying to put all the pieces back together. "We were in Demesne, at the exit gateway. I tried to stop Morgan from using the key, but I guess I was a little too slow," he recalled. "The next thing I knew I was body slamming the hard, rocky ground."

"Sounds like a rough landing."

"Yeah," Joel agreed, stretching out his sore muscles again. "I thought to myself, 'I should get up quick before Morgan gets away.' But then this giant meat hook of a hand grabbed me by the shoulder and hoisted me into the air. My feet were literally dangling off the ground."

"What happened then?"

"I couldn't see the guy holding me, but his massive shoulder had a tattoo of, like, a skull that had been shattered and then riveted back together, if that makes any sense."

"It does, unfortunately."

"Anyway, Morgan was there and she told me I had made a grave mistake. You know, the standard evil villainess spiel." Joel's memory finally came back to him fully and he slumped down on the ground next to the cell bars.

"What is it?" the voice in the next cell asked.

"She told me that I was now a permanent resident of Garda, but, just to show me what a nice person she really was, she would ..."

"She would what?"

Joel hopped up again and ran over to the other side of the cell and called out, "Jules! Jules are you over there?" There was no response.

"Are you looking for Juliette?" Tara asked compassionately.

"Yes," Joel exclaimed, crossing back to the other side of the cell. "The last thing Morgan told me was that to show me what a nice person she was she promised to put me in a cell next to Juliette. But I can't get any response from her over there. Do you know if she's okay?"

"She's fine," Tara answered. "I assume you're Joel? She simply will not stop talking about you."

"So, why doesn't she answer me?" Joel asked, still sounding distressed.

"Because she's not over there, dear," Tara explained. "She's in the cell on the other side of me. She likely cannot hear you at all from there."

"YOU EVIL HAG!" Joel hollered in anger, even though he knew his captor was no longer around to hear it.

"Hold on, just a minute," Tara said politely. A few moments later she returned and with a bit of a giggle said, "Okay, I was wrong. She heard that."

"That's just mean," Joel fumed.

"Did Morgan say anything else before she left?"

"Not really," Joel scanned his memory one more time.

"She just told me Derge would show me to my new accommodations and then I assume the big guy clocked me because the next thing I knew I was waking up here with a five-star headache."

"After he dumped you on the gateway pad and Morgan transferred you to your cell, I heard her instruct Derge to go back to the entry gateway and take care of anyone arriving other than her."

"Does she have other goons around here?" Joel asked.

"Yes, there is one more. Similar to the one you met – big and strong, low IQ. I believe his name is Cazgon. I haven't seen him in a long time though, not since Morgan first sent him and Derge to guard the entry portal. Like I said, he didn't seem that bright, so I'm sure she didn't want him anywhere near us lest we talk him into something." No, just the one as far as I have seen."

"Well, at least we don't have to worry about them doing something stupid while she's gone. It doesn't bode well for any future rescue party though, does it."

"I'm afraid not," Tara agreed. "How is Silas doing? Have you seen him recently?"

"Um, no," Joel answered awkwardly. "I haven't seen him in a while, but last time we were together he seemed to be doing okay."

Welcome Home

"I see, well, you'll have to catch us up on everything."

"Sure, looks like we've got nothing but time, right?"

"Yes. But first, I'm sure you're dying to talk with Juliette. Is there anything you would like me to pass on to her for you?"

"Other than the fact that I feel like I'm back passing notes in sixth grade English class?" Joel chuckled. "Just tell her that I love her. I'm glad she's okay. And that I'm fine."

"Okay."

"Oh and let her know that Matt and Emma are going to get us out of this ... somehow." After Tara had left, he added under his breath, "I hope."

* * *

"Alright, you two," Silas instructed. "Be careful. You've got two worlds left. You know where the boxes are located. Get in. Lock the box. Get out. Meet back here when you're done. After that Morgan and Zander will have nowhere to run."

"Nowhere to hide," Matthew added.

"Good luck you two."

"Good luck, Silas," Emma replied.

"See you soon," the carpenter said as he opened the box on the coffee table and inserted the key to Skalla. Moments later he was gone.

Skalla was a wonderfully bizarre land. When he had first crafted it, Silas had been pondering what it would be like to be an ant or some other bug and how our world must look to them. However, instead of imitating some cheesy CGI movie where humans are accidentally shrunken down to ant size and must navigate a world of giant mushrooms and lawn mowers, he decided to do something different. The landscape and wildlife of Skalla were very similar to that of the American Midwest, however, he designed every living thing, plant, and animal, to be double its regular size. Everything except the people of course. It was a wondrous realm to visit.

But today was not a day for casual sightseeing. He thought it was unlikely that Morgan and Zander would still be in Skalla, but if they were, Silas aimed to reach the exit portal before them. If they were gone, that left only one more world for him to investigate. If he had any luck at all Morgan and Zander would have fled to one of the realms that had already been locked down. Either way, time was of the essence, Silas thought as the gateway light faded away and his eyes adjusted to their new environment.

Silas looked around and groaned, "Uh-oh."

– 22 –
Two More to Go

Matthew and Emma were left standing alone in Joel's living room after the portal to Skalla had closed and the lid to the box had once again flipped shut.

"Is this going to work?" Emma asked.

"It has to, doesn't it?" Matthew answered, sounding not nearly as confident as he would have liked to. "Morgan and Zander have to be stopped."

"Maybe they'll stop now that they are together."

"If that was true they would have stopped when they first returned from Rend. Even if they did retire to some remote area of a distant realm, we'd still have no way to get our friends back."

"Okay, you're right. Let's go."

"Arispe, here we come!" Matthew cheered as he inserted a key into the brass plate and turned.

* * *

"This is not good," Silas murmured to himself. He had anticipated being greeted by a world of oversized things, and indeed he was, just not the things he was expecting. In his eagerness to lock the gateways on the remaining worlds, the carpenter had forgotten a crucial piece of information. He gazed around looking for any opportunity to get himself out of the trouble he now found himself in. He saw no escape. All he saw, surrounding him in every direction, were the remaining criminals Morgan had liberated from Garda. Clearly, this was the realm in which she had been keeping them until their services were needed elsewhere. Although several of them had been dispatched to other worlds, there still remained far more than he could possibly defend himself against or outrun. The thugs were circled around the entry portal, almost as if they had been waiting for his arrival.

"Stupidly predictable, old man," Morgan's voice crowed from somewhere behind the mass of muscle-bound thugs. "I knew it was only a matter of time before you would show up here."

"Sorry to keep you waiting," Silas sneered.

"Oh," she said with a devilish grin as she walked between two particularly beefy brutes and into the open. "It was worth the wait."

"Well done, princess," Zander cheered as he entered the circle behind Silas. "You've got yourself in quite the pickle now, haven't you? You're all alone with no one to do your dirty work for you. No one to risk their own lives to defend you."

"No leverage, no escape," Morgan said gleefully. "You have nothing. Nothing. Not even your young friends. But don't worry, they'll soon join you in Garda, I promise."

"Leave them out of it," Silas implored. "You've got what you wanted. You don't need to chase them down."

"I haven't even begun to get what I want," Zander declared. "You took everything from me! My life, my freedom, my future, my gift, and my woman. I'm going to take it all back from you – with interest. You robbed me of decades of my life, so I'm going to take every miserable minute that's left of yours. I've had plenty of time to think of ways to make you suffer and believe me, I'm going to try out every last one of them."

"Take him," Morgan commanded.

Two of the henchmen closest to Silas grabbed him firmly. One of the thugs held him unnecessarily tight while the other searched him, taking all his possessions, including his satchel. A third goon came over and tied Silas' hands behind his back and tied a second rope around the carpenter's neck to use as a leash.

"Bring it to me," Morgan instructed the thug who had taken Silas' supplies. She looked at the items the brute handed her and then rummaged through the satchel. "Jackpot" she cheered as she pulled out his keys. She tossed the keys over to her partner.

"Is this all of them?" Zander asked. He held each of the keys separately, concentrating carefully on each one. "It's not here," he fumed. "These are all just duplicates of keys you already took from Tara."

"Of course they are," Silas snickered. "You're not dumb enough to think I'd carry around keys that could possibly give you access to any more worlds than you already have…or maybe you are."

"The woodworks key is not one of them." Zander sneered, refusing to respond to the verbal jab.

"Try again," Morgan suggested. "Don't forget, you're looking for the workshop, not the woodworks. Maybe you…"

"I know what I'm doing!" Zander exploded. "It doesn't matter what you call it, it's not here."

"He may not have it," Morgan surmised, staring intently at her prisoner. "But he knows where it is."

"And you think he's just going to tell us?" Zander scoffed.

"Of course not. Not yet anyway," Morgan said thoughtfully. "He's still holding out hope that those kids, will somehow save the day. Perhaps he thinks that if they lock down the remaining worlds we will be trapped." Morgan studied Silas' face and took great delight in seeing his face when he realized his plans doomed to fail.

"Should we take him to Garda?"

"Not yet," Morgan replied, studying Silas' face. "We need to figure out where Matthew and Emma are first."

"How do you suggest we do that?"

"What keys did he have on him?"

"Let's see," Zander held each of the keys again. "Garda, Cumulus, Rend, Nyumbani, Duniya, and here."

"Okay, so it's safe to assume they are in none of those," Morgan deduced, continuing to focus her attention on the carpenter. "I know for a fact the others have been to Arborlada and Demesne. I'm pretty sure they've been to Bhal as well. Which leaves three possibilities."

"But if we guess wrong..."

"Shh," Morgan commanded, intensely studying his facial features. "Where are they, Silas? Serenity, Arispe, or Sliabh? Arispe? Arispe it is."

"Are you sure?" Zander asked.

"I have two PhDs in psychology. I've spent my whole life studying people. I'm sure," Morgan said confidently.

"Alright. They likely left about the same time as he did, so if we hurry we can catch them."

"Exactly. As long as they are there, the portal won't be locked. But if they beat us to the box we're done."

"Then, let's get going. You two are with us," Zander commanded pointing to a pair of lean, but muscular thugs. "The rest of you keep your eyes on him. If he's not here when we return it will be your head on the chopping block and I will personally do the chopping," he threatened.

Morgan, Zander and the two goons stepped outside the circle and moments later Silas saw the bright light of the gateway opening over the backs of the henchmen in front of him.

"Okay fellas, what now?"

* * *

"You okay, Em?"

"Fine, you?"

"Just dandy, now what?"

Arispe was one of Silas' most interesting worlds and one that, on any other day, Matthew would have loved to explore at length. The lush green grass crushed softly under their feet as they walked across a vast field filled with wildflowers, copses of trees and shrubs, small boulders and gravel paths. Off in the distance they could see large ponds and lakes. The field was lined by a heavy stone wall that rose high into the air and, as far as they could tell, surrounded the entire realm, although the full extent of the wall was well beyond their range of sight.

"Check this place out!" Matthew said in wonder.

"It reminds me a lot of Serenity in many ways, but there's something different about it."

Matthew was about to reply when suddenly the ground shook, and a large segment of the earth began to move gently forward. He estimated the moving section to be about as long as half a football field and equally wide. "What's happening, Em?"

"How should I know?" his girlfriend answered, grabbing his forearm for added stability.

After several minutes the ground slowed to a smooth stop. The pair continued to walk along, drinking in their surroundings. Every now and then the ground would move and shift, but after a while they became quite accustomed to it and hardly noticed it happening. An hour into their journey, Matthew, who had been analyzing the tectonic movement since their arrival, came to a conclusion. He had to admit the mechanics of this realm made it particularly fascinating to him.

"I think I've figured it out," the engineer declared.

"Figured what out?"

"This place. It seems like the surface is made up of an enormous network of square plates. Every now and then, however, there is an empty spot. By my rough calculations, I'd guess about one out of every nine blocks is a void."

"A void to what?" Emma pondered aloud.

"Good question. I'm not sure about that, but it seems like random plates move into these voids leaving a new void behind."

"To be filled by another plate."

"Exactly," Matthew concurred. "I don't know if there is a pattern to the movement, but if there is I sure haven't figured it out yet.

Matthew hypothesized that Silas created Arispe with these gaps to provide room for the tectonic plates to move. As such, the terrain was forever changing, making it entirely possible for someone to step onto a plate at one position and, by the time they crossed it, step off somewhere completely different. This made it theoretically possible for one to move across the entirety of the realm simply by staying on one single plate. It would be an incredibly winding and very long journey, but it should be theoretically possible, the engineer postulated.

"This is amazing," Matthew marveled as he observed the movement of the plates.

"Look! There's a bunny," Emma smiled. "I imagine the wildlife here would need to be quick."

"And good jumpers," her boyfriend added. "It makes sense that the local inhabitants, if there are any, would be agile and fast, too."

"Right. The exit gateway is on the far side, so we'd better do some fast moving ourselves," Emma suggested.

The pair had not traveled far before the ground a foot in front of them started sliding to the left. This was the closest they had come to a void thus far in their journey. They stared down deep into what appeared to be dark and endless nothingness. As the plate shifted further it left behind a widening void.

"You don't want to step in there," Matthew stated as he peered down into the dark nothingness.

"If I wasn't in a hurry," Emma grinned. "I'd try it at least once."

"You're nuts!"

"What?" she asked, enjoying the opportunity to rile up her boyfriend a little. "I'm sure Silas wouldn't have designed it to be lethal. You likely just fall for several minutes and then land in a portal that dumps you back out at some other random location in the realm. Kind of sounds like fun."

"Yeah and with my luck it would dump me out into another void," Matthew said cynically. "Come on, let's get going." The gap in front of them had already been filled in by another plate so the pair continued on ahead.

"The important thing is we keep our bearings," Emma stated.

"Right. The exit portal is near the wall on the far side. As long as we keep going in this general direction, we should get to the wall eventually and then we just have to walk along it to find the box."

"Do you think we should have a plan in case we get separated?"

"Definitely. I think our plan should be to not get separated."

"That sounds lovely," Emma grinned, clasping her boyfriend's hand, "but if we do get separated how *do* we find each other again?"

"I guess it depends. If we just get caught on two different plates, that should be easy enough to fix."

"Sure, but what if we actually lose track of each other?"

"Well," Matthew thought carefully, "looking for each other at that point is like an exercise in futility. We could both wander around this place forever and never see the slightest sign of each other."

"For sure. So, then what?"

"I guess we both keep heading toward the wall. We find the box and we wait for the other to show up."

"That seems to make sense," Emma agreed.

"Just don't leave without me," Matthew joked.

"Ha, ha," his girlfriend. "Maybe *I* should hold the keys."

* * *

The pair of travelers had been walking for a couple of hours and were making steady progress, but the realm was expansive. Initially, they had tried jogging in hopes that they could cross each individual plate before it shifted on them. They eventually realized they would not be able to keep that pace up for the entire trek and had slowed to a steady walk. Every now and then they would get caught on a plate that took them backward or would have to wait for a void to be filled, allowing them to continue.

"Agha! I'm sick of this pond!" Emma exclaimed.

"Me too."

The source of their frustration was two plates side by side which were entirely covered by water. They had made several attempts to get around the pond, but each time they were about to round the corner the plates shifted and they found themselves right back at the center of the shoreline. Finally, they decided to just stand and wait where they were. After nearly twenty minutes of waiting neither of the water plates had moved.

"You've got to be kidding!" Matthew moaned.

"They've got to move soon," Emma said, trying to sound optimistic. "It could be worse."

The words had no sooner left her lips when the plate they were standing on started to move backward, away from the water, taking them further away from their goal on the far side of the field.

"I blame you for this," Matthew said in mock accusation.

"This could be our chance," Emma said, ignoring his jab. "Head to that side. We're getting around this pond, one way or another."

The couple hopped on to the adjoining plate to their left. Emma's hunch paid off as one of the water plates slid into the void left by the plate they had just stepped off. The second water plate slid to the side to replace the first and a new water-free plate moved right in front of them. Once the water plates had been successfully circumnavigated, they continued on their trek toward the exit gateway.

"What do you make of this Zander guy?" Emma asked.

"I'm not sure," Matthew replied, "from what Silas says, he's the brute who kidnapped Jules from the apartment. He certainly didn't seem to hesitate to pull out that knife, so I'd say he's definitely not someone we want to mess with."

"Agreed. I imagine a couple decades of exile in a foreign realm would make you a little hardened, for sure."

"True. Then again, it's not like Silas exiled him to Siberia. It was a realm Zander had created himself. If it wasn't a very great place to be he's only got himself to blame."

"In more ways than one. And if what Silas said is true," Emma pondered aloud, "and Zander already knows, at least to some degree, how to create and alter realms, it's more vital than ever that those two snakes never gain access to the workshop."

"You're right," her boyfriend agreed. "It was bad enough when it was just Morgan trying to gain a free pass to visit the realms whenever she wanted to, but now this Zander guy could wreak total havoc in all of Silas' worlds and cause a lot of pain to the people who inhabit them"

"We *can't* let that happen."

"Let's just hope we don't run into either one of them until we've locked down these last two realms,"

Matthew suggested. "Then we can deal with them together, on our own terms."

"And get our friends back," Emma added. "Oh look, another rabbit."

"Man, he's moving fast. Almost like he's running from ... Emma run!"

Matthew pulled at Emma's arm and the couple started to sprint to their left, just as Morgan slipped out from a tree behind them. They didn't get very far before they skidded to a stop at the sight of Zander looming in front of them. Matthew and Emma cautiously backed away as their attackers crept in on them from both sides. They reached the edge of their current plate and found nothing but a fresh void behind them.

"End of the line, kids," Zander taunted. He pulled out his knife and moved toward them. Morgan began inching her way in from the other side. Matthew and Emma were hopelessly trapped with their adversaries closing in from either side and the void directly behind them.

− 23 −
All on Your Own

"Oh, my dear Matthew," Morgan mocked. "I really thought things would be different between us after our little heart to heart by the river."

"How about we have a little fist to face right now," Emma retorted.

"You're right," Zander grinned. "She *is* a feisty one."

"Come on now, you two," Morgan jeered, "this is the part where you bluster on about how we'll never get away with it all and you'll get us for this. It's no fun if you two don't play along."

Those words, almost verbatim, had run through Matthew's head only moments earlier, but he wasn't about to give Morgan the satisfaction of saying them out loud now. "Sorry," he said flatly. "You'll have to live out your B-movie fantasies somewhere else."

"Very well, then," Morgan conceded. "Let's just get this over with. Allow me to give a quick recap of things. I have all of Tara's keys. She is locked away in Garda, as are your friends Juliette and Joel. I have the only key that will release them. You are trying to lock all the realms in hopes of trapping us somewhere, but now that we know of your feeble scheme we will be sure to avoid that little hiccup.

And now we have both of you here. You're all on your own. Cornered – with nowhere to go."

All four people steadied themselves momentarily as the plate they were standing on began to slide forward into the void behind Matthew and Emma.

"I think that pretty much sums it up," Morgan announced cheerfully. "Have I forgotten anything?"

"Just one tiny detail, my sweet."

"Hmm, what could that possibly be?" she asked, feigning ignorance.

"Just before we came here to Arispe, we captured that rat, Silas, on Skalla." Zander snickered. "We got him. We got his keys. We've got it all. And what is it you've got left? Oh yeah, that's right – not a stinking thing."

Matthew glanced behind him. The void was closing, but they were still a long way from the next plate. Much too far to jump. "Hmm, that's interesting."

"What?" Morgan demanded. "What are you talking about?"

"So, you say you captured Silas and you have all his keys."

"Yes. We did, and we do," Zander confirmed.

"Well if that were true, you would have the workshop key already and there would be no point in coming after us."

"The scoundrel didn't have the workshop key on him. We searched him thoroughly. It wasn't there."

"And what? You think he gave it to us?" Emma asked disbelievingly. "Do you really think Silas would trust anyone other than himself with that key? Not a chance."

"Even if you don't have it, perhaps he'll be willing to give it up in exchange for the lives of the four of you and his wife."

"I see. So that's your plan," Matthew said incredulously, glancing behind him once more. "You think that even though he wouldn't give you the key in exchange for his beloved wife, now that you also have four strangers who he's just met and barely knows, he's going to cave? Good thinking geniuses."

"Silas may not have had the workshop key on him, but I guarantee he knows where it is. One way or another, we'll get it wherever it is. And, don't think I don't know what you're doing, kid," Zander sneered. "I see you looking back there. You're just stalling for time until the next plate is close enough you can jump over and make a run for it."

"Wow, Silas was wrong about you," Emma smirked. "You're not dumber than a bag of hammers." She didn't know exactly what her boyfriend had up his sleeve. He clearly had something in mind which involved provoking their soon to be captors, so she thought it best to try and play along. Hopefully he knew what he was doing.

The void was narrowing quickly as the plates slid together. Matthew looked at his girlfriend and with a hint of regret in his voice said, "I really wish I hadn't given you that key."

With a sudden forceful motion Matthew pushed Emma backward causing her to fall into the narrowing void. When Emma entered, the gap was only a couple feet wide. Moments later Matthew leapt across the remaining void and sprinted off toward a section of the next plate with a lot of trees and other visual obstructions. By the time Morgan and Zander reached the edge of the plate, the gap was down to mere inches.

"What do we do now?" Morgan asked.

"We go after them," Zander declared. "There must be a portal at the bottom of the void that returns anyone who falls into it to some other location in the realm. Maybe back to the entry gateway? I don't know. Silas is too much of a softy to make it a death trap."

"Then we should split up," Morgan suggested. "You go after Matthew. I'll try and track down Emma."

"Fine, but don't wander too far off course. We know where they're headed. Eventually, they will both make their way to the box."

"And they are far too tender-hearted to go through the portal and leave the other one behind."

"You better be right, otherwise we'll be stranded here once that box gets locked."

"Trust me," Morgan smiled deviously, "I've got these kids all figured out."

"I hope so," Zander snarled. "Head to the exit gateway and keep your eyes peeled."

The two scoundrels headed off across the realm at a steady pace. They split off from one another slightly, but for the most part, maintained a steady course toward the wall on the far side. Neither of them had ever been to this realm before, so their best hope was to continue on the trajectory they had observed Matthew and Emma traveling. They trekked on with unwavering determination. Both were keenly aware of the fact that one, or possibly both of the people they were hunting, had the ability to lock the exit portal if they reached it first. There was no way either Morgan or Zander were going to let that happen. They had come too far to let a couple of irritating kids ruin it all. They would find the gateway first, even it if meant continuing straight on through the night.

* * *

Matthew sprinted as long and hard as he could but eventually had to slow his pace. As far as he could tell, no one was on his tail which hopefully meant he could afford a short breather. *'Emma's going to be so ticked,'* he thought to himself. He knew her irritation would be less with the fact that he pushed her into the void and more because he had sacrificed himself to get her to safety.

"Better keep moving," he told himself.

He had done his best to keep track of his bearings during his escape, so he was certain of which way he needed to go to reach the wall on the far side of the realm. He wondered where Emma would end up after escaping the void and if it would be possible for her to figure out which direction *she* needed to go.

He kept walking for what he guessed to be a couple hours. He could see evening setting in and decided he should try and find a sheltered place to hunker down for the night. A little while later he came on to a plate that had a grouping of hedge-like bushes clustered together that reminded him of lilacs – if lilacs had orange flowers. He managed to crawl into the middle of the grove and found an open space just large enough to curl up in.

Matthew left his backpack behind and crawled out of the grove again. He waited for a plate with water to pass by and ran over to fill his canteen which had long since been empty. He also filled his pockets with small stones from the water's edge. He made sure not to lose track of the plate with the grove and stay alert for any sign of Morgan or Zander.

He returned to the grove and after a few long sips of water, settled in for the night. Matthew took the stones out of his pockets and used them to create a small arrow on the ground indicating the direction of the far wall. Assuming the plates continued to move all night, who knew where he would be by morning. The last thing he wanted was to get up and head out in the wrong direction the next day.

As darkness settled in and Matthew lay on the soft ground failing to sleep, he pondered a heart-wrenching question. He did not have the opportunity to explain his logic to Emma before he tossed her into the void. He assumed that she would attempt to find the exit gateway. He was now left to decide, however, what to do if he reached the box and she wasn't there. Should he wait? How long should he wait? Or should he use the nullification key and leave before Morgan and Zander had a chance to escape. Of course, he wouldn't necessarily know if the foul pair were still in the realm and he wasn't sure which would be better: to lock the portal and trap Emma in this world with them, or for them to have already escaped to another world. Those were questions he would have to answer tomorrow, as he was too exhausted to ponder them further tonight.

* * *

Emma was startled and disoriented as she tumbled into the void. She could see the light of the open air above her narrowing as she descended into the darkness. She felt a solid bang on one side as her body ricocheted off one of the plates. The force of the collision knocked her tumbling across the gap where she crashed into the other plate. She bounced back and forth at shorter and shorter intervals as the two plates moved closer to one another. The gap closed tighter upon her to where she could feel each of the plates on either side of her simultaneously. She twisted her body sideways creating a little extra room, allowing her to fall deeper into the void, but soon all her breathing room was gone and the plates pressed in upon her from both sides.

Emma tensed up, preparing herself to be crushed by the colliding plates. What a way to go, she thought to herself. Suddenly she realized that the feeling of being completely pressed in and surrounded had been replaced by a feeling of floating weightlessly. Although she was still in complete darkness and unable to move in any given direction, she sensed that she was in a wide-open space. If she were able to somehow propel herself it felt like she could go on forever.

Just as Emma was becoming accustomed to this new and very strange sensation, it was replaced by the very distinct feeling of falling. The light returned and she found herself back above the plates of the world but descending quickly. She glanced down and braced herself for her impending impact with the ground. "Oh, crud."

Emma splashed down into the water. The momentum of her fall pushed her deep below the surface. By the time she managed to swim back up to the top, her lungs were out of air. She gasped as she treaded water for a moment and the tried to assess the shortest distance to shore. The void portal had dropped her in the very center of a plate comprised entirely of water, which as she considered it later was likely a fortunate thing. Emma swam for shore and pulled herself up on to the soft grass of an adjoining plate.

Thankful to be back on solid ground, the young woman rested for few moments and plotted out her next move. She wasn't certain what Matthew's plan had been exactly, but the good news was, Morgan and Zander had no idea where she was now. The bad news was neither did she. Emma replayed in her mind the moments before she fell into the void.

"Why did he say that?" she asked aloud as she sat up. "I really wish I hadn't given you that key," she repeated Matthew's words several times. Perhaps it was all part of the distraction. Maybe he was hoping that if Morgan and Zander thought Emma had the keys it would buy him some time to escape as well. But, then again, he didn't say 'those keys', he said 'that key'. Was he trying to make them believe that Emma had the workshop key? That seemed unlikely. The only reason to do that would be to save his own neck and Matthew wasn't the kind of guy who would do that.

Emma knew there must be a reason for his words. She just had to figure out what it was. Matthew was an engineer and didn't do anything without thinking it through six times. He didn't do random. She replayed the moment again in her mind scrutinizing every detail. He said *I wish I hadn't given you that key*, then he put his hands on her shoulders and pushed her into the void. No, wait, she thought. That's not what he did. He put one hand on her shoulder and the other somewhere lower, more like on her waist. Emma wracked her brain trying to recall the minutia of that moment.

"That's it!" she cried out, and then looked around nervously hoping no one had heard her. When Matthew had pushed her into the void, he placed his one hand down by her waist, but his fingers had fleetingly dipped into her pocket. Emma quickly reached into the front pocket of her jeans, which was no easy feat considering the denim was still soaking wet. Her fingers fumbled around inside momentarily until they found what they were looking for. She retracted her hand, uncurled her fingers and gazed at the key lying in her palm. It was clearly one of the keys Silas had given him, she just had no idea which one. He must have covertly slipped it off the key ring while they were bantering with Morgan and Zander.

She would ponder the purpose of the key later, but for now, she needed to get moving. She would have loved to rest a little longer and more than anything give her clothes a chance to dry out before she started hiking around, but she knew there was no time for that. She rose to her feet and returned the key to her jeans pocket. "Alright," she said, gazing around her. "Where to now?"

Emma knew that the realm was extremely large and therefore just heading out in some random direction was likely not the most productive strategy. She surveyed the terrain and spotted a tree, taller than most, not terribly far from where she was. She set out toward the tree, which took longer than she expected due to the constant shifting of the plates. When she finally reached the tree, which resembled something like a maple, she grabbed a low branch and began climbing upward. Having grown up a bit of tom-girl, ascending the tree came with great ease and soon she was near the top gazing over the rest of the realm.

Emma watched in delight as the plates shifted and moved all around her. It was quite a spectacle to behold from her aerial viewpoint. She also scanned the area as best she could for others walking around. Thankfully she saw no sign of Morgan or Zander. Sadly, she saw no sign of Matthew either. Emma held on tight as the plate the tree was on began to slide forward into a nearby void. As it did, she could see what she thought might be a perimeter wall, right on the very edge of the horizon. She made her way back down the tree, taking special care to stay oriented in the direction of the wall. Once she was back on the ground she started off with a renewed sense of optimism. Deep down she realized that even if she got to the wall it might not be the one she needed to be at, but at least it would be a start.

Emma hiked along for a far as she could. Her still soggy jeans were chaffing something fierce and the sky was growing dim, so she decided to look for a safe place to spend the night. She found a large rock she could lean against and sat down next to it. She considered attempting to start a fire to dry her clothes by but did not want to attract any unwanted attention. Besides, she wasn't entirely sure she could start a fire without matches like they did in the movies.

As she leaned against her rock, weary from the day's events, Emma grasped the key in her pocket. What had Matthew been thinking when he gave it to here. Did he give her a specific key for a reason or simply randomly grab one off his keychain? In the end, she decided that wherever the key led to, Matthew had given it to her so that if she reached the box first, she could escape to safety. She would quite likely be stuck in that new realm, but that would be better than being stuck here with Morgan and Zander. She knew if that happened, Matthew would come back to get her, from wherever she was when this was all over. However, using the key meant leaving her boyfriend here to deal with the renegades on his own, and she had never been one to run away from a fight.

Emma's eyes grew heavy as the sky grew dark. She would have to decide what to do with the key tomorrow, but first, she had to make it to the wall and then, if she was lucky, find the box. There was nothing more she could do until then.

– 24 –
Lows & Highs

Emma was up at first light and eager to get on her way. Her clothes were dry, she had scrounged a power bar out of her backpack for breakfast, and most importantly the wall was in sight. The decision to stop and rest for the night on this particular plate had serendipitously brought her much closer to her destination while she slept.

She set out at a good pace but was consciously aware that the closer she came to the gateway, the greater the chance of being spotted by Morgan or Zander. She moved as stealthily as she could from a bluff of trees around a boulder then behind a tall shrub. As much as possible she avoided wide open areas unless doing so would cost her a significant amount of time.

Her mind raced as she recounted all that had happened and all that she had seen. Such kind and friendly people. Such wonderful and beautiful worlds. She felt her heart growing heavier as she thought of more recent events. The loss of Joel and Juliette was devastating, and if what Morgan said was true, Silas was being held captive as well. Despair crept in and she began to question whether there was any hope of their mission succeeding now – perhaps there never really was.

"Oh! Hello there," she said gently, greeting a fawn of a deer-like species that had wandered out from behind a nearby bush. "And what's your name, little fellow?"

The deer looked at her. She didn't expect it to reply to her, although, she reminded herself, in one of Silas' worlds anything was possible. "I think I will name you Jelly," she stated playfully. The fawn's dark red coat with small white spots reminded her of a jar of raspberry jam. The deer's ear twitched a couple times and then it ran off, leaping over small rocks and bushes as it went.

"Quite right, Jelly," Emma said quietly. As delightful as the momentary distraction had been she knew she must stay on full alert for any sign of her enemies, or of Matthew. She resumed her trek towards the edge of the realm determinedly, but cautiously.

Emma reached the wall by midmorning. She hoped that the wall she was standing next to was the far wall she and Matthew had originally set out for. In truth, she had no idea, and no way to tell. It could have been any of the four perimeter walls. Even if she was at the right wall, it extended further than the eye could see in both directions. She had no clue if the box was to her left or to her right. Regardless of which direction she went, following the perimeter would bring her to the exit gateway eventually, one direction could take a lot longer than the other though.

After several moments of deliberation, she chose to head to the left, for no other reason than it felt like the right way to go. There was a narrow path along the wall that was not affected by the shifting of the plates. Walking this path could make her journey significantly faster. On the other hand, she would be completely exposed, and Morgan or Zander would be able to see her coming from a long way off. Emma chose to compromise by traveling on the plates but remaining close enough to the edge that if the ground started to shift away from the wall she could jump back over to the path.

She continued to cover ground quickly. The anticipation of nearing the box sped her along. Just after noon she slowed her pace and became more cautious. She could see a small shed she was fairly certain housed the portal box. She held her position for some time, observing the area. Not only was this the only structure she had seen in the world, but it also appeared that the plate the structure was built on never moved.

"That has to be it," she whispered to herself. She painstakingly inched her way toward the gateway, scurrying from one place of cover to the next. She did all she could to avoid being spotted by anyone who might be surveilling the area. Finally, she had no choice. There were no more rocks or bushes to hide behind between her and the tiny shed.

Emma made a run for it, key in hand. As soon as she stepped out into the open she heard the sound of someone else moving in the clearing up ahead. "Matthew?" she said tentatively, "is that you?"

"Sorry dear, no," Morgan replied.

Emma shoved the key back in her pocket and peered across the clearing. Morgan stepped out from behind the far side of the gateway shed. "What do you want?" Emma scowled.

"I want your help."

"Fat chance, lady."

"I understand your skepticism," Morgan admitted. "I haven't given you any reason to trust a word I say."

"Look at that," Emma quipped, "we agree on something after all."

"I've made a horrible mistake," Morgan continued to plead her case.

"Just one?"

"No, many of them. You have to believe me! What I told Matthew at the stream was the truth. Well, it was the truth as far as I knew it."

"That's a convenient rationalization," Emma retorted. "And don't take another step."

"Okay, I won't move," Morgan promised. "All these years I thought I was searching for the love of my life. For the noble man who was unfairly exiled by a jealous and vindictive man. The only thing is," Morgan paused as her eyes teared up slightly. "When I finally found him, I realized he wasn't the victim. He was the miscreant."

"My heart breaks for you," Emma replied callously.

"I understand your hostility. I deserve every ounce of it," Morgan conceded. "By the time I realized what kind of man Zander really was I was in over my head with no way out. I knew if I didn't continue to play along, to play my part, he would do unspeakable things to me." Morgan paused again, collecting her thoughts and emotions. "I know you probably think I deserve to reap the consequences of all my many transgressions, but I didn't know what else to do. You don't know what Zander is like. He terrifies me. So, when we split up to search for you and Matthew, I knew this might be my only chance to get away from him and to make things right."

Emma studied Morgan carefully. She was almost certain this was just another one of her ploys, almost. In the pit of her stomach she felt a tiny seed of doubt which was just enough to make her pause momentarily.

"If you have a key," Morgan begged, "please, let me go with you. I don't care where it takes me. If I end up in a realm you and your friends have already locked and I am stuck there for the rest of my days, that's fine. Even if, after this whole thing is over, Silas tracks me down and throws me in a cell in Garda ... anything is better than this! Better than being stuck under his thumb for the rest of my life."

Emma knew the longer she stood out in the open, the greater the chance that something would go horribly wrong. She studied her adversary intently once more. "Well, when you put it that way," she said sympathetically, eyeing Morgan up one last time. "There's not a chance in this or any other world that I'd believe you," she snapped.

"But Emma," Morgan pleaded.

"Save your breath. I'm not buying it."

Morgan's expression soured, visibly annoyed at her counterpart's defiance. "In that case, I'll just have to get rid of you."

"NO!" Matthew shouted as he burst out of a large bush nearby. He charged full speed at Morgan, tackling her from behind. The pair rolled back and forth on the ground each struggling to move into a dominant position.

"Don't move," Matthew commanded, finally pinning the woman to the ground. "Emma, go on. Get out of here, now."

"But what about you? I'm not leaving you here."

"This is more important. Use the key I gave you. I'll be fine. I promise."

Emma moved tentatively towards the shed. Removing the key from her pocket she opened the door, most of her attention still on her boyfriend who continued to fight against Morgan's attempts to slip free.

"It's okay, Em," he reassured, "I'll be ... Look out!"

Before she could even fully turn around, a powerful hand grabbed her by the throat. Zander stepped out of the gateway shed and spun Emma around. After clutching her hair tightly in his meaty paw, almost hoisting her off the ground, he released his grip on her throat. "Let. Her. Go." he demanded.

"Oh, my dear boy," Morgan grinned gleefully, dusting herself off as she stood, "You are nothing if not predictable."

Zander laughed heartily, "I've gotta hand it to you. You sure got these punks pegged. They did exactly what you said they would. Both of them."

Morgan strutted towards the shed with a delightfully satisfied look on her face. She picked up the key Emma had dropped when Zander grabbed her and began searching the girl's pockets and backpack for anything else of value. She handed the key to Zander. He held it tight and concentrated for a moment.

"Serenity," he barked.

"Ah, isn't that precious," Morgan scoffed. "Saintly Matthew was going to ship his sweetheart off to the safety of utopia and take on the big bad villains all by himself." She leaned in close to Emma's face and with a look of disgust spat, "Pitiful."

"Now what?" Zander asked.

"Now we get out of here."

"No! Wait, please," Matthew called out, still ten yards from the gateway shed.

"Don't move," Zander commanded, pulling out the knife he had used earlier to abduct Juliette and holding it close to Emma.

"Just take it easy," Matthew urged calmly. "What do you want?"

"The same thing we've always wanted, you daft boy," Morgan sneered, "the workshop key."

"I don't have it. I don't have any clue where it is. Silas hid it somewhere. That's all I know, I swear."

"I don't know," Morgan said thoughtfully. "I think I believe him. If he had the key he'd give it to us, in exchange for her, in a heartbeat."

"Then what good is he?"

"Not much," Morgan snickered. "Should we take him with us?"

"Why bother? Leave him here. He'll be dealt with eventually."

"Fine," Morgan said. She inserted a key into the box with one hand and rested her other hand on Zander's beefy forearm. She leaned back out the tiny shed just far enough to see the distraught look on Matthew's face again. "Matthew, tell me this and be honest, do you have a key to Skalla?"

"No," he answered in a deflated voice.

"I actually knew that. I just wanted to make sure you did, too," she chortled and turned the key.

"Nooooo!"

Matthew sprinted toward the gateway, knowing before he even started that he was already too late. By the time he reached the shed the light had dissipated and the box lid had flipped closed again. He knew there was likely very little point in it, but he pulled out the device and scanned the brass plate in the box. Zander and Morgan had indeed taken his girlfriend to Skalla, which meant very soon both Emma and Silas would be joining the rest of their friends in Garda. Garda – another place Matthew had no way of getting to.

The young man collapsed back down to the ground next to the shed and laid there staring blankly at the sky for the longest time. He was completely stunned. For the first hour, he couldn't even think. He spent the next hour trying to figure out his next move and how he might possibly get Emma back. He came up with nothing, not even a longshot-off-the-wall-completely-impractical-hair-brained-doomed-to-fail idea. The only thing he could do was travel to the final realm he had a key for and lock the portal box, however, even that seemed pointless now.

Matthew heard a rustling in the bushes near the wall. He assumed it was a rabbit or some other animal as he had not encountered any other inhabitants in this realm. That notion quickly became less plausible as the bushes on the other side of the clearing began moving as well. Moments later two imposing figures emerged almost simultaneously. Matthew didn't recognize them, but he had no doubt that these two brutes must have entered the realm with Zander and Morgan. He suspected they had been sent around the perimeter wall in opposite directions starting from the arrival gateway, but that didn't really matter. They were both in front of him now.

There was nowhere to run and no chance he could fight one of them off, let alone both of them at the same time. Matthew's pulse raced as the two thugs stomped towards him. He scurried to his feet and slid inside the shed. Throwing open the lid of the box he scrambled to find the nullification key and quickly turned it in the lock. He could hear the men approaching. They would soon be upon him. Matthew grasped the handle on the shed door with one hand and held it with all his might.

The henchmen arrived and began pounding on the walls of the shed, shaking it from side to side and trying to pry open the door. It was only a matter of time before they punched their way through or knocked the whole thing over. Matthew fumbled with the keychain in his free hand, eventually managing to grasp the seventh key on the ring. He slipped the key into the box and turned it, opening the gateway to Sliabh just as the shed door was ripped off its hinges and out of his hand.

* * *

Matthew fell to the cold, hard ground upon his arrival. He panted heavily as he tried to slow his heart rate and catch his breath – a task made more difficult by the thin air of a higher altitude. After several minutes of laying on the ground huffing and puffing as he recovered from his nearly failed escape attempt, the young man sat up and took stock of his surroundings. He removed the wool sweater he had placed in his backpack based on Silas' recommendation and slipped it on over his head. Sliabh was a mountainous realm. Although the temperatures were nowhere near as low as they would be at equally high altitudes on earth, he was still plenty cool, even with the sweater.

In light of the mountainous terrain, Silas had purposefully stationed the exit gateway close to the arrival point. As Matthew got to his feet and made his way toward where he believed he would find the box, he considered the futility of his actions. Morgan and Zander seemed to be holding all the cards. There was virtually no way they would risk traveling to Sliabh, unless one of their prisoners was somehow able to convince them this was where the workshop key was hidden.

Of course, they would know if Matthew had the key to Sliabh, the odds of Silas hiding the workshop key here were extremely low. It was also unlikely that either Morgan or Zander would come here themselves in search of the key. As shrewd as they had been, it seemed more likely they would send someone more expendable.

"Well, hello there, lad," a chipper voice greeted.

Matthew, who had spent most of his time staring dejectedly at the ground, looked up and saw a heavyset man with a bushy beard and wide smile standing in front of him. "Hey."

"You seem to be a mite downtrodden, young man. If you don't mind me saying."

"Yeah, I guess," he replied. Matthew wasn't really in the mood for chit-chat. He just wanted to lock the exit portal and move on, although he had no idea to what.

"Perhaps it's because you're traveling alone. I always find traveling with someone to be a much more pleasing experience, don't you?"

"I really can't say," Matthew murmured. "Actually, that's not true. Traveling with friends *is* infinitely better until they get taken away from you." With that, he sank down to the ground again and sat next to the mountain trail.

"Ah, I see," the man said sympathetically as he flopped down next to Matthew. "You've recently lost someone, have you?"

"More than one."

"Goodness, gracious, that must be weighing on you something fierce," the man observed. "Is there anything I can do to help?"

"Not unless you can alter time, speed up the harvest or teleport me off this rock," he said dejectedly.

"I'm not sure I understand ... any of that."

Emma would have got the joke – a line from one of their favorite movies. She might not have laughed out loud, but she would have got it, possibly smiled, and more than likely groaned.

"Thanks for the offer," Matthew replied politely, "but I'm not sure there's anything anyone can do to help at this point."

"Well," the man answered, resolutely determined to remain optimistic. "I may not be able to help you with everything, but surely I can help you with something?"

"I guess so," Matthew said, forcing himself back up to his feet. "I'm headed to the exit gateway, where Silas' box is kept. Perhaps you could show me the quickest route there."

"Indeed I can," the man cheered, jumping to his feet. "My name is Downey, and I know these mountains like the back of my hand."

"Great," Matthew said unenthusiastically, "lead the way."

"And off we go!" Downey started down a winding trail noticeably narrower than the main path. "Why is it that you are looking for the exit portal? Didn't you just arrive? I was sure I saw the gateway's light."

"Yes, I did," Matthew affirmed. "I'm just here to test the portal and make sure it's working properly, that's all."

"Hmm, I see. Was it a broken portal that lost your friends?"

"No. It was a working one actually."

"That seems odd to me, but then again I don't know much about these sorts of things."

"What is it you do know about, Downey," Matthew asked curiously.

"Oh, you know," the man laughed. "A little bit of everything and not much of anything."

"Right," the engineer chuckled. "Well, I'm not sure that's going to help me out much."

"Why don't you tell me your problem and maybe then I could help you?"

"Well, to make a long, and very strange, story short: Someone took something that is incredibly valuable to me."

"Why would anyone do that?"

"Because they thought I could get something of great value to them."

"Ah, I see, a little trade-a-roo."

"Something like that."

"So, what's the problem?"

"I don't have the thing they want, and I can't find the man who can tell me where to get it."

"What is it they want?"

Matthew could tell the precocious man was not about to let any of this go, so he figured he might as well give Downey the whole story. It likely wouldn't get him any answers, but it might get him some peace. For the next several minutes, as they hiked toward the box, Matthew told his chipper companion all about Morgan, Zander, Silas and the workshop key. He told him about Tara, Jules, Joel, and Emma too. Then he explained how, after he locked down the exit portal here in Sliabh, he was completely out of options.

"Hmm, that is a noggin scratcher to be sure," Downey stated with a puzzled look on his face. "Maybe you could…no that wouldn't work. Perhaps you might…nope that don't work either. What if…nah. Wow, you are in a right pickle, aren't you?"

"Yep, that's what I've been saying."

"Well, at least you have the upper hand now."

"What on earth are you talking about, Downey?" Matthew asked in disbelief. "Exactly how do *I* have the upper hand?"

"Cause you've got nothing to lose and everything to gain," the man explained. "Those other folks, it sounds like the pressure is all on them. They've done everything they can but still haven't got the key. They've got to be getting pretty desperate by now."

"I don't know. I still don't feel like I have any cards to play here, at least not any good ones."

"Of course you do, lad. Silas is the only one who knows the location of the key and he'll never reveal that to them no matter what they promise or threaten. He knows they can't be trusted further than a goat can spit them."

"I agree, but…"

"And they have an even bigger problem."

"What's that?" Matthew asked skeptically.

"Even if Silas were to tell them anything, which he won't, but if he did, they wouldn't dare trust him. They know that any information he gives them is guaranteed to lead them into a trap."

"So what option does that leave us?"

"It leaves us you, my boy!" Downey smiled a huge, toothy grin.

"Me? I can't even get to Garda. How can I do anything?"

"You won't have to get there. They'll come to you."

"Why would they do…hang on…because they need me!" Matthew cheered. "Morgan knows I'm the only one Silas will trust with the key's location. She knows I'd do anything to free Emma and the others. She can't risk going to get the key herself."

"And…"

"And the best part is, she thinks she's got the advantage. She thinks she's smarter than me. She thinks she has leverage on me. She thinks she can control and manipulate me."

"But…" Downey asked bursting with excitement.

"But I've got nothing to lose!"

"Exactly, lad. Now, go get your friends back."

"Okay!" Matthew said determinedly. "When will we get to the exit gateway?"

"Oh, we've been here for twenty minutes," Downey smirked. "It's been behind that stone over there all along. You just weren't ready to go through it. But I think you are now, lad."

"Thanks, Downey," Matthew said as he rounded the stone and located the box. "Just one more thing."

"Shoot."

"Exactly what am I supposed to do now?"

"Oh, I haven't got the foggiest clue, but I'm sure you'll figure it out."

"Right," the young man answered, not sounding entirely convinced. "Well, thanks again. I really do owe you one."

"Come back sometime, so I can collect," the man laughed.

"I will," Matthew promised. After using the nullification key, he inserted the only key he had that was still safe to use and opened the gateway back to Earth.

– 25 –
Negotiations

Matthew arrived in Tara's apartment with a soaring feeling of confidence thanks to Downey's pep talk. That feeling was put to the test almost immediately. As the gateway light faded, he could make out the silhouette of something particularly large and muscular. His first thought was that Morgan had sent one of her thugs to wait for his arrival. His first thought was correct.

"Don't move," the brute commanded.

"Okay. Not moving. Now what?"

"I am Derge. Morgan sent me here to give you a message."

The fact that Morgan had sent a beast like Derge to deliver a message and not just clobber him over the head was a very encouraging sign. *'Okay, Sinclair,'* he encouraged himself, *'man up. If you have any prayer for this thing to work out, you've got to be bold, confident, and assertive. You've got to let this guy know who's the boss here. You've got to channel your inner Emma.'* "Okay, Derp, what's the message?"

"Derge."

"The message is derge? I don't get it."

"My name is Derge," the flustered henchman reiterated. "The message is: *'Morgan would like you to come to Garda and discuss a trade'*."

"Yeah, I don't think so, Derp."

"MY NAME IS DERGE!" the brute shouted, stomping on the floor so hard that for a moment Matthew thought his foot might go right through it.

"Okay, whatever," Matthew said as flippantly as he could manage the courage to do so. "Here's the thing, I'm not going."

"I was instructed not to take *'no'* for an answer," the thug insisted.

"Very well, I won't say no then," Matthew conceded. "Just not yet."

A perplexed Derge repeated, "I was told to not take..."

"Yeah, Yeah, I get it. Don't take no for an answer. Well, here's the thing Derp, this is the only answer you're gonna get, take it or leave it. I will come to Garda and talk with Morgan about a trade, but first, you will go back and give her my terms for such negotiations to take place."

"Umm," the brute fumbled for words.

"First, I get to see all of my friends and make sure they are okay. Second, I get to speak with Silas, in private. Third, if I am not permitted to return here alone following our negotiations she will *never* get the key. That last one is more of a threat than a condition, but you get the idea. Would you like me to write those down, or do you got them in that pretty little noggin of yours."

Derge scowled at Matthew. He was clearly seething under the surface, but obviously, Morgan had given him strict limits on what he could and could not do to Matthew. "I've got it, but she won't be happy about this."

"Well, then, that will be something new, won't it. I'll be here waiting."

Derge walked out of the apartment and slammed the door and, presumably, headed to wherever Morgan had stashed Tara's gateway box. Once he was sure the thug was gone Matthew collapsed on the sofa, a complete nervous wreck. He knew for his plan to work he would have to be bold and confident – neither of which were his strong suits. It was tough enough lipping off to a low-level henchman, but he knew it would be infinitely worse when he was standing in front of Morgan and Zander. He couldn't worry about that now. All his mental energies were focused on figuring out how to pull one over on the woman who had constantly been one step ahead of him.

* * *

When Derge returned through the portal into Tara's apartment he looked like a beaten dog. Clearly Morgan and Zander were not pleased he had come back empty-handed. They were undoubtedly even less pleased that he brought a list of demands with him. Nonetheless, that they had sent him back seemed to be promising. As the gateway light faded, Matthew stood up from the couch and affected all the bravado he could muster.

"Welcome back, Derpy. What's the good word?"

Derge growled at the puny young man's smugness, but even more so at his current inability to properly put an end to it. "Your terms are acceptable," the thug spit out the words as though they tasted sour in his mouth.

"Excellent," Matthew replied cheerfully. "Lead the way, my good man."

Derge stood staring blankly at Matthew.

"Dude, I don't have a key," the young man explained. "I'm sure Morgan wants all your muscles and good looks back on Garda for crowd control and what not. Like it or not, we're traveling buddies, Derp."

"But...I..." the thug stammered.

"I don't have a portal box on me, so unless you brought a spare, you'll have to take me to whatever one you used to return to Garda last time."

"You have a box somewhere," Derge asserted. "We will use that one."

"Yeah, right," Matthew laughed. "Do you think I'm an idiot? We do that and then while I'm in Garda negotiating with Morgan and Zander you pop back here and steal my box. Then I'm really up a creek, aren't I?" Nope, either we use your box or I'm not going," he paused for a moment to let the brute's mind catch up. "And let's be honest, I don't' think you want to be going back there without me again, do ya?"

"Fine," the henchman moped. "But, first you call me by my right name."

"No problem," Matthew said with a flourish. "You are Derge, deliverer of messages and possessor of humongous muscles. Now, can we go?"

"This way," Derge headed toward the apartment door, clearly pleased with Matthew's flattery.

* * *

Despite Silas' description of Garda, when he first arrived Matthew was completely struck by the bleakness of the realm. He surveyed the area around the arrival gateway but saw nothing more than jagged black rocks erupting from the ground at random angles. There was a narrow, but noticeable path that, presumably, led toward the prison cells. The hairs on the back of his neck raised as he felt someone breathing behind him. Matthew turned around to see yet another of Morgan's thugs standing there holding a heavy wooden club in his raised hand.

"A friend of yours?" he asked his escort.

"That's Cazgon. My brother."

"Ah yes, I see the family resemblance," Matthew remarked. Aside from their muscular frame and slightly glazed over look, both had hints of canine-like features in their facial structure.

"Cazgon, put your club down," Derge instructed.

"Lead the way, Derge, my good man."

Derge strode along down the path with Matthew following close behind. As they drew near to the cell area he saw Morgan and Zander standing off to the side behind what he assumed was the control panel for transporting prisoners in and out of their cells. As the path widened and opened into the larger area, Matthew moved to walk beside Derge who, up to that point, had obstructed the majority of the view. He saw a large rock face with several rough cut and barred openings.

"You have become bold all of a sudden," Morgan stated in a clearly non-complimentary way.

"Well, you know what they say, right? Desperate people do desperate things."

"Do not make the mistake of thinking you are somehow in a position of advantage here or that further demands will be received well," Zander warned sternly.

"Got it. No problem," Matthew replied politely. "I meant no disrespect, honest. It's just that you guys are clearly holding all the cards, so I had to do what I could to protect myself. You know what I mean? So, can I see my friends now?"

"Fine, but make it quick," Zander said sounding rather inconvenienced. "Straight ahead, I'm sure you can figure it out."

Negotiations

Matthew ran toward the prison block. The first cell he came to was Tara's. They talked momentarily, and she assured him that she was fine and in no immediate danger. She also informed him, to the best of her knowledge, where the other prisoners were located. He moved to the left and found Joel in the next cell over.

"How you doing, buddy?" Matthew asked.

"I've been better," Joel smirked. "Actually, other than being stuck in a cage I'm fine."

"Okay, well, it will all be over soon," Matthew assured his friend.

"Are you sure about that?"

"Yep. We'll either all be free or dead, but one way or another it will be over."

"Gee, thanks," Joel moaned, "I feel so much better."

"Hang in there."

Matthew moved back the other direction again, past Tara. He quickly checked in with Juliette then moved on to Emma's cell.

After awkwardly attempting to hug each other through the bars, Matthew said, "I'm so sorry, Em. It's my fault you're in here."

"It's not your fault," Emma smiled gently. "We all did the best we could. We did what we thought was right."

"Maybe so, but still it ended up with you here."

"Well then, let's all hope this isn't the end," she forced a weak smile.

"I wish it was you out here," Matthew said.

"You don't deserve to be in here any more than I do."

"I know, but I wish you were out here. You're way better at this kind of thing."

"What kind of things?"

"You know – being confident, making demands, sending your food back when the cook doesn't make it right."

"Are you saying I'm demanding?" Emma asked in mock offense.

"Ahh, a little bit," her boyfriend joked. "Okay, down to business. Do you still have the Serenity key I gave you?"

"No, Morgan took it."

"Okay, great. Well, not great, but okay. I love you."

Matthew suspected that Morgan and Zander's patience with the family reunions was likely wearing thin, so he hurried on to Silas' cell.

"Matthew, I'm so sorry for dragging you and all your..."

"No time for that now, Silas," Matthew interrupted. "Where are all your keys?"

"Zander took them all on Skalla," the carpenter stated. "Well, all but one. My nullification key is in a hidden pocket at the bottom of my satchel."

"Where's your satchel?"

"Sitting on the ground over by the control panel."

"Does that mean they don't know exactly how we have been locking the boxes?"

"No, I don't' believe they do."

"That could prove handy," Matthew said. "Okay, I have to ask you one more question, and I need you to trust me on this."

"Of course, Matthew."

"Where's the workshop key?"

* * *

"Are you done with the teary-eyed reunions? Do you need a tissue or something?" Zander said dryly.

"I'm good, but thanks for asking," Matthew replied casually.

"Finally. We've complied with your requests. Now it's time for you to give us what we want," Morgan insisted.

"When you're right, you're right. You held up your end of the deal, now it's my turn. So, let's talk."

"There is nothing to talk about," Zander blustered. "You give us the workshop key and we release your friends. You don't give us the key and they die, slowly, one by one."

"Okay, let's just stop right there," Matthew interjected. "You can skip the whole, do-it-or-your-friends-will-die thing. First, I don't buy it. It would be stupid of you to eliminate your only leverage and you're way too clever to make an idiotic move like that. That's a Derge kind of move. No offense big guy. Second, every one of them has just made me swear that no matter what you do to them, I won't give in. So, let's just bypass that whole song and dance right now."

"Speak to me that way again, boy, and I will slap that smug look right off your face," Zander fumed.

"Noted. Okay, moving on then?"

"What exactly is it that you want?" Morgan asked, stepping in to keep things from getting out of hand.

"Well, here's the problem as I see it," Matthew began frankly. "We don't trust each other. We never have in the past. We will never do so in the future."

"What's your point?" Zander asked, only slightly less irritated.

"My point is that puts us at an impasse. I will never give you the key because I can't trust you to release my friends after I do. You'll never release my friends first because you don't trust that I'll give you the key after they're out."

"So, what do you suggest?" Morgan asked.

"Well let's be honest, you guys clearly have the upper hand here. So, maybe if you give a little something first, and then I give a little something back. Eventually we can work our way toward everyone getting what they want most."

"Go on," Zander agreed reluctantly.

"Okay," Matthew said tentatively. "I'm going to leave here by myself and go get the key."

Negotiations

"Wonderful," Morgan said with mild enthusiasm.

"But first I need all the keys you took from Emma and Silas." He could see they were hesitating to give him any more concessions, regardless of what they were. "Come on," he reasoned. "They're all just duplicates of the ones you already have, and almost all of them are no good to you now anyways – until someone performs the unlocking spell."

"Fine," Morgan started to pass the keys to Matthew, putting them in his open palm.

"You know what, that's going to be really awkward. I'm just gonna throw them in here if that's okay," he said scooping Silas' satchel off the ground.

"Is that all?" Zander asked, growing visibly impatient.

"Pretty much, just a couple more things."

"What is it Matthew?" an irritated Morgan inquired.

"Two things, but they're super simple."

"Go on."

"When I return with the workshop key, there shouldn't be anyone anywhere near the arrival gateway. If there is, I will immediately open a new gateway back to Earth and the deal's off."

"He can't leave without a second box," Zander whispered to Morgan.

"Oh yeah, I also think it would be best if we send ol' Derge and Calzone back to Skalla for now." Derge snickered in the background, clearly finding the mispronunciation of his brother's name more humorous than being called Derp himself. Matthew continued, "You already outnumber me two ..." he looked at Zander's sizable frame, "two and a half to one. I'd feel a lot more comfortable without the extra muscle around." Matthew waited a moment and then quietly added, "Besides, they've got some serious B.O."

"Is that all?" Morgan asked, clearly at the end of her patience.

"Almost. Just one last thing."

"WHAT?"

"When I return, the prisoners will be out of their cells."

"Not a chance!" Zander stormed.

"Hear me out," Matthew requested meekly, "please." Zander simmered slightly, and the young man continued. "You've got the only key to the prison console and I don't even know how to use it. There's no way for me to know if the key works or if I'll even be able to get them out after you're gone. Tie them to the bars if you want. Use a full roll of duct tape on each one of them, I don't care, but they've got to be on the outside. Do that and I will bring the key, you have my word."

Morgan and Zander pondered Matthew's offer for a few moments. They clearly did not like the terms, but if it got them what they wanted in the end, that's all that mattered.

Negotiations

"Alright, Matthew," Morgan finally agreed. "Now it's our turn."

"Fire away."

"We need confirmation that the key you bring us works."

"Right, okay, let me see," Matthew said looking around. "Give me your scarf."

"What?"

"Your scarf. Give it to me. Once I pick up the workshop key, I will pop over there, snap a quick picture of me and your scarf in the workshop and then come back here. You can see the photo and know the key is legit."

"Fine," Morgan agreed, handing over the scarf. "Very well, Matthew. It seems like we have an arrangement. Hold up your end of the bargain and this will all be over soon."

"I certainly hope so," Matthew smiled weakly, stuffing the scarf into the satchel with the keys. "Now, if you don't mind, I have places to go. So, if you would both please step back a little, I'll be going." He slid the Earth key into the black box resting on a small shelf at the side of the console.

Zander stepped forward and leaned in closer. "Don't hold up your end and this will all be over much sooner," he scowled.

– 26 –
The Exchange

Matthew entered the foyer of his office tower in downtown Boston and made his way toward the elevators. He pressed the up button and waited anxiously for the doors to open. He was still on a bit of an adrenaline high from his meeting with Morgan and Zander, but he was also paranoid that they may have sent someone to follow him around and jump him as soon as they knew for sure he had the workshop key. So far his plan had more or less fallen into place, but the line between squeaking through and everything going horribly wrong was paper thin.

The elevator opened, he stepped inside and pressed the button for the 15th floor. The doors slowly closed but were interrupted by a hand sliding in between them at the last second. The doors opened wide once again and a young man in a suit entered the elevator.

"That was a close one," the young man chuckled. "Um, can you press 24 for me, please? Thanks."

Matthew pressed the button and waited impatiently for the doors to slowly slide closed again. Time was of the essence. The longer he was gone from Garda the more suspicious Morgan and Zander would become. Besides, he didn't like being locked in a small confined space with someone who, for all he knew, was sent to take him out. Of course, this guy looked nothing like any of the thugs Morgan had employed, but it would make sense that in this case she would favor blending in over intimidating.

"Floor 15, huh?" the young man asked, noting the only other lighted button. "Who do you work for?"

"Um, Finch and Steele," Matthew answered distractedly. "I'm a, um, an engineer."

"Cool. I'm a lawyer," the man cheerfully replied. "I work upstairs, in the law office… 'cause that's what lawyers do, work in law offices" he explained awkwardly in an unintentionally comical way.

"Uh-huh," Matthew said, not really paying attention.

"My name's Sam, by the way," he said, extending his hand.

"Yeah, Matt. Nice to meet you." Matthew said shaking the man's hand which caused him to look at his companion for the first time. "You ride your bike to work today, Sam?"

"Yeah, how'd you know that?"

"You've got a bike helmet strapped to your briefcase handle and your right pant leg is still tucked into your sock."

"Oh, yeah. I always forget that." Sam gazed at Matthew for a minute which was more than long enough to make him nervous. "Hey, man, are you okay? You seem, you know, wound pretty tight."

"Yeah," Matthew replied trying as hard as he could to sound calm. "I've got a huge deal I'm trying to close today. That's all."

"Man! I know what that's like. Believe me!" Sam smiled reassuringly. "Hey, mind if I give you a little advice? I know sometimes these things can feel like they're life and death, right? But in the long run, a lot of stuff isn't nearly as important as we think it is. Just remember, even if your deal doesn't go well, it's not the end of the world."

"Almost any other day I'd agree with you, Sam," Matthew grinned just as the elevator door opened to the fifteenth floor and he sprinted out.

"Alright, catch you later, Matt. Good luck," Sam called out as the elevator doors slid closed in front of him.

Matthew sped to his desk and started to rummage around the stacks of paper that had accumulated in his absence. The longer he looked the more frustrated he got. He began rifling through his drawers as well, searching frantically.

"Whoa! What are you doing here?"

"I'm not really here, Phil," Matthew replied to the man peering over the top edge of his cubicle.

"Well, you better not let Sayid catch you being *not here,* or you might be *not here* permanently. He is seriously ticked about your extended case of mono or whatever it was you mysteriously contracted."

"Is he here?"

"Naw, not at the moment, but he should be back soon."

"Hey, Phil, did I get any courier packages while I was gone?"

"Just one. I signed for it. Hang on." Phil disappeared behind the cubicle wall for a moment and then reappeared with a small package in hand. "I opened it up just in case it was something important, but it was just some weird key."

"Thanks, Phil," Matthew said, grabbing the package and examining the contents. "I've got to get out of here."

"Well, don't go that way, because the boss just walked in."

"Can you distract him for me?"

"Are you kidding? I'm the master of distraction. I distract myself all day long!"

"Thanks again, Phil. I owe you."

"Yeah, you do," Phil laughed and then headed across the room. "Hey, Sayid," he called out. "This stupid copier is all messed up again. What gives? When are we getting rid of this piece of junk?"

With his boss adequately distracted by Phil's impromptu floorshow, Matthew slipped out the exit and into the stairwell. He went down one floor then walked over and caught the elevator back down to ground level.

The first thing Matthew had done upon his return from Garda was to collect Tara's box from its hiding place, which Derge had so graciously

The Exchange

revealed to him earlier. That left only one more thing to do.

*   *   *

Matthew stood anxiously in Joel's living room. Even though he had searched the entire house multiple times and triple-locked the door he was still nervous about opening the workshop gateway. If there was a moment where his entire plan could go completely off the rails, this was it. In truth, there would be numerous moments where that could easily happen, but this was the one he was most concerned about.

He pulled the couriered package out of his pocket and removed the key. He looked at it briefly. To his eyes, it was no different than any of the others he had on his Mr. Spiffy's keychain, but he knew that in reality, it was infinitely more valuable than all the others put together. The keychain only held three keys now. Matthew had stashed all the others away in Joel's bedroom closet. It would take days for anyone to find the keys, or anything else, in there. After one last glance around the room, he inserted the workshop key into the box on the living room table and let the light of the gateway envelop him.

Moments later when he arrived in the workshop he found himself entirely alone. It was a strange feeling being back in this place. It seemed like a lifetime ago since he and Emma had first stumbled, quite literally, into Silas' workshop. Nothing in the room had changed since that day. He walked over to the workbench where the partially completed door lay. He chuckled at his naivety as he recalled how skeptical he was the first time Silas told him what the doors were created to do. He had come a very long way since then. Everything else in the room was exactly as he remembered it. The workshop key that Emma had originally found in Cat Rock Park still sat on the workbench in front of the midnight blue portal box next to the key rack.

"There will be time for nostalgia later," Matthew told himself. "You've got work to do, and not much time to do it."

Matthew stepped to the other side of the workbench and stood so the circle of completed doors could be clearly seen behind him. He pulled Morgan's scarf out of Silas' satchel and tossed it around his neck. Removing his cell phone from his pocket he snapped several selfies, being sure to capture the scarf and a clear view of the workshop behind him. A few minutes later he was ready to go – at least as ready as he was ever going to be. He removed Tara's box from Silas' satchel and held it open in his left arm. After removing the Earth key from his keychain, he inserted it into the brown box. He then opened the blue box and inserted the Garda key. After one last look around and a deep breath, he turned the key in the blue box opening the gateway.

* * *

Zander paced impatiently as Morgan secured the last of the prisoners to the outside of Tara's cell. "You gave him too much," he complained.

"Trust me," Morgan crowed confidently, "the boy's a pawn. We let him think he's the one in control. Let him think that he's playing us. None of it matters. In the end, if he wants his friends back, he *will* bring the key, and then we'll take it from him."

"I suppose. He just better come through."

"He will. He has to. He has no other play here," Morgan explained. "We just have to humor him a little while longer and I promise you, he'll hand the key over."

"Or we could just take it from him," Zander suggested with sadistic delight.

"We could, but if we move to soon, we might never get it," Morgan pointed out. "I know how this kid thinks – he's a planner. I know how to pull his strings remember. I can see through all his fake posturing. He's trying to look bold and confident, but underneath he's barely holding it together. He's skittish. He's going to make us jump through a bunch of what he believes are incredibly clever hoops. If we keep our cool and play along the key will fall into our laps. If we don't, if we move too soon and he doesn't actually have the key on him, he'll run like a scared little rabbit. Then we'll be right back where we started, hunting for a key that could be pretty much anywhere."

"I know you're right," Zander conceded. "But I just want to wring his scrawny little neck."

"Maybe another time," Morgan chuckled. "Once we're safely in the workshop the world is ours. *All the worlds are ours.*"

"Hey, psycho-chick," Joel called out. "I hate to interrupt your maniacal rant or whatever it is you got going on over there, but I was wondering if you could tighten up these ropes a bit. I can still feel a tiny bit of circulation in my extremities."

Zander wound up to strike Joel's face, but Morgan's hand held him back. "Skittish remember? It has to look like we're playing along with all his demands. We'll have plenty of time to track this one down and pummel him later."

"What are you thinking?" Juliette reprimanded as Morgan and Zander walked back to the console podium. "You're going to get yourself killed."

"I don't have the foggiest idea what Matt's plan is," Joel explained, "but the more distracted and off-balance those two are, the slightly greater chance he has of succeeding."

"What do you think he will do," Tara asked.

"I don't know, he didn't tell me his plan," Silas admitted. "I'm not sure he has any choice other than to give them the workshop key. The best we can hope for is that after he does, they don't leave us stranded here."

"Joel's right," Emma stated determinedly. "The best way we can help now is by keeping them preoccupied and off-balance."

"Off-balanced is my specialty," Joel smirked and then shouted at their captors. "Garçon! Excuse me, garçon! We ordered room service forty-five minutes ago and it still hasn't arrived. I'd like to lodge a formal complaint." Zander scowled but did not respond. "This is going on my Yelp review, you better believe that!"

* * *

The instant he arrived, Matthew grasped the Earth key in Tara's box and turned it halfway. He stared intensely around the arrival area. Initially he saw nothing but jagged black rock, however, he wasn't taking any chances. After several minutes, he was satisfied that he was alone. He hated the idea of having to put Tara's box down because it was his only parachute should things go wrong, nonetheless he knew at some point he wouldn't have a choice. He decided he would hold on to the box and keep the earth key in the slot until he reached the prison area, just in case.

Matthew cautiously followed the path Derge had led him down on his first visit. With each step he could feel his heart beat a little faster. Just around the corner from the cell area Matthew paused and breathed deeply. This was no time to let his nerves get the best of him. With his breathing slowed to an almost normal pace, he wiped a few beads of sweat from his forehead and strolled calmly around the corner.

"Well, it's about time," Zander groaned.

"I'll be sure to let our HR department know of your dissatisfaction," Matthew retorted.

"The time doesn't matter," Morgan argued. "Did you bring it? That's all I want to know."

"I did," Matthew answered standing back at a cautious distance."

"Let me see it," Zander demanded.

"Not so fast," Matthew insisted. "Both of you move around to the back side of the control panel." Morgan and Zander both begrudgingly complied, creating a partial barrier between them and Matthew. "I see my friends are outside of their cells and ridiculously well tied up. Since I don't smell the B.O. bros around I'd say you've kept up you're end of the bargain so far."

"We have been more than accommodating, Matthew," Morgan said sternly. "Enough games. Give us the key."

"First, hand over the control panel key. I'd hate for you to take off and forget that in your pocket."

Zander pulled out the key and slammed it on to the console. Matthew was thankful his friends were already outside the cells because after a blow like that the controls might not work anymore. "Done," Zander growled. "Your turn. Give me the bag." Matthew removed the keychain, stuffed it in his pocket and then handed over the satchel. Zander looked inside and then pulled out a small knife. "And just what were you planning to do with this?"

"That's for cutting my friends loose later. You didn't expect me to gnaw through the ropes with my teeth, did you?"

Zander took one more look inside the bag and then tossed it and the knife behind him. "Now, give us the key or I'm coming over there and take it from you."

"Alright, alright," Matthew agreed. He set Tara's box on top of the console facing him with the lid still propped open. "You wanted proof, here it is. Hot off the press." Matthew showed Morgan and Zander the photos on his phone he had just taken in the workshop. "Satisfied?" he asked putting his phone way. "Oh, by the way, this is yours," he said removing Morgan's scarf from around his neck and laying it on the control panel as well. "It's not really my color."

"My turn," Zander demanded. "Let me hold the key."

"I just showed you the picture, isn't that proof enough?"

"Your photos are lovely, but I'm not stupid, Matthew. You could have easily done that in Photoshop," Morgan snarkily replied.

"Yeah," Zander grunted, "you could have done that in a photo shop."

Matthew reluctantly pulled out the keychain again and took the remaining two keys off the ring. He had purposefully not brought a nullification key for fear it would get used to trap him and his friends in the prison realm. "This one is just for Garda and won't do any of us any good at the moment," he said setting it on the console next to Tara's box."

"Time's up, Matthew," Morgan urged. "Until Zander verifies the key himself, there is no deal."

"Okay, here it is," he said holding up the workshop key. "Here is what all this trouble has been about."

"I don't believe you," Zander accused. "Not till I hold it myself."

"Here's the thing," Matthew explained. "If I let you hold it you're apt to just rip it out of my hand, or maybe just rip my arm right off. So how about this: I'll hold it and you can wave your hand over it. You should still be able to sense if it is the legitimate workshop key without touching it. I've seen Silas do it a bunch of times. Oh … unless you're not as good at that as he is."

"Fine," Zander seethed at the insinuation his power to wield the Heritage was in any way inferior to Silas.

The Exchange

Matthew reached out over the console and extended his hand with the workshop key in it. He held tight to the bow and most of the shaft but allowed Zander to lay his hand just above the bit end.

"That's it," Zander beamed. "That's really it."

Matthew retracted his hand slightly and clarified, "I give you this, you two leave, and the rest of us are free to go on our way, right?"

"Yes," Morgan smiled in glee. "You are all inconsequential to us now."

"Alright," Matthew reluctantly agreed. "I'm so sorry, Silas," he called out looking towards his friends, still bound by the cells. He offered the grip end of the key handle to Morgan. "Here you go. You've earned it," he said spitefully.

Morgan took the key from Matthew's hand with sheer delight. She inserted it in the gateway box stationed near the console podium, "Time to go."

"Not just yet," Zander replied. He lunged toward the console with a grunt, just enough to make Matthew flinch and take a step back, stumbling to the ground. Seizing the moment, Zander reached across and plucked the earth key out, knocking the now empty brown box to the ground. "Enjoy your stay, he snarled.

"Come on, sweetie, you don't want to miss this," Morgan called to Zander. The smug lout stepped over and put his arm around her as she inserted the key into the black box and turned it. The portal opened, and a brilliant light encompassed the sinister pair. When the light dissipated Morgan and Zander were gone.

Matthew laid on the ground collecting his thoughts, overwhelmed by the magnitude of what had just happened. If all six of them surviving had been the measure of victory, his plan had been a complete success. A few moments later he picked himself up, ran to collect the items Zander had tossed away, and then rushed toward the prison cells. He quickly went to work cutting through his friends' bonds and releasing them. Initially, everyone was filled with joy at being free and thrilled at the prospect of returning home. But soon the sober reality of the cost of their freedom started to sink in. Despite all their efforts, Morgan had gotten exactly what she wanted all along.

"Thank you for saving us, Matthew," Silas said, almost in tears. "For saving my dear wife."

"You're welcome," Matthew replied from among the group-hug the four friends were engaged in.

"Unfortunately, Morgan got away with the workshop key," Emma noted.

"And if I'm not mistaken, it looked like Zander stole the Earth key," Joel added. "So, unless you brought a spare, we have no way of opening a gateway home."

"Yeah, that wasn't part of the plan," Matthew admitted. Everyone did their best to be thankful to be alive and free but being trapped in this desolate realm was no one's dream ending.

"The good news is, they left us the key for the control panel," Silas did his best to put a positive spin on things. "Which means we have access to food, water and all the other necessities of life."

"It may not be the ending we had hoped for, but it could be a lot worse," Juliette suggested, still holding tight to Joel.

"All hope is not lost yet," Matthew interjected

"Why's that?" Tara asked.

"Well, when I was at the workshop I saw your copy of the key. The one Emma found in the woods. And I thought maybe I should grab both, so I put the second one in the hidden pocket of Silas' satchel, just in case. Here you go," he said passing the bag to Silas.

"I appreciate the thought," the craftsman said, removing the key from it's hiding place, "but I'm certain the first thing Zander did when he arrived in the workshop was change the encoding on the door which would render all other keys useless," Silas explained sadly.

"I was kind of hoping that wasn't possible.'

"I appreciate the effort," Tara smiled gently. "You all have done so much for us."

"Yeah, don't beat yourself up," Joel consoled his friend. "It was a good plan, it just didn't go your way. None of us could have done any better."

"It's not your fault Morgan and Zander ended up with the workshop key," Emma said wrapping her arms around him.

"I know, but here's the thing," Matthew said with hints of disappointment in his voice, "as it turns out, the key Zander scanned and verified as the workshop key wasn't *actually* the one Morgan put into the box." A slight smirk appeared on Matthew's face as he removed another key from his pocket. He twirled the key in his fingers and passed it to the carpenter.

"What is this?" Silas asked curiously. A look of shock swept over his face as he held the key in his hand. "How is this possible?

"What is it, dear?" Tara asked.

"It's the key to my workshop, *my* key!" the carpenter said in disbelief.

"But how?" Joel asked.

"You used your stupid spoon-fork trick, didn't you?" Emma exclaimed in a joyous moment of realization. "I've always loved that trick!" Matthew gave her a doubtful look. "Okay, but I definitely love it now!"

"You switched keys on them?" Juliette asked in disbelief.

"You sneaky little devil," Joel laughed. "So, if you have the workshop key, what key did they use?"

"Well, in between taking selfies I grabbed a new key off the rack and encoded it to one of the blank doors Silas has in his workshop," Matthew revealed.

The Exchange

"A blank door? What does that mean?" Juliette inquired.

"It means that at the moment, those two scoundrels are floating aimlessly in infinite nothingness," Silas answered, trying not to sound too pleased at the thought. Noticing his wife didn't approve of his level of delight, he added, "As soon as I get back I promise I will give them a place with all the essentials. But for now, it won't hurt for them to dangle a while."

"You have all done so much for us," Tara said gratefully. "How can we ever repay you?"

"You could start by getting us out of here," Joel suggested. "This place gives me the willies."

"That we can most certainly do, Joel," Silas chuckled as he led everyone toward the console. Tara picked up her brown box as her husband inserted the workshop key into the portal box near the console. "Everyone hold on, we don't want to leave anyone behind!"

The Heritage Key

- 27 -
One Last Favor

"Welcome back," Silas greeted the couple as they arrived in the workshop.

"It's good to see you again," Emma smiled and ran over to give the carpenter a hug.

"Good to see both of you too."

"Is Tara here?" Matthew asked.

"Not yet, but I expect her to arrive shortly."

It had been several weeks since they had escaped Garda. Things were starting to get back to normal. Matthew was back at work and had almost worked his way back into Sayid's good books again. Emma was soon to start her residency at Boston Children's Hospital. It had taken some time and effort, but with the six of them working together, and some minor realm adjustments by Silas, all the escapees from Garda had been rounded up and returned to their cells.

"Whatcha working on?"

"I'm just putting the finishing touches on my new door."

"Is that ... *their* door," Emma inquired.

"Yes, it is."

"What kind of world did you build?" Matthew probed curiously.

"Well," the carpenter admitted. "I had several different ideas initially. A foul-smelling swamp. A mosquito infested dome. I even toyed with the idea of a perpetually erupting volcano for a while."

"But?"

"But Tara convinced me otherwise, as she usually does. So, I put them on a nice little island. It has everything they need to have a decent life, everything except a way out. There is no gateway box anywhere in the realm and I have also altered the lock on the earth door to ensure that both of the keys Morgan and Zander took with them are completely useless."

"Sounds fitting to me," Matthew concurred.

"Tara is one sweet woman," Emma noted. "I would have put them in the mosquito world ... and added spiders."

"She is very special indeed."

"So anyway," Matthew said. "We got your message. What did you want to see us about?"

"Well, as you know," Silas began. "Now that all of Morgan's thugs are back where they belong the only thing left to do is to return to the realms she never visited and unlock the portals."

"Of course," Matthew confirmed. "I went back to Sliabh last week and had a nice long chat with my ol' pal Downey."

"That's right," Silas recalled. "Joel and Juliette just headed out to unlock the gateway in Serenity."

"Why those selfless saints," Matthew teased. "Always volunteering for the tough jobs those two."

"Give them a break," Emma chuckled. "They earned a little romantic getaway, don't you think?"

"Sure," Matthew agreed. "Of course, most of the romance will be between Joel and all the fruit in those orchards."

"He did mention something about the apples before they left," Silas chuckled. "Anyways, there is one other gateway that needs to be unlocked, and I was hoping the two of you would take care of that one for me. I need to get this door finished up and then Tara wants to visit Winston and the others in Arbolada."

"Sure, Silas," Emma agreed readily. "No problem, right sweetie?"

"Um, yeah, sure," her boyfriend replied. "I've got no other plans. Why not?"

"Excellent here is the key. And you'll need this one as well to unlock the gateway. The realm is called Rymden. I think you'll enjoy it. Oh, and when you get back, there is one other thing I'd like to talk to you about."

"Okay, hun," Emma said taking the keys and walking toward the blue box on the workbench, "all set?"

"Ready as I'll ever be," he laughed. "See you later, Silas."

"Good luck!"

Matthew put his arms around Emma as she turned the key. The gateway opened and transported them to Rymden. When the light dissipated they found themselves surrounded by a starlit night sky. Emma gazed at the stars above her for several minutes before making a startling realization.

"Matthew, there's nothing below us!"

"Nope, there definitely isn't," her boyfriend confirmed.

The pair seemed to be floating in the middle of space. Unlike the space around earth, which is void of oxygen and icy cold, Rymden was idyllic. There was plenty of air to breath and the temperature was perfectly moderate.

"This is incredible!" Emma gasped as she looked dumbfounded at the starscape encompassing her on all sides.

"Yeah and here's the best part," Matthew grinned broadly. He made a gentle swimming motion with his arms, slowly propelling himself forward. "Come on, Em," he encouraged. "It's just like being in the water."

Emma tentatively copied Matthew's motions and began to float upward. She moved slowly at first, but soon she was speeding around, spinning, rolling and somersaulting through space. "This is incredible!" she repeated. "Never in my wildest dreams have I imagined a place like this. Not even after all the things we've seen, which is saying a lot," she giggled.

"Yep, Silas really outdid himself on this one," Matthew agreed.

"Hey, Matthew," she said, drifting over close to him. "You know, we don't have anywhere else to be."

"I guess."

"Maybe we don't have to head straight to the gateway and unlock it. Maybe we could just spend some time here, together." She gazed around once again, literally starry-eyed. "We deserve a little us time, don't you think? The gateway can wait."

"Actually, I have a confession to make, Em," Matthew admitted. "The exit gateway in this realm was never locked."

"Then why would Silas have sent us here?" she asked, continuing to stare awestruck at the sky around her. "Not that I'm complaining, that's for sure!"

"Well, there is one really important thing that does need to be addressed."

"What is it?" she asked turning back to face her boyfriend.

Matthew calmly slid his hand into his pocket and grasped a small, velvet-covered box. "Emma, I have a question for you ..."

Also from Mike Parker:

When physicist Carl Ryan and his friend Nick Jones set out to realize their dream of inventing the world's first teleporter they had no idea their machine would have some incredible and unexpected results.

Together with fellow scientist Dr. Stevens and Carl's sister, Ainsley, the friends embark on an adventure that could not only change the future but rewrite history.

They soon discover that things are not always as simple as they seem. Unknowns and uncertainties lurk behind every corner and they begin to wonder if they will ever get back home ... in time.

Also from Mike Parker:

Overnight Sam's world has been turned upside down. The realization that every time he falls asleep he wakes up somewhere else has the young lawyer questioning everything, including his own sanity. His desperate search for answers will pull him into an adventure that is beyond his wildest dreams.

BELL THE CAT
PUBLICATIONS

CPSIA information can be obtained
at www.ICGtesting.com
Printed in the USA
LVHW041549311019
635967LV00003B/461